They'd only moved a few steps when she caught her fingers in the waist of his sagging wrap and jerked. The wrap fell to the floor.

He stopped cold, making an indistinct sound that sounded like a garbled "fuck me." His buttocks were as solid, though nicely round, and not quite as muscular, as the rest of him. He looked back over his shoulder, and she saw his high cheekbones were red. She knew his dilemma. If he turned she'd see all of him in full-frontal glory. She watched him weigh modesty and duty.

For the first time that night, she smiled.

While he debated, she tugged her wrist, and finally was free. She couldn't help it; she slapped his buttocks with her gloved hand on her way to the door, delighted with the meaty echo against all the fancy marble and woodwork.

Her own smile showed perfect white teeth as she flung open the door. "Next time, I'll bring a twenty."

Also by Colleen Shannon

Foster Justice

Sinclair Justice

Travis Justice

Colleen Shannon

LYRICAL PRESS
Kensington Publishing Corp.
www.kensingtonbooks.com

To the extent that the image or images on the cover of this book depict a person or persons, such person or persons are merely models, and are not intended to portray any character or characters featured in the book.

LYRICAL PRESS BOOKS are published by

Kensington Publishing Corp.
119 West 40th Street
New York, NY 10018

Copyright © 2016 by Colleen Shannon

All rights reserved. No part of this book may be reproduced in any form or by any means without the prior written consent of the Publisher, excepting brief quotes used in reviews.

All Kensington titles, imprints, and distributed lines are available at special quantity discounts for bulk purchases for sales promotion, premiums, fund-raising, educational, or institutional use.

Special book excerpts or customized printings can also be created to fit specific needs. For details, write or phone the office of the Kensington Sales Manager: Kensington Publishing Corp., 119 West 40th Street, New York, NY 10018. Attn. Sales Department. Phone: 1-800-221-2647.

Lyrical Press and Lyrical Press logo Reg. U.S. Pat. & TM Off.

First Electronic Edition: September 2016
eISBN-13: 978-1-60183-762-2
eISBN-10: 1-60183-762-3

First Print Edition: September 2016
ISBN-13: 978-1-60183-763-9
ISBN-10: 1-60183-763-1

Printed in the United States of America

Chapter 1

Tarrytown, Austin
Present Day

Hana Nakatomi dropped silently down from the high stone wall. Going very still, she appraised her surroundings with that sixth-sense awareness drilled into her since childhood. Dressed entirely in black, right down to the hood, with night-vision lenses, she was one with the night. Even in the bright moonlight she'd seem but a shadow if someone had looked out the mansion window. She sliced her gaze from side to side, not turning her head. All seemed quiet. Safe.

As safe as it could be to break into the house of the deputy director, law-enforcement operations of the Texas Department of Public Safety. John Travis was operational chief of the Texas Rangers and head of the famous Travis family. Not the wisest choice for her first felony breaking-and-entering job, but she hadn't picked the target.

He had something she had to have. Period.

The prestige the Travis name bestowed was on display everywhere she looked.

The grounds were immaculate right down to the small gazebo centered in the lawn. The enormous red brick mansion had a rear-covered porch accented by a white painted balcony that belonged in a southern gothic novel, and a lacy black balustrade perfect for her needs. A gaping window on the second floor reassured her that at least she wouldn't have to cut the security system.

She tried closing her eyes and slowing her breaths, but the Zen state eluded her as it had for the past few years. She was dishonoring her samurai heritage by literally being a thief in the night. William Barrett Travis himself would have made a good samurai, dying fighting at the Alamo against vastly superior numbers for the quaint notions of liberty and honor. He'd even wielded a sword against his enemies. He'd be the first to brandish the blade at her for daring to break into the home his blood had founded.

Inside the second-story bedroom, Zachary William Barrett Travis—Junior many times over—was having another nightmare. He'd left the window open because even so many years after Afghanistan, he preferred the Texas summer heat to the closed-in feeling he got when he was locked in an air-conditioned room.

He tossed and turned in the big antique bed that had belonged to his great-grandmother, hearing only "Look out!" His buddy Tyler shoved him inside a doorway, away from the hail of gunfire from the insurgents who'd surprised them in an alley while they were on patrol. Tyler was cut to pieces. The machine-gun fire grazed Zach's body armor, just missing his legs. He'd walked away without a scratch. At least, a visible one.... He'd been on point as they searched house to house and missed the nest of fanatics on a flat rooftop disguised by camouflage netting.

Still in the midst of his dream, Zach threw the thin sheet off and reached out as if to pull Tyler inside the doorway. In his thrashing, Zach hit the bedpost with his ankle.

She wished she didn't have to do this. She wished her grandfather wasn't dying.

She wished she'd never been such a wild child in her youth.

And most of all she wished she'd kept up her Shotokan karate training. She could use the calmness it engendered right about now. Cautiously, she opened her eyes to search for red motion sensors. The house was pitch-black.

Even as she crept silently forward, keeping to the plush grass instead of the loose stone pathway, she had a feeling once she invaded this bastion of Texas pride and power, her life would never be the same. Careful step by careful step, she reached the balustrade. The iron, cool under her gloves in the warm, humid evening, tangibly warned her of the hard choices forced upon her.

Squelching her guilt, she nimbly boosted her slight weight onto the porch railing. She used the height to pull herself up the lacy ironwork to the second story, toward the open window.

* * *

Zach hit the post again, harder. The pain jolted him instantly awake. He sat up, sweaty but still clammy from the dream. A shadow drifted past, and he blinked rapidly, trying to focus, but when he looked toward the door again, it was gone.

Great, now he was seeing things.

Still shaken by his recurring nightmare, he got out of bed to pour himself a glass of water from the cold thermos beside his bed. Leave it to their housekeeper, Consuela, to anticipate his every need. Of all the things he'd missed over the years of wandering, she had topped the list. Even, he admitted to himself guiltily, over his own mother and father. He also knew a more immediate reason for his restlessness: He was wearing out his welcome. He took another gulp as if to wash down the unpalatable knowledge that he had to make up his mind or book. As usual, his dad was on his ass to complete his application to the Texas Rangers, but Zach knew his mental fitness wasn't on par with his physical readiness for such a demanding job. Besides, he hated all the sideways looks, the hidden smiles from other Texas Rangers and Department of Public Safety troopers. "Daddy's boy," they said without saying it.

If they only knew... he was as far away from a daddy's boy as circumnavigating the globe three times since college graduation could take him. He took a couple of deep breaths from his diaphragm as the Zen lessons had taught him, but he was too tense to drop back to sleep. He robed his hips in the terry-towel half wrap, which was his only concession to decency when he was home. He hated most signs of domesticity: fluffy robes, slippers, recliners, and cookbooks.

The patter of little feet? Dear God, he'd rather face the Taliban again. However, since he also hated upsetting his mother by walking around nude, he made sure his snaps were secure. He'd go down and watch Netflix for a while in his dad's study, one of those inane sitcoms that would instantly bore him and stultify the memories.

Hana had crept downstairs into the study and already scoped out her surroundings. The tiny but bright LED flashlight zipped around numerous display cases. They were loaded with World War II memorabilia: maps, helmets, old compasses, armaments of every kind. She recognized a Japanese-supplied grenade. A dud, she hoped, or at least one with its firing pin removed. She spotted a type 1 Tera .38 carbine by

Nagoya. Produced late in the war in 1941, they were reputed to have been constructed in a run of less than a thousand. The carbine folded up and was intended to be used by paratroopers. From her grandfather's tutelage, she knew how valuable this weapon was because of its rarity and strange design.

But she skimmed over it and other tantalizing memorabilia, looking for the sword. She'd been assured it was kept in these glass cases with the other cherished memories of a victorious war for the Americans, and a humiliation unforgotten for seventy years by the Japanese. The Japanese half of her wanted to smash these cases and every valuable relic, but the prudent Norwegian side kept her calmly searching.

As she searched, that calmer half wondered what William Barrett Travis would think of the modern dynasty he'd founded by siring two small children before dying at the Alamo. He'd probably be nonplussed to know that his descendants seemed to grow richer with every generation, spreading their influence far beyond the Texas vision he'd died for, with their media-empire profits many years ago poured now into more lucrative cattle and oil.

It wasn't here ... the maid she'd bribed had claimed she'd dusted the priceless fourteenth-century samurai sword and returned it to its place, alone in a wide, temperature-controlled glass case in the director's private home study. Desperately, she searched again, a bit more jerkily this time. She'd looked for and not found surveillance cameras in the study, but they lined the staircase and the entry. While her disguise would prevent any facial-recognition software from identifying her, her slim form was still distinctively female, even in the head-to-toe black attire and tall, soft boots.

She had to hurry. . . .

Moving with that quiet assuredness he'd learned in years of football, baseball, and Army Ranger military training, Zach strode to the landing and descended the stairs. Not wanting to wake his parents, he automatically avoided the creaky floorboard that had been there as long as he could remember. He'd reached the ground floor, the black-and-white marble tiles cool against the soles of his feet, when he saw a tiny flicker of light dancing under the closed study door. There, then gone. Like the fireflies he remembered from his youth, but never saw anymore.

There it was again—not a firefly, more like a small but very bright flashlight waving about in the darkness. Instantly, he was on alert. His weight raised to the balls of his feet in readiness, he eased forward.

Finally, Hana's light found a long case that held a sword, but she knew a split second later it wasn't a samurai katana. It had the long, curved blade of a Turkish scimitar and though the hilt was laden with gold and jewels, she felt only dismay. It wasn't here!

What would she tell them?

She'd failed. Panicked, she bit her lip so hard through the mask that she tore a tiny hole in the nylon. Unless... maybe there was a safe room? She began feeling along the bookcases. She couldn't crack one, but she knew people who could, and if need be she'd return. Her presence had gone unnoticed so far. With no evidence of an intruder, maybe they wouldn't take time to view the surveillance footage—

The thought barely fired through her brain before she heard the slightest noise. She spun toward the sound, waving the flashlight. The study lever handle, the heavy ornate kind, turned. One way, the other. Almost soundless, but her senses were unusually acute. Thanking the caution that had made her lock the heavy door, she ran toward the French doors leading onto the patio before she remembered she'd not deactivated the alarm, intending to ease out the way she'd come in. She spun around, frantic as she wondered what to do. No closet to hide in; the drapes were sheer. Hana heard a slight pause, then a key in the lock.

Her searching gaze swept upward.

Warily, Zach paused on the threshold. That sixth-sense awareness the special forces training had drilled into him tingled from his nape to his spine. The room was dark—no evidence of a light of any kind. He put one foot over the threshold, feeling, not seeing or hearing, a presence.

He eased forward another foot, 20/10 vision acute eyes scanning carefully from one end of the room to the other. Nothing. He tried the French door. Still locked. Even the security alarm stayed a steady red. Was he imagining things as a remnant of his nightmare? How could they have a home invasion with the alarm still active? Then he recalled that shadow... the one that had slipped past his bed upstairs.

Dear God, the open window...

He looked up. Even his good night vision took a moment to distinguish between the black shade clinging to the study crossbeams and the dark wood. Holy crap! An intruder clung to the rafters. He'd leaped toward the alarm pad to push the alert button when a weight dropped on his back and knocked him off balance enough to lose his footing.

As tackles went, it wasn't fierce and Zach knew the person attacking him couldn't weigh much. He easily turned his body mass sideways as he fell, landing half on the intruder, surprised at the slight but soft feel of the body under his. He heard breath *oof!* from his weight. However, though the attacker wasn't big, the figure was incredibly lithe and nimble. Before he finished turning, his hands reaching out to grasp shoulders, arms, legs—whatever he could reach—the attacker had writhed away and risen, running toward the open study door.

Zach was a bit slower, but his strides were much longer, and he caught the fleeing black shape by the back of the hood. He heard Velcro tearing and then the hood came away. Even in the darkness lit only by weak moonlight from the window, Zach saw long, glossy dark hair fall over narrow shoulders. He wasn't really surprised to be confronted by a woman when he caught a hank of hair. He'd sensed her gender the second their bodies touched.

Yelping, she came to a stop, not resisting when he tugged on her hair, forcing her to face him. With his other hand, he snapped on the light switch.

Hana blinked at the sudden wash of light and for a second, the tall, muscular figure towering over her was a blur. She quit tugging, trying to get away, hoping the grip on her hair would loosen, but instead the man facing her wrapped his hand around her long hair and tugged her toward him.

"Who the hell are you and what do you want?" the man growled.

Hana was mute, staring up. She knew who this was: the reluctant scion of the family, Zachary William Barrett Travis the gazillionth or whatever it was. She'd seen his picture in her research. He'd upset his entire family by wandering all over the world, then joining the Army Rangers for eight years, then wandering again. He'd refused to take up his family responsibilities, reportedly to the extreme frustration of his father, who, according to the maid who'd given her firsthand knowledge of the family, wanted Zach to join the Texas Rangers.

She'd made a mental note of how handsome he was the first time she Googled his image, but a static photo couldn't do his vitality justice. His hair was tousled from the nightmare she'd seen him thrashing in as she slipped past his bed. His chiseled features, with that perfect cleft chin that held true generation through generation in the Travis family, reminded her a bit of Brad Pitt in the movie *Troy*, one of her favorites with its warrior ethos and battles to the death... Hana kept her black gaze steady on his upper half, but in her peripheral vision she noted one of his snaps had slipped open.

"Start talking or I'm calling the police." He pulled her a bit closer as his gaze scanned the study, looking for open cases or signs of theft, she knew.

What should she do now? If she were discovered and sent to prison, Kai would have supreme authority over the most important person in the world to her. She had to avoid that at all costs. Hana's heart galloped, but she kept her expression calm even when the man began running his free hand over her, as if to frisk her. But he paused where he shouldn't; she was used to that, but it still pissed her off. She was close enough that if she'd leaned forward she could have nuzzled the light spattering of blondish-brown chest hair that matched the thick, unruly locks shining even in the dim study light. The hairs on the back of her neck and her arms stood up.

She'd never been much attracted to blonds, but she'd never been in such close quarters with a half-naked one before. Instinct told her to wait, to let him think he had the upper hand—quite literally, because this time his hand stroked up her side dangerously near her breast. When she stayed silent, he pulled her even closer, until she could feel every sinewy inch of his fit body. Given the way he touched her, she'd already picked up on the fact that the reluctant, instant attraction she felt was mutual. She stayed docile, silent, waiting.

She expected it, and when he finally released her hair to reach around her to shackle her wrists, she used his slack grip against him. Supple as an eel, she slithered sideways, using her hips and all her body weight, Tae Kwon Do–like, against him, to pull him slightly off balance. He was tall and solid, but when she kicked him in the shin as she moved, his loose grip broke and she twisted free.

He stumbled, recovering quickly, but it was enough to allow her to reach the hallway. This time he tackled her, catching her about the hips to force her to her knees. The marble smacked into her patellas, but she had no time for pain. As she fell, she caught her weight on her hands and bowed her back, using the leverage it gave her to straighten, smarting knees spread for stability, and smack her head backward. She had a very good idea that he was bent over her, that arrogant cleft chin offering a nice bull's-eye. Sure enough, she felt the point of his chin and then his own gratifying grunt as she caught him obviously off guard. She scrambled to her feet.

When he recovered enough to grab again, he reached for air. She'd gained the front door. However, she was slowed as she had to unlatch two very solid locks. She was reaching for the knob when he whacked her hand away and trapped her, both hands flat against the door framing her head.

A smile lifted those arrogant lips, allowing her to see the rim of his perfect white teeth. "What now?"

She was pretty sure now he wouldn't call the police since he'd searched her and visually scoped out the study, so he knew she hadn't stolen anything. But she had a feeling his father would make a more critical audience, so she had to finagle her way out of here and she had to do it quietly.

"I didn't take anything. Let me go," she finally said.

"Oh, so you can talk. Why did you break into my house?"

"Your house? Your father would probably have something to say about that—Zachary." His blue eyes, the exact deep turquoise color of the Aegean Sea she'd sailed once with Kai, narrowed. "Who the hell are you?"

"No one." She fingered behind her with her hand again, feeling for the knob.

"We'll let the police decide that." Snatching her hand away from the knob, he caught her wrist to pull her back toward the study.

So much for her reading of his character.

She acted on instinct. His towel shower wrap had lost another snap in their struggle. If she hadn't been so desperate to get away she would have enjoyed the sight of so much unfettered male power. His years in the Army Rangers had sculpted him into pinup status, except there was nothing airbrushed or fake about his six-pack abs and pure symmetry, broad shoulders angling down into his lean waist. He was primal, powerful, and a fitting adversary; the tingling at her nape and other inconvenient places might have intrigued her at a less critical moment.

She hadn't felt this inconvenient sensation in a long time. Since Kai, really, but then she'd been a foolish child. No longer... As it was, she pretended to let herself be pulled behind him back toward the gaping study door. But they'd only moved a few steps when she caught her fingers in the waist of his sagging wrap and jerked. The wrap fell to the floor.

He stopped cold, making an indistinct sound that sounded like a garbled "fuck me." His buttocks were as solid, though nicely round, and not quite as muscular, as the rest of him. He looked back over his shoulder, and she saw his high cheekbones were red. She knew his dilemma. If he turned she'd see all of him in full-frontal glory. She watched him weigh modesty and duty.

For the first time that night, she smiled.

While he debated, she tugged her wrist, and finally was free. She couldn't help it; she slapped his buttocks with her gloved hand on her way to the door, delighted with the meaty echo against all the fancy marble and woodwork.

Her own smile showed perfect white teeth as she flung open the door. "Next time, I'll bring a twenty!" The alarm sounded as she spoke, but she saw the shocked look in the blue eye she could see, and she realized few women ever challenged a man so bounteously gifted with money, power, and sex appeal. She was still smiling when she made it halfway over the wall by the time he reached the porch, his hips sheathed in the towel again.

On top of the wall, she looked back at him. He'd never reach her now and they both knew it. Somehow, they also both knew they'd meet again. He was lit by the motion-activated porch light and she was shocked to see a half smile about his lips. He blew her a kiss that promised retribution and a continuation of the strange competition that had begun this night.

Hoping he could see her in the darkness, she blew a kiss right back. She saw him wave something black like a battle flag.

Then she'd dropped to the ground and was sprinting toward the nondescript car she'd parked several streets away. As she sedately drove off, she looked down the street at the Travis mansion. She heard the alarm cease, saw more lights come on, and knew he must be explaining to his parents what had happened. She'd thankfully reached the freeway entrance ramp by the time she heard distant sirens.

Back to square one ... her gloved hands tightened on the wheel as she pictured going to Kai with empty hands. Only then did she realize her hood was gone. Zachary had ripped it off and she'd not had time to retrieve it. A chill ran up her spine: hair samples. She should have worn a stocking cap over her hair, dammit ... they were almost certain to have at least one of her hairs to test for DNA.

And she was on file because of her priors.

An hour later, across town overlooking the Loop 360 bridge in the Buckhorn Estates, several athletic black shapes, garbed like Hana, slipped inside a large mansion. They'd deactivated the alarm with the tools in the small backpack one of them had strapped to his back. One held an iPad and the other two looked over his shoulder at the display, which showed the plan of the mansion. Two of them slipped up the long, curving staircase, pulling the swords they carried on their backs, while the third one stayed downstairs, scanning every window and door he could see from the central corridor. Standing guard. Just in case.

As the other two disappeared above, he looked at the black Hublot watch on his wrist, activating the timer. *"Ichi seichi,"* he said under his breath, Japanese for "one minute." A few seconds later, a woman's scream was choked off. A man's guttural grunt came next, full of both pain and outrage, followed by a few sounds of fists landing. A second choked scream, male this time. Then silence.

The waiting man checked his watch again, snapping off the timer at exactly 58 seconds when the swordsmen came back down the stairs, their soft shoes eerily silent, as if they were wraiths ... or demons. One sword still gleamed sticky red and the swordsman, with an adroit movement of his wrist, flicked off the blood, leaving a spatter stain on the wall.

The waiting man didn't chastise him; instead he looked at the stain and nodded approvingly. As the three gathered together again in the spacious front hall, the man with the expensive watch pulled a hood from his zippered pocket. It was exactly like the one Hana had worn. He dropped it in a crumpled heap in a corner. Then all three of them walked out the front door.

The next day, Hana was still shaken from her close escape as she parked at the sprawling hospital complex. She hurried up the stairs, the local paper folded under her arm. Since he'd been here, she'd tried to read to her grandfather Jiji every day, and she was glad she had the paper. This time she'd read all the local news buried in the third section she usually ignored. She was glad that, so far at least, her intrusion hadn't been noted in the papers. Then again, she imagined even enterprising reporters would keep her raid quiet, given John Travis was so respected in the state. It wouldn't do for the public to learn the second-in-command of the Texas Rangers was susceptible to home invaders at his own residence. She'd counted on that inconvenient reality. So far she'd been right, but it was early yet.

She went up to the third floor, hating the smells and sounds of people dying all around her. She knocked cursorily on her grandfather's door, but he had an equally sick older man sharing his room, so it was a needed courtesy. The other bed was empty. When she moved aside the curtain around her grandfather's bed, she was shocked at his gray pallor. This place seemed to leech the life out of him by the day. She wished she could take him out of here to die in peace at his own nice little home in Hyde Park—a bungalow, really—with the huge Japanese garden in the back, complete with a koi pond and raked sand garden that her grandfather changed with his moods.

But the little house was lost to her too. Like her mother, like her father, like... Knowing she couldn't let her grandfather see her cry, she bit back tears and took Jiji's hand. So papery, the skin, and even though she cradled it between both of her warm hands, he didn't stir. She saw his thin chest rising and falling and noticed all the instruments that monitored his vitals appeared to be functioning. Still, this pile of bones and covers in the bed was little reminiscent of the man who'd shaped her into who she was. He'd saved her from her own foolishness more times than she could count. Despair almost overcame her, but she smoothed her expression and sat next to his bed, unfolding the paper.

The print swam before her eyes, coalescing into an accusatory finger. Jiji had given her everything and she couldn't give him the one solace he'd asked for before he died. She'd failed him. Again. For the moment, all she had to offer was the love brimming over in her heart; all she had to say were words strangely comforting in their banality. One hour led into the next as she read the paper to him; the ritual, even though he was asleep and didn't hear her, slightly soothing her own anxiety.

But even as she read, other thoughts tormented her. Who did she go to now to try to track down the sword? Would Kai give her another chance? Would the Travis family be angry enough at her intrusion to demand DNA testing? Would she see Zachary Travis again?

Most of the questions had no answer, but one certainty stood out: The strange attraction she'd felt toward Zachary Travis was a distant memory now, as it should be. It could quite literally get her killed. It was best—for both of them—that their paths didn't cross again. The sun was lowering in the sky, and still she sat there, reading the comics now. Her grandfather never stirred, though his breathing was peaceful. He seemed genuinely asleep. But she'd seen his pain when he was awake, so she was careful not to disturb him. As she turned the paper to the last page, she saw she'd come to the obituaries. She swallowed down acid and crumpled the paper into a ball, tossing it into the garbage can against the wall. She closed her eyes. Like these lost souls, soon enough he'd be but an image, a life that defied description synopsized to a few lines of terse text. His only future now lay in these pages.

The tears were too strong this time, even for her iron will. She rested her forehead gently on the side of the bed and wept, holding his frail hand. She felt caught between two nightmarish realities: fear that Grandfather would die—and fear that he wouldn't.

Chapter 2

That same morning, Zach came downstairs fully dressed in his leather chaps, boots, and jacket. It was still early, and even though it was a Saturday, he knew his parents would both be on the terrace eating the elaborate breakfast Consuela prepared come hail or drought, peace or war, famine or plenty. Zach winked at his favorite senora, ignoring his father's glare at his attire. Consuela, who had helped raise him and taught him fluent Spanish, winked back.

He kissed his mother's unlined cheek, wondering yet again how she managed to stay so young looking; blond hair blended gracefully with gray, a bit stout around the middle, perhaps, after two kids, but still lovely at sixty. She tilted her half reading glasses up to gauge his expression. The glasses fell back down her nose again as she glanced nervously at her husband. Gently shoving the glasses back up for her, Zach gave her shoulder a reassuring squeeze as he sat down.

"*Buenos dias*, Consuela. Mother, Dad . . . sorry for the ruckus last night." Zach tossed his jacket off over the back of his chair in the morning sunlight. It was spring in Texas, but today the temperamental weather was sunny and Zach had dressed accordingly, for a long ride on his Harley. He needed to blow the cobwebs out of his brain. In retrospect, last night had been fun, and it had also helped relieve his restlessness. He couldn't keep hovering, half in the family bastion, half out. It wasn't fair to his father. So he'd come downstairs resolved to inform them of his decision on whether to begin the lengthy process of applying to the Rangers or not.

Not. . . . At first. Zach ate his hearty breakfast of eggs, biscuits, bacon, sausage, and fresh orange juice silently, ignoring his father's seething glare. In reality, despite what people thought, and despite his stellar military career, Zach knew that even if he applied, he'd have to wait to see whether he was accepted. His father would take it as a point of pride not to grease the wheels.

His movements speaking volumes to Zach, who knew all his father's mannerisms, John Travis carefully folded his morning paper and stuck it under the orange juice pitcher so it wouldn't blow away. "You never explained to my satisfaction why your almost perfect memory failed you last night when you tried to describe the intruder to the police." The elder Travis quoted from memory: "'Height: average, or maybe tall. Hair: dark, don't recall if it was black or brown. Kinda nondescript, don't know the length. Eye color? Her eyes were shielded by the hood.'"

John glared at his eldest child. "Care to try again?"

"It was dark most of the time, Dad. Besides, since she didn't take anything, surely there are plenty more compelling cases that require time-consuming police investigation than an abortive break-in—no damage, no theft, by some young thing on a lark. Probably a sorority initiation." He took a hasty sip of coffee to wash down the lie. He knew exactly what the girl looked like and felt he could have sculpted that tall, willowy body with his eyes closed. But she'd studied martial arts too, and she was good, very good. She had to be to so easily squirm away from someone twice her weight. There had never once been any panic in her mannerisms even when he caught both her wrists to pull her toward the phone.

That meant she was disciplined.

Which meant she had a very specific reason for climbing through that open window. He also, after some thought, had a suspicion of what she'd been after.

He was pretty sure she'd been in the study awhile by the time he caught her, but she'd only scoped out the place, not snatched anything of value. She'd acted like a woman on a mission, in other words. While he was curious as to what that might be, he wasn't quite sure why he felt the urge to protect her, other than the obvious testosterone boost. But he knew he had to get his father to drop this. Since nothing had been stolen, the case would move to the bottom of the police files if the family didn't pursue it, and for a reason he couldn't define, that's the way Zach wanted it.

When John opened his mouth again, Zach used his reserve ammunition. "Besides, if we proceed with prosecution and they assign it to detectives for a full-blown investigation, won't that look pretty bad downtown? That our own security is so full of holes?"

Zach's mom, Mary, lost her glasses this time, so quickly did she turn back to her husband, as if she dreaded his reaction. They plopped into her plate right on her sunny-side up egg, which was soft enough to squirt yolk onto her husband's crisp white shirt sleeve as he smacked down his coffee cup.

Quelling a grin at his father's rare muffled curse, Zach retrieved his mother's glasses and dipped his cloth napkin into his untouched ice water, polished them thoroughly, and handed them back to her. With a soft "sorry" to John, she put them back on and shoved her plate out of range. John was using his own napkin to rub at the stain on his sleeve.

During this familiar ritual—for his mother could be a klutz when she tried to mediate between her son and husband—Zach stuffed the last of his biscuit into his mouth to give himself time. Damn, this was hard, and his dad was already in a foul mood. Maybe he should wait to tell him he'd decided to accept his friend Jeff's offer to join him on a Gulf oil rig for a few months. Roughnecking would provide the physical activity he needed. He was getting soft in Austin. And while enrolling in the Texas Rangers would include some physical training, it wasn't enough and it came with too many rules. He'd had enough of that after eight years in the military; he wasn't ready to devote the rest of his life to a position of such gravity and responsibility, especially given his last name. No one would admit it, but he'd be held to a higher standard. He had no yen to live in a gigantic petri dish.

Finally satisfied he'd dabbed away all the stain that he could, John gave his wife a reassuring kiss. She caught the back of his head to deepen the kiss and for a long moment, heat at the dining-room table came from more than the bright sunshine.

Zach looked away, feeling like an intruder, but he'd seen many times the passion his parents shared. He also knew there was much more to Mary than anyone realized. In a strange way, the Japanese girl had reminded him of his mother. Just thinking about the would-be thief gave him a semi–hard-on. Society girls bored him to tears.

Breathing slightly faster, John pulled away, giving her a last, brief *later* kiss. He cleared his throat, but his soft expression hardened as he looked back at his son. "Well, it happens your memory lapse isn't pertinent, because I pulled the security footage from last night. There are several great shots of a tall young woman garbed head to toe in black. Her face was hooded, as you said, but since her hood came off I assume you saw her when the two of you tussled in the hallway. At first the angle was wrong to pick up on her features—until she reached the door." John hit *play* with the remote next to his plate. The small flat-screen TV on an adjacent table flickered to life.

Zach couldn't help it: He felt his cheekbones go warm when the girl jerked his towel wrap away. Even his stern father's mouth quivered a bit at Zach's on-screen automatic reaction of covering his genitals, all captured beautifully by the security camera. His mouth flickered into a grin when the girl slapped Zach on the buttocks, but Mary frowned in sympathy with her son's obvious embarrassment.

John's blue eyes, the exact azure shade of Zach's, sparkled for an instant as he goaded, "Want me to erase this part?"

"Yes, especially if you plan to show it to anyone," Zach growled.

"Might be a bit tricky to edit," John said smoothly. "I could take it to the lab—"

"No!"

John relented when Zach moved to eject the DVD. He waved him back down. "Never mind . . . I guess we can let it slide for now. But if she tries again. . . ."

Zach was a bit worried about that too. The long, straight dark hair, her exotic black eyes—she was at least part Japanese. And he'd been stationed in Japan for one tour, even spoke a smattering of Japanese. Their culture was very foreign to Americans, but one attribute was clear: the most valued family heirloom in Japan was weaponry. Specifically swords. Especially samurai swords.

John nodded at his expression. "Yes, I think there's a very good chance she was after the Masamune katana. Good thing we had it sent out for verification."

Zach had been with his father when he flew to New York City to purchase the famous blade. It had recently come up for auction at Christie's, part of the collection of a billionaire recluse obsessed with World War II arms. It was rumored that he got the blade from a renegade Marine guard at a Japanese internment camp set up during World War II in California. It was one of many blades confiscated when the Japanese were imprisoned during the height of war hysteria.

They were supposed to be smelted, but even then Masamune blades were legendary.

It was commonly known now that some of the finest blades were kept by American servicemen while their superiors looked the other way. However it came into American hands, Christie's listed the blade's provenance as *in the style of Masamune, early 1300s, perhaps by one of his students*, but would not stake its reputation on full authentication. Nevertheless, the mere possibility it was a Masamune, who was perhaps the finest swordsmith the world had ever known, drove the auction price well over a million. The blade was not just a sword; it was a work of art. Even a Travis heir to oil and gas prudently formed an LLC with several other oilmen to buy it.

They were all collectors, and the idea was to endow a wing at the Harry Ransom Center at the University of Texas with war memorabilia going back as far as they had items to donate. The sword they believed had been forged by Masamune in the early 1300s would be the key display and the earliest artifact. But first they had to prove he'd forged it. Masamune had a unique style of firing the steel, then folding and cooling it, firing and cooling to make many different tempered layers, the steel composition changing between the tip of the blade, along the length of it, to the haft, all varying compositions to accommodate the warrior's moving battle stance from thrust to parry to blow. The blade would bend, but not break. However, it was also well known that Masamune usually didn't sign his blades, so proving this undoubtedly ancient and rare sword one of his was a challenge in itself.

Zach asked, "When will they be finished with it?"

"You know the Japanese. They will not be rushed. Even on American soil." A Japanese-born samurai weaponry expert at a California Asian museum had agreed to try to track the blade's origin for the LLC, but only at a princely sum and with no time deadline, John explained to his son. "He's had it now over six months. Our lawyer told us the expert's billed for the final payment, so I'm hopeful he'll get it back to us soon."

Zach said grimly, "So if she is after the blade, she's risking herself for nothing."

John smiled, his teeth wolfish in the bright sunlight. "Yep."

While Zach was trying to keep his father from making her his latest investigation, Hana was vetting all her contacts again to try to figure out why the sword had not been in the study after all. Finally, the maid admitted under close questioning that she'd been fired for pilfering and the information she'd given Hana was more than six months old.

Hana gave her that dead-black stare Kai had taught her many years ago when she'd been a wild, homeless teenager recruited by him as a drug mule. No condemnation, no promises of retribution, just intellect and assessment, much as a forensic scientist would appraise his subject at an autopsy, one dissected organ at a time.

The maid backed a step. "I'm s—sorry, *madre de Dios*, I'll pay you back, I promise, I needed the money for my *niños*—"

"Get out," Hana said flatly.

The maid got.

After the maid left her day hotel, Hana paced the small open space, up and down, until she could see her own tracks in the thin carpet. No matter if she paced a million miles, she'd end at the same destination: She was at a dead end in seeking the sword without more inside information. She stopped at the window overlooking a dumpster and an uneven parking lot badly in need of new asphalt. But she didn't see the ugly scene. Her visions were far more horrific. How long had it been now? Hana put her hands flat against the grungy glass. It became literally a dirty window into her past as the memories she seldom allowed subsumed her.

For a weak instant, the strength of her mind was helpless against a rush of emotions. She pretended she could feel those warm little hands pressing back in the patty-cake she'd taught him. She didn't need to look at her watch or her phone to know the date. He'd been missing for exactly three months and five hours because it was ten a.m. on a Saturday three months ago. Kai had snatched him from day care while she worked an extra shift as a waitress at a popular breakfast spot in south Austin because she needed the money to help save her grandfather's house from foreclosure.

Another useless exercise.... Resting her head against the grimy windowpane, Hana asked herself yet again how she had ever been stupid enough, even at a rebellious, impressionable seventeen, to get involved with Kai?

Her practical, stable father had just died in a car wreck, and her Japanese mother, a high-strung traditionalist, was trying to groom her only child for marriage into the small Japanese community then in Austin. Hana's dream of winning the world women's karate championships was just that, a foolish dream. Years later, she could recite her mother's nostrums now almost verbatim: How could such a strange ambition for a respectable female prepare her for a prosperous future? Even karate masters who opened their own dojos usually went broke in a few years. Since she had no interest in business or engineering or medicine, what else was she to do but marry well?

Then, after Hana got involved with Kai and even became an illegal drug courier, Hana's aggrieved mother took her scanty life-insurance proceeds with her back to Japan, leaving seventeen-year-old Hana with her grandfather. Hana had refused to admit—then at least—how much she missed her mother, even when she was relieved of her nagging about character and appearance. Jiji never nagged her; he only loved. And it was his sole, loving support that drew Hana back to the straight and narrow after she was arrested for intent to deliver illegal substances. The fact that she'd been pregnant at the time had no doubt contributed to the judge's decision to be lenient, especially since it was her first offense and she was barely seventeen. But he'd forced her into hours of community service and rehab even though she'd never used any of the drugs she carried, including marijuana. Not because she had any moral scruples—but because they affected her karate abilities... and because she knew the use would harm her unborn child.

Hana kept her condition secret as long as she could. She'd broken all ties with Kai while she sat in jail awaiting her hearing where he'd left her to rot instead of paying her bail.

The windowpane grew tangible again as a much wiser Hana now quashed the unhappy memories. They only made her feel lost and alone and hopeless, especially now that Jiji was dying. She washed her face at the sink, drying herself off thoroughly and methodically. Very well, then. If the sword was not where it was supposed to be, it was only logical to make a list of possibilities of where it could be. And in that case, it was best to start with where the Travis family acquired the weapon.

Hana opened her browser and went straight to Google, reminding herself of one of the most important guiding principles of Shotokan karate: *The art of mind is more important than the art of technique.*

As he approached the bed-and-breakfast stuck into the hills outside Austin, Zach slowed down. From here, the quaint Victorian looked like a country-girl wallflower at a debutante ball, surrounded by sleek, modern mansions. Leave it to Ross and Emm to pick the nicest boutique hotel in town to stay in. Zach didn't much care for modern monstrosities like the JW Marriott, either. He parked his bike under a tree and kicked down the stand, leaving his helmet locked in a special tie-down attached to his tiny rear saddlebags.

As he approached the antique glass door up several flights of steps, Zach knew his father would not be happy with him if he knew whom he was visiting, but his father was never happy with him these days, full stop. Zach had three weeks before he was supposed to join his army buddy Jeff on the coast. He had the contract in a drawer in his room and while he hadn't signed it yet, he intended to.

But first he had a mission to accomplish, the first mission he'd felt obligated to complete since his last tour in Afghanistan. He couldn't explain it, but he'd felt in that slim, athletic girl a kindred spirit. He'd felt her ambivalence and desperation. As if her mission were onerous. As if she didn't want to invade their home, more as if she *had* to—which was why he'd advocated she not be pursued. Before he could work himself to exhaustion, he had to find her and ask her point-blank why she needed the sword. And if there was anything he could do short of giving it up—because it wasn't his to give—how could he help?

Zach told the desk clerk, a matronly woman with an apron and streak of flour on her cheek, that he was there to see the Sinclairs. She picked up a desk phone. The bed-and-breakfast was so tiny he could hear a phone ringing at the top of the stairs. The next thing he knew, Ross was halfway down the wide staircase. At the bottom, they shook hands. After the pleasantries, in which Ross explained Emm was too busy renovating the second historic building they owned in downtown Amarillo to tag along on his business trip, they got down to brass tacks, the way both liked it.

Wordlessly, Zach handed over a tiny Ziploc evidence bag. Inside was one long, black hair. Ross held it up to the light and set it on the small table between them with no comment other than a long, appraising look at the young man he'd known since his diaper days.

Zach hurried into speech. "Look, I know I'm putting you in a difficult position, but this is not official Texas Ranger business, Ross. This is me looking for a girl who's in trouble before she gets herself in even more trouble. Dad agreed not to pursue the case this morning as long as she doesn't try again. So he wasn't going to do anything with this sample, anyway."

"Does he know you brought it to me?"

Zach shook his head.

Ross sighed heavily. "He's my boss, Zach. Why don't you give this to your dad instead of me? Then it's officially in the chain of evidence if it ever becomes pertinent."

"You know what a huge backlog there is at the state labs. Even if we pursue the case, it will be low priority. Why add to the workload? Nothing stolen, no one hurt."

Ross's mouth curled into a smile and Zach knew his dad must have spilled the beans about his towel incident, so he admitted, "Except maybe my pride. But this girl is in trouble, and I want to help her. It's that simple."

"Doesn't sound simple to me. It sounds quite complicated. You've never been the kind of guy to tilt at windmills. If you were, you'd have joined the Rangers years ago."

Zach ignored that remark and barreled on: "I put out some feelers, but I don't trust most of the private labs. And they don't have the latest databases to cross-reference, anyway. This needs a pro to handle it." Zach took a deep breath. "I haven't told Mom and Dad yet, but I'm due on an oil rig off the Gulf in three weeks so I have limited time to get the results."

Ross picked up the sample and held it to the light, eyeing the long black hair that even behind the thin plastic glowed with blue-black health in the sunshine coming through the casement windows. "If I do this, your father will not be happy with me."

"I know. But strictly speaking, this is personal. Dad knows how persuasive I can be."

Ross's lips quirked wider this time. "Yes, so Yancy is always telling me. She likes you. So does Emm, though your lukewarm reaction to her matchmaking has put her off a bit."

"I like them too."

To Zach's relief, Ross finally put the baggie inside his jacket pocket. "I'll talk to a consulting forensic scientist I know. She's the best. But she's not cheap."

Zach pulled out his checkbook, but Ross waved him away.

"I don't know what she'll charge, but she'll bill you when she gives you the results. She's based in Austin, so that part is easy, anyway. Her name is Abigail Doyle."

Zach whistled. "I've heard Dad speak of her, and how the conviction rates in district C skyrocketed after y'all engaged her services. Wasn't she involved in that business down in Mexico with you and Emm?"

"Yes. I trust her implicitly." Ross glanced at his watch and stood. "I have to get ready for a dinner party tonight. I hate this political BS, but your dad wanted me here to talk to the legislature reps, so I came. We're asking for an increase in funding for the Ranger Reconnaissance Team. With these new Asian gangs muscling in on the drug trade all over central Texas, we need the additional funds. Most of our resources have been deployed near the border."

Zach nodded. "Yeah, I heard that. Hope you get it."

When they reached the lobby, Ross shook Zach's hand. "I only have one request—two, actually."

"Name them."

"Please tell your dad you asked me to do this. That I agreed only because the case is no longer official business. I don't need him any more pissed at me than he usually is over my 'confounded propensity for not keeping him in the loop,'" Ross quoted.

Zach grimaced but nodded.

"And secondly, give some serious second thoughts to whether to take the oil rig job or apply with the Rangers. You're perfect Ranger material, whether you realize it or not—"

Zach was shaking his head before Ross even finished. "I don't know why y'all keep saying that. I'm not going to be the butt of every daddy joke on the Internet, and I'm sick of having to toe the line on rules I didn't write. Plus I'm getting soft staying in Austin—"

"We have a new position opening up at the state level. It's security for state officials, including DPS execs and director-level Texas Rangers. Your special forces background makes you perfect for the job."

Zach frowned. "Why didn't Dad tell me about it?"

"Because he wants you to make your own right choices."

"Yeah, his."

Ross sighed at the bitterness in Zach's tone. He'd opened his mouth to retort when his cell phone rang with an "Eyes of Texas" ring tone. "Sorry, official business." He pulled two phones out of his pocket and put the iPhone back, holding the BlackBerry to his ear. He moved aside and Zach went over to a display rack of gaudy tourist brochures to give him privacy.

The call was short, but when Zach turned back toward Ross, he saw that Ross was pale beneath his tan, almost ashen. "What's wrong?"

Ross replied, "That was dispatch. The cocktail party is on hold but I'm called into a meeting at headquarters. Sam Taylor and his wife were found dead in their beds this morning by their maid. Not ten miles from here. They were... eviscerated. By the looks of the cuts, the examiner thinks it might have been done with a samurai sword."

Chapter 3

Zach was shocked. He'd been to that lovely home in Buckhorn Estates more than once and he liked Sam Taylor, who was a director-level Ranger, reporting to John Travis. "In his bed? How can that be? Theft?"

"It doesn't look like anything was taken. It looked like a hit. With extreme prejudice. We don't know many details yet, except they're pretty sure the weapon was a sword. A very sharp sword. It's almost like... the Taylors were—that is, the coroner thinks..." Ross took a deep breath and finished rapidly, "The coroner thinks the Taylors were used as target practice, but he's still verifying."

Zach went totally still as Ross added grimly, "The stab marks showed a pattern in multiple strikes on both bodies of a long, thin blade with one sharp side—like a katana."

"Oh my God..." Zach was so stunned his stomach roiled. He groped for a lobby chair to sit down.

Ross handed over the hair sample. "I can't help you with this now. You have to take it through official channels. How many experts with samurai swords can there be in Austin?"

Zach swallowed back his gall. Their eyes locked, but neither voiced the same conclusions they'd reluctantly drawn—was John Travis next? And was the mysterious female intruder involved?

Two days later, Hana hung up the phone, excited that she was, after many hours of digging, close to tracking down the blade. She knew the date when the katana had changed ownership at Christie's auction house because the announcement of the offering was still on the internet. The maid had also told her that the sword was in a joint-ownership interest, the paperwork for which she'd come across one time while dusting the study desk. That had led Hana to the Texas Secretary of State web site and a search for John Travis as a managing member of an LLC formed around the time of the auction. She hit on the tenth try.

The name they'd chosen for the LLC was hardly surprising or original: Masamune Limited Liability Company. The formation papers listed the attorney of record. Hana found his Austin office easy to break into, and there, neatly in the file, was a budget with a recent disbursement to a well-known samurai sword expert in California marked *final payment*.

Gloved the entire time, Hana put everything back as she found it, right down to arranging the paperweight in the exact spot, and ducked out the second-floor window she'd used to enter, closing it securely.

Back at her hotel, she put the facts together coolly, logically, with no emotion, considering all her options.

Hana knew why they'd hired this particular Japanese-American samurai expert. They were trying to prove provenance. Good luck with that, Hana thought grimly. The blade had been passed from generation to generation in the Nakatomi family for untold centuries, but only word of mouth proved it was a gift from Masamune to the samurai who supposedly saved the sword maker's life back in the mists of early Japan. Even the Nakatomi family had no actual documentation.

However, if final payment had been rendered to the historical expert, the sword was surely on its journey back to the military men who'd stolen it. The only question was: Where would they store it? Given her abortive break-in, if the Travises had figured out her target—and she did not underestimate their intelligence—they'd probably secret the sword in a vault somewhere.

Wonderful. Hana had been trained in bypassing sophisticated surveillance systems, but she had no skill at safecracking. She knew someone who did, though . . . but she'd not spoken to him in months and their last parting had not been cordial. Hana had also seen a bill in the attorney's files on the LLC that paid a private, secure transport agency to ferry the blade to California. It was logical they'd use the same service to bring it home. She'd snapped pics of the entire file in case she needed them for later perusal. She called them up on her phone now and stopped on the bill from the private security firm.

She knew the address of the transport company. It was in a row of warehouses along Dessau Road, and while they probably had very secure cages, perhaps even safes, they had to be easier to circumvent than a bank vault. Now she only needed the date of arrival. Hana set down her cell phone and used the old-fashioned hotel landline to call another old acquaintance, one of Kai's allies on the West Coast distribution line for his drug smuggling. If the Travises were seeking her, it would be easy for them to trace her cell phone, so she had to carefully think through every step.

She made a mental note to buy a burner phone with cash later today. The hotel landline could also be traced, but Hana had paid cash for her lodging and not signed any registry. She was listening to the first ring on the other end when the noon news came on the television. She'd turned the volume down low, but when a brief image of a samurai katana flashed on the screen, she slammed down the phone and jacked up the volume.

"Sources say a similar sword was used in what police are describing only as an execution-style killing of central Texas Ranger chief Sam Taylor and his wife. Evidence was recovered at the scene, and state and federal agencies are working the case. Meanwhile, security among DPS and Texas Ranger ranks has been tightened, though details are sparse at this point. In other news..."

Hana turned the volume back down, fear congealing like slush in her veins. Dear God, had Kai done this? Did he really hate her that much, to do this to deliberately implicate her? Or was this related to his grand plan to take over the entire drug trade in central Texas?

Zach sat on his bed, still wearing his chaps and biker boots from his drive on the winding-hill country roads. It would probably be his last for some time. He'd taken it to clear his mind and be sure he was doing the right thing.

He held the contract for the roughnecking job in his hands, turning it this way and that. Since high school, when the prom queen and most of her court had pursued him, he'd known that sure, his looks and intelligence were part of the reason for their attraction, but mostly they wanted his legendary name tacked onto theirs. And the growing family wealth didn't hurt any, either. So he'd proved himself in the best and only way: by joining one of the most elite and toughest military training programs in the world. He could be George

Washington reincarnated and his drill sergeant would still grind his face into the mud if he didn't finish his reps on time.

The stint on the rig would have given him the anonymity and freedom he craved to make his own mistakes. But he'd listened to the news reports about the slaying, and he didn't need crime-scene photos to picture what the bodies looked like. Petrie dish or not, he had to officially apply for the new security position the DPS had created to protect its upper ranks. No matter how complex and sometimes adversarial his relationship with his father, he still loved him and would lose his own life before he'd let him be eviscerated like his former colleague and his wife.

Methodically, Zach tore the contract into fourths and tossed it into the trash. Then he pulled out his cell phone to call his buddy. As he did so, he thought again in the back of his mind of the tall, slim Japanese girl who seemed to know just about every self-defense move he'd been taught. He couldn't quite believe her capable of such a horrific crime, but evidence against her was piling up. He had a sinking feeling in the pit of his stomach that he would, indeed, come across her again. . . .in the line of duty.

A few miles outside the Austin city limits, Hana pulled up before a strange structure, turning off her car but sitting there for a second to weigh her approach. After hearing the brief news report, she'd dialed her West Coast contact again. She'd coaxed and flattered him into agreeing to use his sources to hack into the secure transport-delivery database, so now she had an arrival date when the sword was due back at the warehouse. The man had warned her he'd tell Kai about her inquiry, but she didn't care about that. Kai not only approved of her quest; he was blackmailing her to do whatever it took to get the sword, including risk her life.

Still striving for that elusive calmness of mind that karate espoused, Hana appraised the pile of cantilevered shipping containers stacked on top of one another like giant Legos. Ernie Thibodeaux was one of the oddest men she'd ever met, but also one of the most talented. She saw that he'd added to his domain in the months since she'd been here. He was a closet architect, an art historian with a PhD, a gourmet chef, a martial-arts expert with a grandmaster red belt in judo and the corresponding black belt, highest-level tenth

Dan, in Shotokan karate. He was also a wiz at playing the stock market, his current primary source of income. And he was a man who loved skirting rules, including the law, which he considered an imposition on the god-given liberties he'd enjoyed in the swamps of Louisiana, where boys were self-sufficient—or dead.

When she'd been friends with him before her break with her mother, she'd often tried to find a blind-date candidate for him. She'd never come across anyone else with his diverse skill set, range of interests, and flexible morals. His on-again, off-again relationship with her mother had dissolved precisely because he skirted the law with impunity, but so far his check kiting and securities fraud hadn't landed him in jail. However, the authorities didn't know he was also an expert safecracker, a legacy of his days as a ragin' Cajun with New Orleans mob ties.

If she was right about his character, Hana suspected he'd kept up his skills with the increasingly sophisticated digital safes most secure institutions now used. At least, she hoped so.

Banging the incongruous brass lion-head door knocker she knew he'd pilfered from a vacant, crumbling British estate in Northumberland, she admired yet again his unusual front door. It was massive, stainless steel, but it still pivoted easily and quietly on divots when opened. He'd designed and built it himself. But when he wanted his privacy, she knew the giant bars on the other side of the door would require an arc welder to penetrate.

Looking up, she noted he'd also added to his elaborate security system. Tiny cameras blinked at her from all around the porch, and, she was sure, from the entire first floor of the complex structure. Ernie wasn't paranoid; he just liked nice things. Very nice things. Thus, she knew he'd appreciate her quest for an item of immense value and beauty. It wasn't really theft considering this most cherished of family heirlooms had been stolen from her grandfather when he was forced into a Japanese internment camp.

She was about to wield the knocker again when the door opened. In his stockinged feet, wearing his usual ensemble of cargo shorts and hippie tie-dyed T-shirt with a gaudy Hawaiian surfing overshirt of eighties vintage, he was still somehow imposing. His pulled back long, dirty-blond hair showed some gray, but aside from that and a few more laugh lines in his chiseled, tanned skin, he looked exactly the same.

"You look like hell," he delivered with his usual bluntness. He swung the door wide. It pivoted in place, all thousand-plus pounds perfectly balanced. "Come in and I'll fix you some peppermint tea."

Just like that, as if the last six months had never happened. He didn't even ask the obvious question of why she'd come. In his kitchen, which took up most of one of the storage containers and looked exactly like a kitchen from *Architectural Digest*—complete with quartz counters, stainless-steel Thermador appliances, and decorative tile in the backsplash and underfoot—he immediately turned on the rear burner to heat the bright copper kettle. He kept up a conversational flow that seemed banal, about politics and weather and the latest celebrity scandal, but she knew he was really giving her time to collect herself. Of all his sterling qualities, his ability to read another person's moods and motivations was most amazing, at least to her. She tended to react first and figure out later, whereas he could tailor his actions to the situation. He'd tried to teach her to read body language, not words, but she hadn't been a good pupil except when it came to reading opponents in the ring.

For the first time since she'd broken into the Travis estate, she began to relax. The old routine of sitting at his bar proved as comforting as the aroma of the tea he set before her. She sat on the plush, comfortable bar stool, swiveling from side to side as she had from about the age of ten, when he had become her black-belt karate coach. He made himself another cup and stood across from her, elbows on the quartz, chin in his hands, appraising her with pale gray eyes that missed nothing.

After she'd taken a few sips, he said, "Okay, spit it out."

She carefully set her cup back in the saucer, getting directly to the point. "I need your help. I have to break into a local warehouse to retrieve a family heirloom and I suspect it will mean some safecracking."

His expression didn't alter; in fact, she might have asked him to help her change a tire. "The Nakatomi blade."

She nodded, but no matter how she tried to contain herself, her eyes began to fill with tears as she added, "Jiji is dying. He's only asked for one thing. To hold our family legacy once more..."

"And then?"

"He doesn't want me to go to jail again, so he says I'm to give it back to the Travis family after he—after he..."

"But you don't want to give it back."

She took another deep sip, almost glad of her scalded tongue, for it made her croak a bit easier, "No, but I would have. Except for Kai."

She saw the tiny flare of alarm in his flickering eyes and flared nostrils, but he only looked down and picked up his cup to blow on his steaming tea. He was obviously waiting for more, letting her set the pace.

"Kai knows I'm trying to retrieve the blade. And he wants to do a swap. The blade for..." Her voice broke and she couldn't even get her son's name out.

This time, Ernie's usual adept movements were so clumsy his cup went sideways in his saucer and tipped over. He caught it but not before some of the tea spilled. He grabbed up a towel and dried the splash, taking several deep breaths. When the counter was clean, he looked at her with those incandescent quicksilver eyes, his dislike crystal clear. "The unregenerate piece of pond scum."

Hana stared over his head at the sparkling stainless-steel vent hood, but she was seeing in her memories something far less attractive. After Kai took her son, she'd demanded to see Takeo and Kai had acceded, but only when she agreed to be hooded and transported by his own men.

Her hood wasn't removed until she was inside his impregnable compound, a warren of tunnels and caves attached to, she was pretty sure, some type of sprawling mansion over the Edwards Aquifer. The water table was porous with limestone and easy to excavate. The elaborate tunnel system El Chapo had used to escape his Mexican prison had been his model. Kai was nothing if not thorough; the authorities would never catch him. From birth, he'd been tutored in two of the most arcane but disciplined credos on earth: Japanese perfection by practice in everything, and Yakuza tactics.

That night Kai had baited her, rejecting her pitiful offer of ten thousand dollars in ransom, all the money she had. He'd told her he knew she was after the Nakatomi katana to give to her grandfather before he died. He wanted it as soon as the old man passed. Just carrying the sword at his side would give him status among the three competing Asian gangs in central Texas. Even the Chinese with their roots in the Triad lusted for Masamune blades....

With little choice, Hana had agreed to the devil's bargain. Then he'd allowed his men to abuse her just short of rape. They were all products of the Yakuza, right down to their tattoos, but had also taken on the characteristics of the worst Latino gangs in their new American home.

Only when she was able to swallow her rage and hatred and pretend submission, did he allow her to see her son for a brief moment. Long enough to hug him and dry his tears and promise she'd come back for him as soon as she could.

Ernie hauled her back to the present. "Let it go. Quiet your mind. Hatred is not your friend."

Hana gulped down the last of her tea, savagely glad of her scalded lips and throat. The pain brought her back from her vision of using her family blade for its most exquisite purpose: to kill Nakatomi enemies. Kai prided himself falsely on his samurai heritage as a Japanese; she knew his lineage was full of fishermen, not samurai. Her own lineage could be traced to a major samurai clan all the way back to the 1200s. She'd often wondered if that was why he'd chosen her as his Pygmalion-like teen mistress so many years ago. How charming he'd been . . . at first.

Thankfully, Ernie interrupted her painful memories.

"You can't give him the sword, Hana. No matter what. He's already got an edge over the other gangs, if you'll pardon the expression, and the symbolism of that blade will give him even more authority."

Hana nodded. "I'm aware of all that, but if it's my only option to get Takeo back, I'll take it. His compound is virtually impregnable. From what I saw of it, which wasn't much." She shook her head.

"I know. I've been there."

"You have?" Hana was surprised, for Kai had only finished the compound in the last couple of years. "Hooded and escorted?"

"Yeah. Kai contacted me, asking me to train his men in karate and swordsmanship. I declined. I have no illusions about who he really is and I was still livid with him for . . . leading you into a life of crime, then deserting you when you got caught. And he was such a promising student. . . . You didn't let your talent spoil your character. He did."

Hana was touched. Few values got between Ernie and his bank account, but her heart leaped in her chest as she contemplated his news. "Do you think you can get into the estate to check on Takeo?"

"Possibly. But getting him out would be very difficult. You know how many guards Kai keeps around."

Her tea finished, Hana propped her chin on her hands, glum again.

Ernie didn't mince words. "Hana, if you keep going after the sword and get caught.... Kai will have full control of Takeo then."

Hana sighed heavily. "I've already made plans to disappear as soon as I have my son."

"And you'll raise an impressionable five-year-old alone, as a fugitive? No family, little money?"

Hana slammed her hand down on the quartz counter, her palm tingling. "What the hell else can I do?"

Later that evening, in exactly the same manner, Zach slammed his hand down on the counter before his father in the family kitchen. "Dammit, I can't perform my job if you don't listen to me."

"You're not official yet." John Travis finished making his huge sandwich, set it on a plate and cut it in half, offering a piece to his son. "And we have no idea yet if it's a sole slaying or if there will be a pattern and a broader message."

"And you want to be the next message?"

"I can't hole up and still do my job. It's a public position and I won't set an example of fear. Surely you know me better than that."

Zach looked down at his sandwich. He usually loved his dad's sandwich concoctions, but this time it was unappetizing. He shoved it away and propped his elbows on the counter, swiveling his bar stool back and forth because he couldn't be still. "How much longer before they make a decision?"

"I'm told another few days. A rush decision. There was some talk about nepotism and conflict of interest in having you guard me, but you're clearly the most qualified candidate on paper and that should carry enough weight to get you hired. And since it's a brand-new position contingent on budgeting, a direct appointment from the governor's office rather than Ranger management, they're being more lenient in their findings." John took a huge bite of sandwich, chewing with a relish his son eyed sourly.

"Dad, how can you eat at a time like this?"

"Starving won't give me any elucidation or insight into forensics." John took another big bite.

However, when his official encrypted cell phone rang, John gulped down his food and answered immediately. "Yes, do you have the results?" He listened, then tapped up a secure e-mail account on the iPad sitting next to him on the counter. "Thanks, I have it." He used his forefinger to page through what appeared to Zach to be a criminal file.

He was about to leave the kitchen when he glimpsed, upside down, a photo: a long fall of dark hair. He skirted the counter and looked down at the iPad. He saw an arrest record attached to a top sheet with a photo and the usual stats of height, weight, and gender. Hana Nakatomi was the name at the top. His father shoved the iPad in front of him, *I told you so* on his face, if not his lips.

Zach wasn't surprised he'd rushed the hair sample through the lab, but his heart sank as he paged through the girl's arrest record. She'd been a mule, arrested for shoplifting while in her teens, and was a known gang member of the worst Asian Yakuza offshoot that had set up shop in central Texas in the last few years, the self-named Edo Shihans. Roughly translated: respected old Japanese experts.

Zach read on, relieved to see that at least she was twenty-three now and he didn't see any charges in the last few years... but what did that prove?

His father's eyes were a dark, steady blue as he appraised his son's expression. "Why are you so drawn to this girl? She's totally inappropriate for you, quite aside from the fact that she may be a murderer as well as a drug pusher and shoplifter."

Zach snapped off the iPad. "I don't deny I was attracted to her briefly for the obvious reasons. But now my only interest is in seeing her detained and questioned."

John nodded. "Good." But he still watched his son very closely.

Zach turned away and walked toward the kitchen door, glad his father couldn't see his stomach was tied in knots. "I'm going to the gym to spar in the ring. Text me if you get the go-ahead from HR and I'll show up at the office first thing in the morning to sign everything."

Inside Ernie's kitchen, Ernie and Hana crouched over his laptop, reviewing all the news info they could Google about the Buckhorn Estate double murders. When they were done, they both plopped down into Ernie's plush armchairs in the attached, spacious living room.

Ernie fired up his pipe. Hana inhaled tentatively, relieved when she smelled only the sweet scent of expensive tobacco. Above all, she had to stay clearheaded. Besides, she didn't really like illegal drugs, not even marijuana or prescription-strength painkillers. She'd tried them all while dating Kai, but they only dulled her passions and made them more unmanageable when she came back from the high.

Finally Ernie tapped out his pipe into a crystal ashtray. "You think Kai did it?"

"I don't know."

Ernie frowned. "Surely Kai's too smart for that. He has to know offing someone at that level in the Texas Rangers will bring enormous retribution down on him."

"Yes, but if he implicates one of the other gangs in the process, he wipes out a major competitor and disrupts the state-level leadership of the various task forces trying to stop the Asian gangs from further infiltration. To tie up their resources at the least, because I'm pretty sure he's expecting a massive shipment. It may be a distraction tactic and this will be the only murder."

"Wouldn't he start with the DEA instead of the Rangers?"

"They may be next on his agenda. If I know him, his true goal is chaos, especially if he keeps moving up the chain of command." Hana took a deep breath. "And plants some of the blame on me. After I get the sword I'm expendable."

Ernie put his pipe down, the words obviously distasteful in his mouth. "Hana, it makes me sick to my stomach to say this, but you need to go to the authorities. If you help them intercept this shipment, they'll know you're on the right side of the law and you'll be safe. Plus, if another murder occurs, obviously you'd be in their custody."

Hana looked away. "And Jiji? Takeo? You know they'll probably throw me in jail until they figure out whether my intel is any good. I can't afford any delay, Ernie. If you saw my grandfather . . ."

Ernie stood. "As usual, you refuse to be sensible. One thing at a time. Let's pull up some plans on this warehouse."

Chapter 4

Two days later, after his swearing-in to his newly created position of Chief of Personal Security, Texas Department of Public Safety Executive Offices, Austin, Texas, Zach was trying to get used to the typical Ranger uniform-not-uniform. Like his dad, he wore a crisp white shirt, jeans, tie, and Stetson as he stood at attention at the closed door in the governor's mansion. Zach was in the process of vetting applicants to the newly created department he headed, but for now he was it. Where his father went, he went. Almost all of John's meetings these days were with other high-level officials, so Zach was in protective mode for everyone in the room.

The governor's office had been renovated a number of years back with extensive security measures installed. However, he still warily eyed the hallway outside the ornate salon that was used mostly as a conference room. He appraised every entrance and exit for the umpteenth time before he relaxed slightly. More security personnel patrolled the grounds and exterior, so they should be fine.

The low rumble of male voices behind the door occasionally grew heated. He knew they were discussing the most recent developments in the Asian gang incursion into Austin. The operational heads of the central Texas DEA, the FBI, and the Austin Chief of Police were all at this meeting. They were trying to create their own joint-response team with shared intel and security protocols in case the assassins planned to strike again, but in Zach's experience, these well-intentioned alliances seldom worked: Too many different priorities, budgets, and constituents, not to mention big egos all around.

He was still considering that point when a familiar figure entered the hallway outside the meeting room. Ross Sinclair was accompanied by a tall, regal woman of indeterminate age whom Zach had never seen before. However, Ross had an easy manner with her, and she wore a visitor's badge, so he knew she'd been vetted by gate security.

"Hey, Zach," Ross said. "We have some new data I felt should be shared immediately, as it's extremely timely. Do you know how much longer they'll be?"

Zach glanced at his watch. "The meeting was scheduled for an hour, but they've obviously run over."

Ross nodded. "Zach, this is Abigail Doyle, the forensics expert I mentioned to you. Abby, meet Zachary Travis, former Army Ranger, the new head of personal security for the executive officers of the DPS and Texas Rangers."

After Zach and Abigail shook hands, Ross added, "Abby has new information about Asian gang activities. She thinks part of the escalation is competition over control of the new designer drug that just hit the streets."

Abby hoisted her laptop bag over her shoulder as if it weighed heavily on her, in more ways than one.

"I know we're not scheduled to be in the meeting," Ross said, "but I think everyone will want to see this evidence for themselves as it may impact their tactical response. As you know, your dad asked me to take a temporary assignment managing the various response teams until we catch these murderers. I brought Abigail in because she's the best at putting together complex arrays of evidence."

Zach smiled slightly. "Yeah, he told me last night. How does Emm feel about you being away so long?"

A twinkle turned Ross's blue eyes even brighter. "A few weeks away is OK while she works on the new building in Amarillo. After that... well, I'd rather face the murderers single-handed than explain to her why I can't come home when scheduled."

Zach nodded, smiling, while Ms. Doyle laughed as if she too knew Emm.

Zach responded, "I'll see if I can get their attention," and knocked lightly on the heavy door. After a muffled "come in," he walked inside. He was uncharacteristically nervous as, for the first time, he faced the heads of the major law-enforcement agencies investigating Asian gang activity in central Texas.

As everyone looked curiously between him and his father, obviously knowing his background, Zach murmured in his dad's ear.

John Travis glanced inquiringly at his own boss, Chief Jeremy Porter. Nodding, Porter made a beckoning move with his hand.

Zach ushered in Ross and Abigail, turning to walk out again, but Chief Porter called him back. "Stay for this, please, Zachary, as it may impact our protection detail. John was going to brief you after the meeting but this will save us all time." The ghost of a smile crossed his tanned, lined face when Zach hesitated as if he didn't want to desert his post. "Relax. If we're not safe at the governor's mansion, where *would* we be safe?"

Nowhere, Zach wanted to retort, but of course he didn't. He sat as indicated, but he still felt confined in the jeans and Stetson, especially laden with weapons as he was. He'd gotten one stipulation through all the bureaucracy: He was allowed to pick his own arms. After they were approved by the DPS he could even carry them at his discretion, government issue or not.

His discretion was simple: 24/7 vigilance. Sleeping with his weapons near to hand. No more open windows, and at night his bedroom door stayed wide so he could hear the slightest sound. Even the motion detectors inside their house were activated now at night. And he seldom sat down during his duty hours.

He half listened to the introductions going around the table, adjusting his bristling arsenal by shifting his body weight. Standard-issue Glock in his visible hip holster, six-shot featherweight revolver strapped to his calf beneath his jeans, fifteen-round custom Browning .45 in the hidden holster under his armpit. His last backup was a Silver Trident sheath knife with a double-serrated edge strapped in the small of his back. It weighed over a pound and because of its supreme balance, it was perfect for throwing, which was why he stored it where he could grab it easily.

As Ross recapped the forensics conclusions based on the remains of the victims, facts he'd already heard, Zach still couldn't get comfortable. Even in one of the most secure buildings in the state, he was on edge. But as Abby took center stage, he began to listen.

After Abigail hooked her laptop to the room's projector system, she began flashing PowerPoint slides. "These are some of the samples of this new designer drug we've sourced back to China. It's only been on the streets in Austin for a couple of months. It started in Europe and has since moved to the East Coast and is now spreading through the South and Midwest."

Zach eyed the bright, appealing packaging, tilting his head to read the label: *Blue Moon incense.* Or *Zinger tea,* and so on. All innocuous home products.

"I'm sure I don't need to tell this audience how hard these drugs are to interdict," Abby said. "The distribution is different from any of the usual illegal pipelines: mom-and-pop stores, raves, independent gas stations. Sometimes the proprietors don't even know what they're selling. And increasingly, people buy them on the Deep Web, often using digital currency like Bitcoin that makes the transactions difficult to track."

The next images were even more troubling. She flashed through them quickly with obvious distaste: people of every shape and size, but mostly young, in various states of illness, hooked to IVs. Some looked as if they were in comas and more than a few looked as if they'd overdosed.

"These designer drugs hit the streets before we even know what's in them," she continued. "All too often they mimic the highs of heroin, or cocaine, or methamphetamine. Equally addictive; in a few cases, even more so. They obviously have no quality controls so one packet can be much stronger than the next on the same rack. Users are taking enormous risks without realizing it. As soon as the labs identify the chemicals used to make these drugs, and we get the legislation through to ban them, they reformulate and add plant products that are used for such things as tea and incense and release them with new packaging under innocuous new names."

DEA chief Dexter Rhodes was nodding impatiently. "We know all of that. We tried banning them several years back when they had the all-encompassing label *bath salts,* only to have them reformulate, exactly as you said . . . But what does this have to do with the murders of our people?"

Abigail switched to a different picture: A muscular man of medium height. A chill crept up Zach's spine. He'd seen a similar apparition before, though the black nylon had molded a much different form. He was looking at a male version of Hana, the Japanese girl. Like her, this man was garbed head to toe in black. He wore a samurai sword strapped to his back, and another shorter one in a belt sheath. His hood looked very similar to the one the girl had worn the night he'd fought with her. The photo had a grainy nature, as if it had been taken from a distance, but the man was still imposing in his menace.

"We believe this is the leader of the Edo Shihans gang, which as I'm sure you all know, seems to be winning the wars with its rivals. We know him only as Kai. We think he grew up around Okinawa, the son of a prominent Yakuza boss. He tried to take over his father's gang and was disgraced and banned. That's when he came to the U.S. He keeps a very low profile, obviously aware the DEA is trying to track him."

Abby switched screen shots yet again, flicking through various major U.S. ports: Los Angeles, Miami, New York, Houston. She shared her detailed research as she switched slides. "We think Kai had an ally in his father's gang who helped him finalize connections in China with the source of this new drug known as Blue Moon. He outbid his rivals for a massive shipment. He's spent the last few years setting up his trade routes and distribution channels, though he was a minor player in the hard stuff like heroin. However, rumor on the street is this new product is much stronger and more addictive than previously, so it's priced higher."

She switched screen shots again, showing prostitutes plying various streets. "Until recently he stuck to nonviolent ventures like identity theft and prostitution. However, his rivalry with the Green Gang, the Chinese offshoot of a prominent Shanghai-based former Triad group, has heated up recently. They pride themselves on their roots as Friends of the Way of Tranquility and Purity." Abby continued over Dexter's scoffing sound, "In the last week, we've found the remains of two Green Gang members, or I should say former members." Taking a deep breath as if she had to brace herself, Abby flipped to a new slide.

Even the most hardened cops among them had to look away. Zach's stomach roiled as he stared. Good God, he'd known their foe must be ruthless and brutal . . . but this. This was a message.

The corpses were hardly recognizable as human, as they'd been butchered into pieces, like cattle. Zach had seen more than his share of dead bodies, mostly blown to bits by IEDs or machine-gun fire. These pictures, disgusting as they were, had an almost clinical air. The shots had obviously been taken well after exsanguination. The cuts on the torso where arms and legs had been attached were smooth diagonals, as if the blade that severed them had been very sharp and wielded with both power and experience, cutting through in one stroke. Zach recalled the feel and touch of that female ninja-like figure. Surely she couldn't be involved in this? Was she even strong enough to do something like this in one stroke? His lunch bubbled in his throat and he had to force himself to concentrate on the presentation.

Abby's voice was soft. "The bodies were scattered. The coroner had a difficult time... reassembling, but when he finished we ID'd them as Green Gang from their tattoos. No next of kin came forward so their remains were cremated. The examiners had never seen anything like this, but I had once, in Japan, where I was called upon to investigate the Yakuza. These cuts are taught to those who profess to follow the way of the samurai. Each cut even has its own name, such as *Do* for the abdomen cut and *Kiriachi* for the lateral thorax cut."

Zach asked, "Are you saying they use humans as practice dummies?"

Abby tilted her head slightly and eyed him with steady gray eyes so acute and assessing they might have looked through him to the wall behind his head. "If you mean is this barbarism, a twisted test of their artistry in battle, absolutely. Only the most advanced samurai can make such clean cuts and it requires a very sharp blade and a great deal of strength and accuracy. The medical examiner believes these cuts were each made with one blow."

Zach and his father exchanged a look.

"So you think this Kai had some of his rivals terminated like this to send a message?" interrupted Porter.

"Yes. While we have no proof, these two bodies turned up two days after one of the Edo Shihans was beheaded. Beheading is another ritual of the samurai. In the middle ages, samurai were judged on the number of heads they took in battle." She flashed another slide. Grisly as it was, the one-stroke killing seemed merciful in comparison to the other blows.

"The final indisputable point is," Abby concluded, going back to pictures of the new drug, "these two gangs are in a fierce turf war over the distribution of this new drug, and probably over other criminal activities we haven't identified yet. And their violence is obviously escalating." Abby's tone lowered until they all had to strain to hear. "And most troubling of all, both gangs seem to have twisted the original honor the samurai historically held for their shogun masters into allegiance to their gangs. Which means most of the members, if not all, will die before they betray their leaders."

The FBI chief scowled. "We've never had gang wars this bad before, even between the Crips and the Bloods. What the hell is going on here?"

Ross spoke up. "That's why I thought it critical you all hear this as soon as possible." He stood, nodding at Abby. She popped up a new screen, showing a rising graph depicting the growing Asian population both in Texas and nationally. "Analysis of recent census data shows a sharp rise in Asian immigration. As you can see, Asian immigrants are projected to be the largest minority in the U.S. within the next thirty years or so. Unfortunately, with their good influence comes the bad ... and obviously there are huge cultural differences between them and our fiercest Latino criminals. These gangs already have ties in the Orient. As you can see, some of their tactics put the worst Mexican cartels to shame. It behooves us to figure out their methodologies now, before they become deeply entrenched. This isn't just a murder investigation—it needs to be an interdiction. We need to capture the leaders of these gangs before they spread their influence."

DEA chief Rhodes nodded as he listened, confirming their facts. "I've been trying to tell everyone this for over a year, but our resources were mostly deployed near the border."

John Travis scowled as he glared at Abby's final screen shot: the figure in black. "Isn't there enough evidence to at least bring this Kai in for questioning?"

Before Abby could answer, Rhodes elaborated: "The few informants we've arrested with ties to the Edo Shihans are going to prison rather than talk. We're not sure if it's from loyalty or terror of the consequences." He looked to Abby to continue.

Abigail nodded. "Probably a bit of both. The Yakuza has survived as one of the oldest criminal organizations on the planet partly because of its strict code. And from the evidence I've reviewed thus far, Kai has blended that structure he learned from his father with the samurai mystique and ninja terror tactics. He's suspected to offer a generous bonus system that rewards loyalty, yet his retribution tactics rival the Zetas cartel ... ritual sacrifice."

"Yeah, we've never linked him personally to any of the distribution channels," Rhodes added. "Whatever else he's involved in, he's one smart son of a bitch. Plus, we have no idea where his base of operations is except that it seems to be in the area."

"Do we know where the shipment is coming into the state?" asked Chief Porter.

Abby shook her head. "Nothing is surfacing on any of our tracking mechanisms." She looked inquiringly at Rhodes. He also grimly shook his head.

The room was silent for a moment.

Zach had listened carefully to the presentation. He looked around, but when no one else voiced his concern he spoke up. "Did you show these pictures to the forensics lab that analyzed the remains of the Taylors to see if there's a possible weapons match?" Zach asked.

They all eyed the full-length picture of Kai, appraising the swords he carried. Abby responded, "Yes. Inconclusive, though the head of the lab agreed these swords, as far as cutting angles and splatter pattern, could match the gashes on all four victims."

Zach absorbed that. So far, they had no proof linking the Japanese girl to the Buckhorn murders other than the hood that was found. It was identical to the hood he'd ripped off her head the night she broke into their house, the one they used to match her DNA and identify her. But it had been clean of any DNA, as if it had never been worn. A plant, perhaps? But Zach couldn't voice that gut feeling because he had no proof. Besides, what motivation would the real killers have to try to implicate the Japanese girl?

All latent DNA residue they'd tested from the murder scene had been male and had not hit any of their many databases, including the one the Japanese authorities had on Yakuza activity in Japan, which they'd been good enough to cross-check. However, the single hair sample recovered showed a strong correlation to Japanese DNA markers around Okinawa. Kai was from Okinawa. The girl had been born in the U.S. Thus, there was only one apparent link between Kai and the girl, and it was literally staring them in the face.

The katana.

With a look at his dad, who nodded, Zach stood and walked to the screen, using his pen as a pointer. "I was stationed in Okinawa for a year. The Japanese value swords, especially family samurai swords, beyond anything we can claim as Americans. The oldest ones are tied to their national identity and the clans who hold them. Whoever is strong enough to acquire one revered from the Edo period, has an advantage in any power struggle. Since there's only one link between the girl who broke into our house and this Kai, other than the obvious fact they're both Japanese..." He traced the outline of the katana blade with his pen. "Follow the sword. I'd bet my Harley they both want the Masamune blade. Let's use it as bait."

The next night, Hana was back perched on the Tarrytown fence, once more garbed in black so she could scope out the Travis mansion. She and Ernie had formulated an action plan for the following night, when the sword would arrive in Austin. But just in case, she wanted to investigate the Travis mansion so she'd have a backup plan to snatch the sword if for some reason they failed at the warehouse. She used the expensive night-vision binoculars Kai had supplied her with when they'd made their devil's bargain, along with a sword and various other weaponry, which so far she'd refused to carry.

Sparring with swords had always been her favorite part of her training in the ring. She normally trained with *bokken*, the wooden sword, and was only allowed to use a real katana when Ernie deemed her ready. She'd never used any blade to render harm, and she wouldn't start now. She only wished Kai had the same compunction but knew he didn't. That was another reason she didn't want to leave him with the sword. If there was any other way to get Takeo back, she'd find it.

Immediately, even without the binoculars, she saw the new security: hired guards in uniform leading dogs around. Not just any dogs, but Belgian *Malanois*—the favored breed of the armed forces and large police departments because of its intelligence, protective instincts, and loyalty to its trainers. They were much more alert and well trained than the family Rottweilers. She also noted that the upstairs windows were all closed. New motion detectors blinked from all quarters as they moved from side to side.

Yikes! One arc of movement almost included her position. She vaulted down, she hoped, in time. She ran to her car, her mind moving even faster than her feet. Hana had her answer as to potential backup: none.

It was the warehouse or nothing.

The Travises wouldn't be fooled twice.

The warehouse had digital-dependent security, according to her contacts. The valuable items the transit service handled were seldom there more than a few hours and they counted on their high-tech security and safe more than costly security guards. She trusted Ernie to get past that. Her own skills in breaking digital security usually ended with snipping a few wires, but Ernie was a true Renaissance man. She turned a corner and stopped abruptly, certain she heard pounding feet. She listened: Background noise of a busy city.

She hurried on. She was panting slightly when she finally reached her car. Unlocking and opening it, this time she was certain . . . someone was following her. She spun in time to meet a large shadow in the dim streetlamps.

A very solid shadow. The minute the long, lithe body crashed into hers, forcing her body weight flat against the car and slamming the door, she knew who it was despite not being able to make out the face. No one else she'd ever met had made her nerve endings tingle head to toe like he did.

Hana tilted her head back to allow the dim streetlight to illuminate her face. "Zachary Travis. Somehow I knew I'd see you again." She gave him a sweeping glance. "But I liked the way you were dressed better the other way."

He reared back slightly, as if insulted, and even in the dim light she saw his cheeks flush. "Ditto. I figured you'd be back at some point. Scoping out our new security."

"So you were watching?"

"Always. It's my new job as head of security for DPS and Ranger execs." He settled against her so she could feel the holster at his shoulder.

She tried to squirm free, but he held her arms at her sides and let her struggle, his cold smile widening. She stopped and used a better weapon—her tongue. "Go ahead then, take me in. But a charge of trespassing won't keep me locked up very long, and I also have powerful friends with ties at major media outlets."

He lockstepped her out of the shade of the tree directly beneath a streetlamp so he could see her face more clearly. "Oh, we know a lot about you now, Ms. Nakatomi. Enough that we'd much rather catch you red-handed with evidence that will stick than bring you in on a misdemeanor. Go on with your malfeasance."

She was tempted to reach for his weapon, but then she saw the feral gleam in his blue eyes and thought better of it. He wanted her to go for his gun. No doubt that would have some serious penalties attached now that he was an officer of the law.

She tilted her head back and thrust out her pointed chin, as she did when she was cornered. "I had nothing to do with the murders."

His grip went lax, but then he caught her, more tightly. "At least you get straight to the point. But why would I believe you?"

"Uh, a little thing like *motive*. I had no reason to kill two people I've never met."

"Yes, well, that's why you should come in for questioning. Only you can clear your name."

She made a scornful sound. "Like you don't know anything about me, huh? You'll believe me despite my priors?"

That feral gleam softened a bit. "It's obviously not my call, but I can tell you we'll all listen to your side of the story. Good enough? Do us both a favor and come quietly." He moved back half a step, preparing to shove her in front of him. "I'm decent this time."

Hana smiled up at him, long and luxuriously. "Pity, that."

When his gaze caressed her lips, she struck, stamping her booted foot down on his toe. His grip loosened enough for her to get one arm free. In one fluid movement, she twisted sideways and brought her elbow up sharply into his jaw. He staggered slightly, but still had presence of mind enough to keep her other wrist manacled, so she was pulled with him. With a growl of anger, he brought his other hand up to latch it around her hair.

She saw it coming. Rather than pull back against gravity as most people would, she used the fall as her friend and followed the curve, pushing with her toes to overbalance them both, hard. He fell backward into the street with her on top. Then she heard his teeth snap together and the grip on her hair went lax. She'd landed on top as she'd devised. She felt a twinge of guilt as she saw blood gush from his lip, now realizing Zach bit his lip when he fell.

No time for recriminations or apologies... she was up and running. He scrambled up a split-second later, and then he was in hot pursuit, blood dripping down on his white shirt.

She was half his weight, and faster, so at first veering through cars and leaping over shrubs allowed her to pull ahead, but she'd already exerted herself and her breath soon was labored. She dared a look over her shoulder and wished she hadn't.

Even in the moonlight she saw the blood on his shirt and that familiar gleam in his eyes, much brighter now. He wasn't even breathing hard. She realized she might be faster, but he was fitter and stronger.

She ran harder, knocking over a trash can as she went, but he only leaped over it and kept coming. Could she make it back to her car? She veered around a block in the right direction but her legs were tiring. She refused to heed them, pumping harder. She had to get away—Jiji only had a few more days. He was in and out of consciousness now. The sword was coming in tomorrow night.

Everything was set up with Ernie. She had to get away, or Jiji would die while she was in prison. And Takeo... despite the stress of the moment, tears filled her eyes at the mere thought of Kai raising her son.

Then she heard sirens approaching.

Chapter 5

Hana's breath was wheezing now in her chest, and as hard as she tried to keep ahead of Zach, she knew he was closing the gap. Even as she ran she was reviewing potential escapes in her head because she'd scoped out all the streets surrounding his house before she made her first home invasion.

A culvert was coming up on her right, she recalled. It had a large drainage pipe, big enough for her to crouch inside and hope he missed her. But if he did find her, she'd be trapped. And she wasn't certain whether he was close enough to see her or if he was still rounding the other block. It would slow her too much to turn and look.

She turned another corner and there, to her shock, was Ernie's van. He was leaning against it, as if waiting for her. Without a word he slid open the side-panel door and she leaped inside, so out of breath she managed only a garbled, "Thank God." He didn't bother to ask for direction; he just got in the driver's seat, fired up the engine, and drove away sedately.

"I thought you might need a backup getaway vehicle," Ernie said as he turned his blinker on and turned a corner as if he hadn't a care in the world: A boring citizen who'd never missed paying a parking ticket.

Hana was lying flat on the floorboards in the rear and she stayed there. "Do you see him?"

Ernie turned his head toward the sidewalk and slowed a bit as he looked in that direction, but he sped up immediately, taking the corner. "Yep. He's staring straight at us."

"Oh God, Ernie, he'll take your plate number."

"You know me better than that, baby girl. This isn't my van."

Hana closed her eyes in relief and did what did not come naturally: She was happy, for once, to put her fate in the hands of a man.

Outside the van, Zach was indeed memorizing the plates. He'd turned the corner too late to see how Hana had disappeared into thin air, but the van was logical as her escape route. He'd heard it fire up right before he took the corner, and the driver had turned to peer at him curiously. Zach couldn't see his face that well in the darkness, but the red, ancient Volkswagen van was a relic from the 1970s, so it was distinctive enough. Just in case, he used his cell phone to snap a shot of it as it drove down the block and disappeared.

He started walking home, not happy that he'd have to tell both his dad and the police he'd summoned on his cell phone that he'd lost the girl . . . for the second time.

Once they reached the freeway, Hana sat up. "I can't thank you enough, Ernie."

"What about your car?"

She sighed. "I'm sure it will be impounded and thoroughly searched. I parked it farther away but it's registered in my name."

"Did you sweep it clean?"

"I think so. They won't find anything incriminating or that would link me to you."

"Did you find more security at the Travis house than last time?"

"It's a fortress. New motion detectors, armed guards with Belgian *Malinois* . . . I won't be able to get near it again without my own little army."

"OK, kiddo, time to hunker down and plan our little adventure for tomorrow. With no plan B, plan A has to be flawless."

Hana climbed into the seat beside him. "Ernie, I have a bad feeling about this. Zachary Travis was obviously expecting me. How do I know they won't be guarding the warehouse too?"

"You don't. But maybe we can do our own little reconnaissance first."

Hana eyed him, not liking the little smile flickering at his lips. In her experience with him, it usually accompanied reckless behavior. Ernie's biggest flaw, other than his petty larcenies, was his feeling that he was invulnerable to the downfalls of most mortal men, criminals in particular.

"Ernie..." she said in a warning tone.

He only winked at her and drove the old VW as fast as it would go. Doing what he did best—pushing limits.

The next morning, the mood was somber as two simple caskets sat draped by the Lone Star flag at the Texas State Cemetery. On their final passage to eternity, the Taylor couple would rest after death as they had in life: side by side. It was unusual for a wife who was not a state employee to be interred next to her husband but the state facilities director had bent the rules to allow it. The graveside service was crowded with high-ranking Texas Ranger and Department of Public Safety officials. The Taylor family sat under an awning, adult children and grandchildren openly in tears.

As he watched the ceremony, Zach was uneasy. Two hours before the event, he'd reconnoitered the site himself. All the muckety-mucks gathered here would make a prime target for anyone who wanted to eliminate top state law-enforcement officials. Several police officers, astride their motorcycles, monitored the perimeter, but Zach was still on edge.

While he knew he wasn't the only bodyguard sprinkled around at the ceremony, he kept to his father's side, continually scanning the surrounding trees and gravestones, looking for anyone who might be skulking around, as the minister quietly gave his eulogy. After the eulogy, several older men wearing typical cowboy garb of chaps, boots, and vests, lifted old Colt revolvers to the sky and gave their version of the twenty-one-gun salute, a ceremony unique to Texas Rangers, Zach knew, having attended such services before.

The crowd slowly dispersed, but John Travis stayed rooted by Sam Taylor's casket, which was slowly lowering into the ground on hydraulic lifts. Zach was moved when his father knelt and picked up a clump of dirt to drop gently down on the casket. "Rest, old friend," he said quietly, turning away.

But not fast enough. Zach saw the tears in his eyes. He could only clasp his father's shoulder in sympathy, but as usual, John Travis recovered quickly. He patted his son's hand and then went to talk to several reporters who'd asked for an interview.

Zach half listened as he continued to scan his surroundings. His eyes narrowed as he thought he saw a blur of movement near a huge, shady oak, but when he moved sideways to get a better look, he saw nothing but leaves restless in the wind. Still, the hairs rose on the back of his neck and he instinctively moved a bit closer to his father.

Meanwhile, John forestalled a battery of questions about the killing with a raised hand. "I'm sorry but you know I can't give details of an ongoing investigation. Suffice it to say that every law-enforcement agency in central Texas is working on solving this crime—"

An aggressive reporter with the *Austin American Statesman* interrupted. "But the DPS is obviously worried this isn't a single instance. They've hastily created this new position of Personal Security Director and hired someone named—" he looked down at his notes "—Zachary Travis. Is he any relation to you and if so, isn't this a bit unusual? Is this appointment a direct response because the threat is greater than anyone lets on?"

John replied curtly, "That's all for now." He stalked back to his car. Zach skirted the group of reporters, ignoring their requests for a brief word, and joined his dad. As they sped off, driven by a DPS trooper trained in escape maneuvers, Zach said quietly, "Maybe this wasn't a good idea. The last thing you need is more political heat—"

"Zachary, we already had this conversation. You're the most qualified. Period. They can deal with it until the next hot story distracts them." John leaned back, his face still drawn as he stared into the distance.

Zach left him to his memories. Now that they were safely in the armored vehicle, he could give in to his own preoccupations. He mentally listed all the steps he'd taken to prepare for the coming confrontation at the warehouse tonight. A smile lifted his lips as he visualized Hana's expression when she saw him. This time, she wouldn't escape. They safely rounded the drive, turning on to a major street, and for the first time since he awoke that day, Zach relaxed.

Outside, a stocky male figure in green camo waited, legs crossed, perched in the lowest branch of a huge oak. Like the ninja he revered, he wore the stillness of his ancestors as easily as the camo. At any distance beyond a few feet, he was virtually indistinguishable from the tree. He held a powerful Nikon digital camera and used its zoom to snap close-ups of John Travis and his guard as they got in the armored limo. Calmly, his breathing very even, he waited for all the cops to disperse before he sought his own Kawasaki motorcycle hidden in the thick shrubbery. He replaced the camera in its case and drove away.

That night at precisely 2:00 a.m., Hana and Ernie, lithe figures in black, clung to the side of the three-story warehouse on Dessau in east Austin. Hana had received a curt text from her contact that would be gibberish to anyone but her. It stated the blade had arrived on a late shipment and was due to be delivered to the Travis household tomorrow morning. She and Ernie had followed their prearranged plan.

They'd circled the entire building, looking for any telltale signs of a stakeout, but the warehouse district looked deserted except for trucks in the transit company lot, all marked with their logo. They felt the hoods... good. None of them were warm. No new arrivals.

Ernie then disabled the external security system that controlled the motion detectors and window sensors while Hana rigged up their gear. The climbing gear, complete with wall anchors, would allow them to climb the slick brick exterior and then rappel down. They knew the vault holding the most valuable transit items was on the third floor, and only one window was dimly lit. They also had monitored the building several times, enough to know that only two men were on guard: First, at the entrance; second, outside the vault. Easy pickings for two martial arts experts.

They'd briefly debated as to whether it was too easy, but the Travises would have no way of knowing she had contacts familiar with the building security. They probably thought a supposedly impregnable vault and two armed guards were protection enough for the brief twelve-hour period during which the blade would be stored there until the planned delivery in the morning.

They didn't know Ernie had studied the same model vault several times. Her contact had given her the model number and Ernie had a friend out in Spicewood on his own land who was a former welder at a safe manufacturer. His hobby was collecting safes—or at least that's what he told the authorities on the rare occasion he was questioned.

This model was a couple of years old and like many of the newer digital safes, seemed impregnable. It was designed to lock down after two abortive passwords and not open again without a special security code known only to the owner of the company.

Ernie didn't intend to use a password.

Hovering on the side of the building, Hana held her breath as Ernie soundlessly raised the windowsill. She sighed in relief when no alarm blared, then followed him inside. Carefully, they appraised every corner, using the night-vision goggles inserted in their hoods to appraise the room. Sure enough, a man in a security uniform sat in a desk chair in front of a massive vault door. However, he leaned against the wall with his cap tilted down over his head, looking half asleep. He held a shotgun, but it had fallen down into his lap. The only light in the room was a lamp on a desk on the far wall, too far away to burn their lenses.

Easy-peasy... the guard barely startled awake as they pulled a gag around his mouth. He began to struggle to lift his gun, but Hana snatched it away and stuck it against the opposite wall, racking out the shells, while Ernie tied the man up with zip ties.

"Sorry, pal," Ernie muttered. "We'll never tell anyone you were asleep."

The guard was very quiet. Very calm. He didn't even struggle. Hana was taken aback by his reaction. She'd been uneasy from the moment they'd arrived and the guard's nonchalance raised her apprehension a notch. This was going far too smoothly.

Ernie took off his backpack, pulling out a reciprocating saw to begin cutting a hole, not in the huge, thick steel-plated door, but into the reinforced Sheetrock it was embedded in. Hana still appraised the room. But she bit her tongue on the concern she wanted to voice to Ernie, not wanting to interrupt or distract. The sooner they got out of here, the better.

Just in case, she went to the desk phone and checked the dial tone: none. It was dead. She put it back in its cradle, a bit reassured. The security-system cut had worked.

Ernie had a huge, neat rectangular hole cut in the Sheetrock quickly enough. Next, he cut through the wall stud to get deeper into the cavity. Over the soft *whir* made by the muffled drill, he said, "Relax, it's not a support beam."

She wasn't surprised that he'd picked up on her unease, even as busy as he was.

"I'll watch out the window... hurry, please," she responded. Walking to the window, she kept to the side so her shadow wasn't visible outside and looked down at the street.

A car passed slowly, but it was a sports car that looked nothing like a security or police vehicle. It soon disappeared around a curve.

Finally, she heard the sound she was waiting for: the bite of a very powerful and fine diamond bit into steel. The door of the vault, as Ernie had explained to her, had a thick layer of glass. The minute it was penetrated, its shattering triggered the secondary locking system that slammed a second lever into place over the door and required the special security code to open.

So Ernie didn't go through the front; he bypassed it to the side of the vault. From there, after measuring carefully, he made an angled cut that left a wide hole: wide enough for him to slip inside a flexible tube with a tiny video camera and light at the end. Ernie eyed the small-view screen attached to the tube, tweaking it into the premeasured position he'd practiced on the other safe.

He made a satisfied sound somewhere between an *ah* and a grunt. "Come hold this for a second."

Hana complied, glancing again at the guard. He was very quiet and watchful, barely moving a muscle. She frowned beneath her hood, thinking again that he reacted strangely. Typically guards in such a position had two emotions: fear or anger, or a blend of both. This guy just watched... as if waiting. But there was nothing to do but help Ernie so they could get the heck out of there.

She held the tube steady while he fed another thin, flexible wire down the tube's length, slowly and carefully, using the viewing screen as his guide. The wire had a hook on the end that popped out and widened once it reached the opening in the tube. Ernie maneuvered the wire slowly, slowly, feeding it to a location mystifying to her but obviously premeasured to him. Finally, he stopped pushing and turned his wrist to a pulling position. The hook caught on a small release lever she could barely make out in the gloom of the safe interior on the tiny view screen.

Ernie pulled, slow and gentle. When the hook was firmly caught on the lever, he tugged harder. With a slight scraping sound, the latch moved. The safe door opened with a soft *whish* of air, gapping an inch. No alarm, no glass breaking. Lights automatically came on in the interior.

She knew Ernie was smiling behind his hood because she heard it in his voice. "Release mechanism in case someone gets stuck inside. The safer they make these things, the easier they are to break into."

Ernie took a swaggering step to push the door wide. He froze. Slowly, his hands lifted in the air. He backed up.

Hana was standing to the side, distracted. Her heart was leaping as she visualized holding the katana for the first time, this sword her ancestors had died to protect. But when Ernie raised his hands, she snapped to attention. Her gaze frantically scanned the room, and then she bolted toward the window. She looked out, preparing to grab the nylon rope she'd anchored.

It was gone. She looked up at the anchor bolt she'd shot into the side of the building. She saw a neat inch of rope still tied to the bolt. It had a straight edge—it had been cut. By a very sharp knife.

The little bravado she'd retained deflated instantly. She ducked inside. As she slowly turned toward the safe, she knew whom she'd see. Ernie had backed up until his tall form blocked her view, but she recognized the voice.

"Hello, Hana." Zachary Travis stepped outside the safe, where he'd obviously been waiting. He held a Glock on them. With his free hand, he used a wicked-looking special forces knife to cut the guard free. "Nice to see you again." Somehow, despite his pleasant tone, his voice dripped with contempt.

Slipping the knife back into a sheath at his waist, he pressed the mike on the side of his head. "Situation secure. Backup requested."

Feet stormed up the hallway outside. The door they'd locked lost its bolt as it was rammed to the ground.

Then a SWAT team wearing DPS insignia crowded into the room.

Zach eyed Ernie's tall form. "And you are?"

Ernie shrugged. "Smart enough not to answer without my lawyer present."

Then they were both handcuffed, hands in front. One of the men pulled Ernie's hood off. The head of the SWAT team moved to shove Hana ahead of him out the door, but Zach stopped him.

"Wait a minute." He disappeared inside the safe and exited, holding a long bundle wrapped in red silk and gold cord. "Is this what you were looking for?" He jerked his head at the SWAT commander. The man pulled off Hana's hood and stepped back, grinning.

She blinked, her vision adjusting to the dim lighting. Then she focused on the long object. Her eyes filled with tears. She bit her lip rather than give him the satisfaction of her despair.

Snapping on the overhead light, Zach unwrapped the sword, reverently holding it out toward her. "Beautiful, isn't it?" He turned it this way and that. The many layers of lacquer on the highly glossed black sheath made it gleam. He pulled the sheath off. The elegant sing of the blade as it came free sent a shiver down her spine.

She knew what the Nakatomi katana looked like because she'd seen multiple family pictures taken before the blade was lost to them in the 1940s. This sword was even more beautiful because then the blade had been dull, slightly pockmarked on the edge, its fine silk-woven hilt, in the traditional diamond-shaped pattern, a bit frayed.

It had been totally refurbished by experts. The diamond-shaped triangles were now sharp in that distinctive samurai form, allowing a firm grip on the long hilt designed to be wielded two-handed. The sheath was simple bamboo, she recalled, but it was black as ebony, glossy now with many coats of lacquer. The hilt was a stylized hawk, the heraldry symbol of the Nakatomi family, slight flecks of the original gilding remaining. And the blade... It looked as if it had recently been polished. It shone, reflecting every tiny ray of light as Zach moved it from side to side. A slight hazing of the steel made a very faint pattern of feathers. Hana knew if the blade was removed from the fittings, the Nakatomi *mon*, or crest, would be imprinted on the steel: A crossing hawk in a circle.

The edge was obviously very sharp, which Zach demonstrated on a piece of paper from the desk. With one small stroke, the paper fluttered to the floor in two distinctive pieces.

He turned to Hana with a cold smile. "Sharp, isn't it? Would you like to test it out yourself on your next victim?"

Zach and the SWAT team leader both watched her expression and body language, but Hana barely heard the taunt, focused only on the katana. Her fingers itched and she had to clench them into fists to avoid the urge to grab it. Which was impossible, considering her hands were cuffed, but for now, she was focused only on the katana.

It was the blade that made the sword so unique and valuable. In fact, samurai swords were sometimes displayed with only the blade showing. Masamune swords, seven centuries after his death, were still strong and flexible, almost invulnerable to breaking. Made by hand in three different consistencies of tempered steel, the Nakatomi katana had been forged, turned, and cooled many times so that the sword was of different tensile strengths depending upon the strike:

body blow with the side edge, stab with the tip, or sword-to-sword locked in battle near the hilt. Masamune swords had been hugely prized even in the heyday of the samurai before modern imperial Japan. Now, they were literally priceless . . . but it wasn't money she and her grandfather wanted.

This blade belonged to them.

Their ancestors had used it in battle, generation after generation. Nakatomi tears had blessed it, forging a bond reaching across the ages as strong as the steel. Automatically, for she felt it her birthright, she reached out without thinking, her hands still cuffed. "Give it to me."

Zach looked at her as if she were crazy. "I don't care to be gutted too." He stuck the sword back in the sheath and rewrapped the blade in its red protective covering.

What was he talking about? Hana knew he was accusing her of something awful, but she had no idea of the specifics. This would be her only chance to get the sword to Jiji in time . . . before he . . .

She gnawed at her lip so hard she tasted blood. "Please, may I borrow it? For just a day?" She debated telling him her family history.

Zach gave her a cold glance before he handed the sword to the armed head of the SWAT team. "My dad is expecting it. You'll take it in the armored transport?"

The man nodded. He held it reverently as he exited.

Hana swallowed back her tears as yet again, the blade was taken far beyond her reach. She knew it was useless, but still she tried. "I've never cut anyone with a sword in my life. I did not kill your friends."

"Yes, well, you can tell that to the brass. My job is done." Zach turned on his heel and left her to be shoved down the hallway to the elevator, her hands still cuffed.

Chapter 6

As she sat in her holding cell awaiting interrogation, Hana reflected glumly on all the key concepts of karate she'd violated on the second transgression that landed her in a jail cell: Free the mind; support righteousness; karate begins and ends in respect. And most of all, never attack first.

Yet how could she obtain the sword without attacking? Perhaps she should have just gone to John Travis and thrown herself on his mercy, asking pretty please to borrow the sword. But she suspected his reaction would have been the same as his son's—scorn and disbelief. And always, Takeo's stalwart little figure hovered above every karate precept. She'd had no choice but to give Kai the blade if it was the only way to free her son.

With time for nothing but reflection, she stopped in front of the tiny window, looking at the patch of blue above her head. It reminded her of the porthole that had decorated their cabin on the yacht they'd used to sail the Aegean. How many years ago now? Six, at least. One of Kai's allies had loaned it to them shortly after they became lovers. She usually avoided thinking of that time, for that was when she'd fallen deeply in love with the boy who seemed as wrongly outcast as she felt. She couldn't reach the window, but she put her palm flat against the wall beneath it, tears coming to her eyes despite her best efforts.

How had they come to this, when she'd loved him so in the beginning? She knew the answer: Because he let his resolve to prove himself better than his father twist him beyond recognition. The Yakuza were not known for paternal excellence, but they drilled the concept of duty and loyalty into their offspring from a very early age. Hana knew that Kai had been lucky to escape with his life when he violated all his oaths to gain control of his father's empire. He was twenty-two, an illegal immigrant, she a sixteen year old American born and bred, when they became lovers. They'd been sparring in the ring together as Ernie's two star pupils since she was twelve.

And yet... she'd made excuses for him then. He was so strong, so smart, and so charming. She understood that he'd felt stifled under his restraints, for her mother continually tried to make her into her image of a proper Japanese girl—complete with kimono and wooden clogs. It was their mutual rebellion that brought them together. Initially, at least. But Kai had been a tender lover, already much more experienced than she because he was six years older and she was a virgin.

On that particular voyage, the world was as limitless and new as the horizon. Kai helped her look past duty to see the possibilities of a life without such restrictions. She had been his sole focus of attention.

She remembered their first morning in the sun-streaked cabin. The scent of their long night of lovemaking still wafted from the silk sheets. Kai was insatiable, and she so enjoyed everything he was teaching her that she ignored her soreness because she wanted only to please him. Afterward, Hana had always suspected Takeo had been conceived on that morning when Kai bent her backward over the side of the bed, tilting her hips up, and took her over and over; not violently, but with his firm stamp of possession.

Only when they were both sweaty and panting did he let her rest. He'd teasingly brushed back a damp tendril of hair from her temple. "A fitting woman for the new leader of the Edo Shihans never tires of her master's touch."

Even then, Hana recalled, she'd inwardly balked a bit at his arrogance, but his smile made his face so beautiful that she'd merely circled his strong mouth with her fingertip. "Yes, master; anything you say, master." And when he lowered his mouth to kiss her, she squirmed free and leaped up, running with a taunting laugh to the tiny head to lock him out and shower. He made a pretense of banging on the door, but she heard him laughing too.

And so it had gone for two glorious weeks. They stopped at island after island, making love in every possible position on the ship, on the islands. Once Kai even bent her over a tree branch. By the time they returned to Austin, he might as well have been her master in deed as he was in name . . . and so she'd violated every lesson her mother and Jiji ever taught her. She let him turn her into a drug mule.

At that moment, a cloud blocked the brilliant blue sky, turning it gray, tainting her memories gray too. That past of shadows and brightness had brought her to this uncertain future. While she was chastising herself and swearing never again would she be so vulnerable to a man, a uniformed female warden came and fetched her, putting her in cuffs, and most humiliating of all, in ankle chains.

As they were attached, Hana mused, "I don't know whether to be upset or flattered that I'm considered so dangerous."

The woman shoved her hard between the shoulder blades down the hallway, forcing Hana to stumble to catch her balance. "Rangers don't take kindly to butchering, especially one of their own."

For once, Hana obeyed every karate precept and held her tongue. This was the second time someone had implied she was a butcher, and smart or not, her temper was beginning to simmer.

When she arrived in the interrogation room, three people sat there. She recognized John Travis, but had no idea who the other two were: A woman, tall and imposing even sitting down, and another man in a ranger's badge with iron gray hair and bright blue eyes. Hana barely glanced at them, instead fixating on the long, wrapped object on the table: the katana, still in red silk.

After the gray-haired man read her the Miranda warning for the second time, John Travis took charge. "We will be recording this conversation. You waive your right to an attorney?"

Hana nodded. "I can't afford a good one and a bad one is worse than none. Besides, I honestly believe the evidence will prove my innocence."

Travis began. "Zach tells us you only wanted to borrow the blade. You'll forgive me if I find that a bit incredible, given we have your DNA match after you broke into my home. Doesn't sound like someone looking to borrow anything. Sounds like someone out to steal."

Hana forced herself to look at him instead of the blade, making sure her face was calm. "How do you know I was after the katana? You have many other valuable things in your study."

John Travis leaned across the table, his eyes so narrow and menacing it was all she could do not to shrink back into her chair. "Young woman, I suggest you dispense with the stalling game and answer me yes or no, and a *sir* tacked on would be nice. Otherwise, I'll let my upper ranks have their way and urge the DA to give you maximum charges for B and E. Given the value of this sword and that you were caught red-handed twice, that's first-degree felony—sequential sentencing sounds good to me. You'll be considerably less sassy by the time you get out in, oh, twenty years or so."

Hana couldn't sustain his gaze. Staring over his head at the wall, she said, "Yes, I was trying to get the sword back. But not for the reason you think. I'd never sell it . . . sir."

His stiff spine relaxed slightly and he looked at the gray-haired man.

The man leaned forward with a tentative hand extended. It was as close to a peace offering as she'd get in this room, so Hana shook it as firmly as her cuffed hands would allow.

"I'm Captain Ross Sinclair, on temporary assignment as investigative lead in this matter," the gray-haired man said. "This is my associate Doctor Abigail Doyle, a forensics expert. We're compiling the evidence against you for presentation to the DA. We'll be doing the majority of the questioning today."

Hana nodded stiffly.

"Ms. Nakatomi, Zach told us you asked to hold the blade. Would you like to do so now?" Ross asked.

Hana's eyes flashed with eagerness as she looked back at him. "Yes, please."

With a questioning look at Travis, who nodded, Ross removed the handcuffs, leaving her in leg irons. John Travis stood and carefully unwrapped the blade. He offered it to her, still sheathed. All three of the interrogators then stood and moved back, well out of range, John and Ross with hands hovering above their pistols.

On some level, Hana realized two things: These tough men obviously considered her dangerous, and they were not just being kind in allowing her to handle the blade.

They were testing her.

Even knowing she was being watched, Hana couldn't stifle her emotions as she touched her family legacy for the first time. She stood and moved aside from the table for room to maneuver. The sibilant *hiss* as the steel escaped the sheath sent goose bumps down her spine. Hana had held many katanas, but never one that felt as right as this one. Not just the balance, nor the shining blade that went beyond deadly artistry to something sublime. For the first time in her life, she understood the concept of Bushido—the Way of the Warrior.

She was the last of the Nakatomi line and had taken her grandfather's name when he adopted her. The blade was hers. It felt like hers. The rightness of this hilt in her hand.

It fit. It belonged. The sword awaited her bidding because she was the last Nakatomi.

And every one of her blood cells, only half Japanese though she was, fired at the touch of the hilt that had been imprinted by fifty or more previous Nakatomi heirs, many times in battles to the death. Tears sparkled in her eyes, but since she refused to give in to her emotions, especially in this company, she stalled to minutely examine the steel. She slowly turned it blade-up so it caught the light.

Holding it with both hands gripped around the long hilt, she moved it from side to side, lunging from the waist as far as she could, constrained by the leg irons, going through each of the eight samurai blade stations. Even limited as she was, the air whistled with the force of her fluid movements. Never had the ingrained movements felt so precise, but never had she held such a worthy weapon. She went through the stations that were second nature to her after so many years: left-right thrusts, right-left thrusts, left-right diagonals, right-left diagonals, rising diagonals both sides, and finally the head strike, the sword poised above her head and arced straight downward in a move designed to decapitate the enemy in one blow.

She was totally unaware of the steely glare exchanged between the two men standing watching her, hands on their weapons. Or that behind the two-way window, Zach cursed at her amazingly fluid and practiced movements even in the leg irons. When she performed the head blow, he moved back a step from the window before he realized it. Yet at the same time he stared, rapt, for there was a terrible beauty about her movements. Had he not known the sword was her birthright before she touched it, he knew it now. It was almost as if the priceless, shining blade cleaved to her, rather than she to it.

Finally, Hana glanced their way, saw their grim scrutiny, and realized she'd only confirmed their darkest suspicions. She froze mid-strike.

With a slight, very Japanese bow, she sheathed the blade and offered it back to Travis, the hilt resting on her elbow. "Thank you, Mr. Travis. It's the first time I've ever touched the Nakatomi katana and I could not resist. It was confiscated from my grandfather in 1943 after Pearl Harbor."

When they all settled at the table again, she said calmly, "What you see as a supreme example of the art of warfare, I see as a legacy bearing the blood and tears of many ancestors. So while the law may be on your side to possess the blade, given the huge sum you paid for it, I'd argue there is a moral duty that clouds that right because it was stolen from my family in a time of paranoia. I'd further point out the federal government has acknowledged the internment camps imprisoning Japanese-American citizens were so wrong they've paid restitution in recent years. I cannot help but wonder... in this new age of strife and paranoia how would a jury of my peers view my supposed theft?"

When John scowled, this time she stared right back. Her voice went very soft. "And lastly, I wonder what your own esteemed ancestor, Colonel William Barrett Travis, would say if I tried to purchase his pocket watch at auction after it had been confiscated from you in a time of war?"

That mark hit home. For the first time, John Travis looked hesitant as he too stared at the disputed antique.

Without pause, she added matter-of-factly, "And no, I did not murder either the Taylors or anyone else, despite my ability with the blade. I've trained with every weapon imaginable since I was a small child. From the time I could walk, my grandfather encouraged me in it to keep my Japanese heritage alive. I've sparred many times with both wooden *bokkens* and real blades." She leaned forward and emphasized, "But I've never killed anyone with a sword or anything else."

Looking skeptical again, Travis turned to Ms. Doyle. She opened a thick file, but didn't glance at it.

Hana had the feeling she knew every line in the file.

The woman said softly, "Ms. Nakatomi, we know your background. We know this katana was once owned by your family. There was no evidence during your prior... incursion at the Travis home that you wanted anything but the sword. What we don't understand is why it was so urgent that you obtain the sword. Urgent enough to risk capture a second time at the transit agency. Can you explain that?"

Hana was glad to shift her attention from John Travis to meet the clearest gray eyes she'd ever beheld, clearer even than Ernie's... Ernie. Hana swallowed hard, but the guilt she felt at drawing him into this hurt far more than the shackles chafing at her ankles. Just tell the truth. Maybe that would help. She'd never been good at lying, anyway.

So she told them about Jiji, how the sword was so important to her family, not mentioning Kai. Limiting her information wasn't the same as lying, she told herself.

When they began to grill her about her alibi on the night of the Taylor murders, she had none, because she'd gone straight back to her hotel room to continue her research when the sword was nowhere to be found. She noted all three of them watched her body language very closely as she spoke. Hana recalled reading about the newest interrogation methods, where exhaustive study had yielded very strong predictions of guilt or innocence by careful attention to tells. Just like in poker, human beings tended to fidget in an interrogation room when they were bluffing.

So Hana stayed very still, hands clasped before her, answering *yes, sir, no, ma'am*, as Travis had requested, her gaze steady as she answered each question. All the while she stifled worry about Takeo, hoping, praying that Ernie was facing a less stringent inquisition. Perhaps he could at least get out on bail and find a way to get Takeo back.

In a separate interrogation room, Ernie kept his cuffed wrists resting on the table in front of him, looking quite at home. The two Austin detectives before him both recorded him and made handwritten notes in his file as he amiably answered their questions as briefly and truthfully as possible.

Where did you learn to open safes like that? New Orleans.

What else have you broken into? Nothing much lately. I'm reformed.

What did you and Ms. Nakatomi intend to do with the blade? Ask Hana that.

If you've reformed, why did you help her? She's my friend and she needed me.

And so on. At the end of the interrogation, the lead detective looked down at his notes. They were thick across the page, but he shoved them away in disgust. "You haven't told us a damn thing we don't already know."

Ernie smiled. "I answered every question I was asked, did I not? Was it my elocution or was my word choice a bit problematic for you?"

The detective looked as if he wanted to hit him, then blew a bitter breath. "I think he just insulted us."

The other detective said, "I know he did." They exchanged a look. "Time to call in the cavalry."

His colleague nodded.

In the adjacent interrogation room, Ms. Doyle reached into the file and pulled out a picture to shove on the table before Hana. "What can you tell us about this man?"

Hana glanced down. Kai. She stared for a long time, debating what to say. They already knew from her previous arrest record that she'd worked for him, so lying would only exacerbate their suspicions. Yet, she didn't dare tell them the truth: How could she claim she'd always intended to give the sword back if they knew Kai was blackmailing her to hand it over by kidnapping her son? Surely they'd believe she was still his paramour if they knew about Takeo.

Takeo... the picture wavered before her eyes as she wondered what tender mercies his father would subject him to before she could rescue him. Above all, she had to get out of here. If she couldn't obtain the sword as a bargaining chip, she had no choice but to invade the compound and rescue her son or die trying. If she could find it... she'd been forced to wear a hood when she was allowed inside several months ago to see Takeo.

She shoved the file back across the desk toward the gray-eyed woman. "I'll tell you everything I know... but only if we can make a deal that gives me total immunity from prosecution."

When John Travis's eyes flared in rage, she stared right back, her spine as straight as the katana still lying on the table next to her.

In the rugged hills outside Austin, a cool, dank cavern was lit only by occasional walkway lamps and overhead fluorescents. They illuminated an uneven path through the labyrinth. The sub-chambers leading from the main path like rough rooms were partially carved by erosion in the limestone, but tunneled deeper by excavation. All had heavy metal doors with locks and key-card readers firmly anchored into the limestone.

From above the main cavern, Kai's stocky figure was, as usual, garbed in black as he came down two levels of precarious metal circular stairways. He was holding a small boy. Kai wore his usual arsenal: katana strapped in a sheath on his back, short blade, his *tanto*, fastened at his side, and a leather satchel holding various other weapons, such as throwing stars, attached to his belt.

The little boy was restless and squirmed to be put down. "*Otosan*, let me go. Where is my mama? You promised you'd take me to her." Kai soothed the boy with a quick pat on plump little buttocks. "Soon, Takeo, soon. But first you must get better in your lessons so we can impress your mama with your skills."

As Kai carried him, Takeo looked around at his surroundings, as if still getting used to this strange place. While most of the sub-chambers were dark, they passed one bright room bustling with activity. Glass insets revealed a sparkling clean room and white-coated figures wearing masks working over what looked like chemistry benches. They were laden with beakers, burners, huge vats, vials, and other drug-making paraphernalia. Above them, lining the walls, shelves held bottles and boxes. Some were marked *flammable* or *poisonous* in bright red.

Takeo couldn't read the words, but he knew the universal symbol of a skull meant bad things were inside.

As they passed, Takeo looked inside curiously. "What do they do in there, *Otosan*?"

Kai said sharply, "Nothing that concerns you, Takeo. Mind only your lessons. Everything important begins in your mind, my son. You must learn this if you are to be a good samurai. Get into the ring." Kai plopped Takeo down. "Walk yourself, little inquisitor."

Takeo planted his feet and looked back at his father curiously, but he was not upset despite the fact that his little feet smarted from the abrupt contact with the stone walkway. In that moment, though he did not know it, he was a tiny replica of his mother as he stared up at the figure looming over him. Even at five, he had Hana's inherent common sense and logical mind. "If only my mind matters, then why do you teach me to fight?"

Kai's eyes narrowed. "Get into the ring. Now."

Sighing, Takeo turned toward their destination in the center of the large cavern: a full-sized martial-arts ring with a padded mat, ringed by elastic ropes that would bounce combatants back as they fell against the sides.

A strange look of both resignation and eagerness on his face,

Takeo grabbed a short *bokken*, a wooden sword longer than Kai's to give him equal range, from a rack against the wall. Then he willingly climbed through the ropes into the ring.

Kai paused to pull off all his own weapons, glancing at the guards hidden in various dark corners of the vast chambers, wordlessly warning them to stay on alert. Then he chose a thickly cushioned *bokken* from the wall rack before climbing into the ring.

With a little bow of salutation, they squared off. And for the next hour, Kai painstakingly trained his son to use the *bokken* in all the stations of Shotokan karate. Every time Takeo missed his mark, Kai tapped him with his own padded weapon, not hard enough to hurt, just enough to remind Takeo who was master. At the end, during their last round, he only had to correct Takeo once. He praised his son effusively. "Harder this time, Takeo. Hurt me."

Takeo stopped, the tip of his *bokken* wavering, as he breathed a bit heavily. He wiped sweat from his brow on his sleeve. "But you are my father. Why would I hurt you?"

"In this ring, I am your opponent. Show no mercy. Mercy is weakness. You must learn to fight without hesitation, someday even to kill. Such is the way of the world. You are a leader, Takeo, not a weakling. Show me."

And thus did Kai breed in his five-year-old son the twisted values Hana had spent the last five years unlearning: Anger. Aggression. Feelings of superiority. Pride. By the last round, Takeo's *bokken* hit Kai's with such force that Kai had to juggle his stick to keep from dropping it.

He gave his son a huge grin. "Excellent, Takeo!"

Clambering out of the ring, Takeo wiped his *bokken* off and carefully put it back in the wall enclosure. Then he looked expectantly up at his father. "I can see Mama now?"

Hana was tired of all the questioning, but she maintained her composure. They kept hammering on the same line, her relationship with Kai: Did she know where his compound was or how he was distributing his product, always coming back to the motive for the murders. Finally Hana said, "My relationship with him is nonexistent. I avoid him when I can. But we still have some common interests."

"What are those?"

She said reluctantly, "He also wants to hold the katana. He allowed me to use his connections to track down the blade only if I agreed to take it to him after I showed it to Jiji."

All three questioners went still.

"And what does he intend to do with it?" John asked the question this time, his voice very quiet.

"Keep it, but I would have done all I could to return it to you, Mr. Travis, even if I had to fight him to get it back."

"You've fought him before?" asked Captain Sinclair.

"Sparred with him, yes, many times, but it was years ago. I've never faced him with a real blade. I think he wants the blade as a status symbol against his rival gang leaders. I don't believe he'd ever use it to kill anyone." The words almost stuck in her throat, but since her fears were conjecture, she owed the father of her child some loyalty, at least.

The three interrogators exchanged a look. Travis and Sinclair both gave slight nods. Ms. Doyle went back to her voluminous file and flipped through to something. She shoved several black-and-white pictures across the table to Hana.

Hana looked down, and all the color left her face. She had to cup a hand over her mouth to gag back bile. "Oh my God... you think I did this? That's what Zachary meant when he said I might butcher him."

"And the Taylors were murdered not quite this horrifically, but after extensive retesting in the lab, forensics has confirmed the weapon could only be a long, single-edged sword. Like a katana," Ms. Doyle said, watching Hana through a hooded gaze that missed nothing. "You recognize the pattern of these cuts?" Closing her eyes against the grisly pictures, Hana turned her head away. After a moment, she swallowed hard. She said dully, "It's an ancient samurai ritual. Test a katana's sharpness against an enemy. The better the blade, the easier the cuts. The best katanas are called five-body blades because they remain sharp even after several cuttings."

Then she looked back at them, gripping the edge of the table. "I did not do this. I cannot believe Kai did it, either. I know he's been warring with a rival Triad gang and I recognize the victim's tattoos as one of the Triad gang members. Perhaps one of his men did it, trying to gain status?" This last was almost to herself, for Hana had retreated to the privacy of her thoughts, not even hearing the next questions.

Travis exchanged a look with Sinclair—if she was acting, she deserved an Oscar. She looked genuinely revolted to think that any man she'd once loved could do something like this.

Ms. Doyle said gently, "I'm sorry, but please look at the . . . uh . . . face of the person who was decapitated and tell me if you can identify him. We have no record of his prints or DNA in our databases."

Hana gave a tiny shudder before she steeled herself. She picked up the photo of the head, carefully examining what remained of the face. She put it back down. "I don't know him. But as I've said many times, I'm not involved in any of the gangs any more. I've been working two jobs and going back to school—"

"Yes, we've verified that," Sinclair interrupted curtly. "That doesn't mean you're not a person of interest in these murders and, at least, aiding and abetting the criminal activity that foments this sort of thing. You have a record as a drug mule, Ms. Nakatomi. Given the horrific nature of these crimes, you'd be wise to cooperate with us in any way we ask."

Hana cried, "What else can I say to convince you my only interest was the sword?"

John Travis leaned forward. "Ingratiate yourself with Kai. Then become our informant. Help us get enough evidence to put him away for a long time, and we'll drop all the charges against you." His smile showed the sharp intellect behind his aristocratic face.

In that moment, he looked exactly like portraits of William Barrett Travis, right down to his cleft chin. "It was your idea, right, Ms. Nakatomi? You want immunity? We aim to please."

Chapter 7

While Hana was blinking in shock, for she'd never expected such ready agreement to her impulsive plea, a knock came at the door. Sinclair opened it, conferred with the Austin police detective standing there, and went back to whisper something to Travis. Travis looked at Ms. Doyle, his mouth twitching before he controlled it.

"You're needed in the other interrogation room, apparently."

Ms. Doyle frowned, looking at Hana's pale face.

John said, "We won't torture her much longer. I promise."

Ms. Doyle flushed slightly, obviously not realizing her compassion for Hana was showing. "Do you want the file?"

"No, you may need it in the other room."

Ms. Doyle exited quietly.

Hana had regained her composure during the interval. She gnawed her lip savagely and then burst out, "You don't know what you're asking me to do. I despise Kai and everything he stands for. He knows that. I don't believe he'd even want me back. There is too much... strife between us for him to trust me."

John Travis shrugged. "Well, it was worth a shot. I guess we don't have a deal—"

Hana leaned forward, her black eyes sparkling. "But I can offer something else. I might be able to show you where his compound is. It's also the place where he makes his product. I've seen his drug-making paraphernalia. If you catch him there, you'll have evidence aplenty against him and all his men."

Now she had their acute attention.

Inside the other interrogation room, Ernie's long, untidy figure moved from its habitual slouch to bolt upright when Abigail Doyle entered the room. The lead detective accompanied her, but Ernie didn't even glance at him. His gaze, almost the exact silvery shade of Abigail's, appraised her from her sensible heels, up her severe pantsuit, lingered on the gentle flare of her bosom in a white silk blouse, down her long form to her toes again. When his gaze locked with hers, his slow smile widened until it ended in a grin of pure appreciation that was so male the ever-calm professional shifted nervously, from foot to foot.

He winked, his Cajun undertone pronounced. "Now, this is more like it. I'll share all my sweet nothings with you, *chere*. You must be the indefatigable Ms. Doyle. I've heard of you from my . . . er—colleagues. Such words as *brilliant. Tenacious forensics expert.* So on." The cocky male grin spread to his pale eyes, darkening them. "But now I've seen you, I think other appellations would be more appropriate."

Ignoring his compliments, or trying to, Abigail sat down across from him and made a show of straightening her already straight papers. When the high flush on her cheekbones had faded, she looked at him severely. "Mr. Thibodeaux—"

"Ernie."

"Mr. Thibodeaux, with your background in prior, shall we say, illegal activities—"

"Safecracking. Kiting checks. Securities fraud. But the key word there, *chere*, is *prior*."

"Hardly a defensible position, given you were caught red-handed breaking into a vault—"

"And I wasn't going to keep a thing. We only wanted the sword."

"So you can confirm Ms. Nakatomi's statement that she only wanted the sword to let her grandfather hold it one last time and then she intended to return it?"

He hesitated, finally nodding.

She pounced on his hesitation. "There's something you're both not telling us. And frankly, if we can't trust that you're telling us the full truth so we can assess your intentions, we have no other option but to ramp up every charge we can legally justify—and they are many—to keep you both off the streets."

Ernie eyed her closely. Her nose was a bit prominent, but there was character in every patrician line of her bone structure. He looked at the detective, and back at his interrogator. "Hana won't tell you why she really needs the sword because she's protecting the person she loves most in the world."

Ms. Doyle's busy pen froze as she made notes in the file. "Yes?"

Ernie hesitated. "She'll be very angry with me if I tell you."

"She'll be in jail for a very long time if you don't," Abigail retorted. "As will you."

When Ernie still hesitated, Abigail said coldly, "Given the evidence we have that the Taylor murders were committed with a very similar sword to the katana, someone with Ms. Nakatomi's training performed that heinous crime." She shoved over the same pictures of the dead gang member that she'd shown to Hana. "There are similarities between the Taylor murders to this gang slaying. Even the angle of the strokes, their depth, not just the type of blade. Only someone trained in cutting techniques could leave such carnage."

Ernie stared down at the photos and for once in his life, was rendered speechless.

Ms. Doyle enunciated, "Correct me if I'm wrong, but it takes extreme skill and practice to be able to butcher a human body like this. The same skill was used in a slightly less revolting way on Sam Taylor and his wife. Coincidentally, the deaths occurred a few nights before you and Ms. Nakatomi—for the second time, in her case—went to great lengths to steal a priceless sword that's revered precisely because it was so well designed for these very cuts. And you wish us to believe the two acts are not linked and neither of you know who committed them?" She made a harsh sound in the back of her throat that was decidedly unladylike, but very to the point.

Still looking a bit sick, Ernie shoved the photos back toward Abigail. "Very well, I'll tell you everything. But you have to promise both Hana and me immunity."

Abigail waved a dismissing hand. "That will not be my decision. I cannot promise a thing. But the more valuable your information in solving these murders, the more generous the prosecutors tend to be."

Ernie looked at the detective. "You're recording all this?"

The detective nodded. "Do you wish to change your mind about a lawyer before we proceed?"

With the reckless, go-to-hell grin Hana would have recognized with dread, Ernie propped his cuffed hands on the table before him as if they were diamond bracelets. "Nope. I'm of Shakespeare's persuasions when it comes to attorneys: *The first thing we do, let's kill all the lawyers.*"

When he finally won the flicker of a smile from Abigail, he leaned forward as if he and she were in a cozy booth in a French café conducting their own little tête-à-tête.

"First off, you're right about the cuts. They probably are similar because the angles are almost perfect examples of samurai practice cuts. I'm pretty sure Kai is responsible, but I can't yet prove it. However, I'm going to tell you everything you need to understand Hana's motives. But only in the interests of clearing Hana of any wrongdoing. Let me tell you a story about two young lovers. The boy was a new illegal immigrant from Japan, the female half Japanese, but an American citizen. They were both wild and rebellious, but of uncommon martial-arts ability. I know, because I trained them. Unfortunately that's how they met. At my dojo. They became lovers when he was twenty-two and she was sixteen—"

Inside the other interrogation room, Hana read the brief and very conditional immunity agreement the DA's office had drawn up after hearing her offer.

John Travis warned her, "For the third time, I'd suggest you let us get you a pro bono criminal attorney before you sign anything binding."

Hana signed the short document. "Lawyers took my grandfather's house away. And they'll only delay my release if we can come to terms now. Besides, I have nothing to fear because I've told the truth. I'm pretty sure I can find the compound if we duplicate the conditions of my other trip. A hood, a van, darkness, starting from the same place. Martial arts teach one to listen to one's senses and I counted between turns. I can't promise I can find it, but I won't know if I don't try."

Hana shoved the document back across the table. A cop took the papers out with him. Hana turned back to John Travis. She nibbled at her lip, hesitating, then burst out, "But there are other people there. Young children. Workers. Innocents. If you storm the compound, Kai is not above holding them hostage. This must be done very delicately."

"Understood," Travis agreed. "First, let's see if you can find it and then we'll figure out the logistics." He smiled at her—really smiled at her—for the first time since the interrogation began. "Even Texas Rangers can show finesse, from time to time."

Hesitantly, Hana smiled back. She wanted to believe him. Desperately. But all she saw in her mind's eye was Takeo, dragged with Kai as he deserted his men. She'd not seen it, but she knew it was there: He'd disappear down his escape tunnel, her son his key to freedom, the minute he realized he was being raided.

Immunity agreement or not, on the day of the raid she had to get to Takeo first. If it violated her agreement, so be it. She would somehow convince her mother to take Takeo if she had to do jail time.

The next day, released on bond after Ernie posted bail for the two of them, Hana chafed at the ankle monitor and its blinking red light. It was hidden beneath her jeans, but it felt more burdensome than leg shackles. And if Kai ever saw it, he'd know instantly she had betrayed him.

Ernie said, "My van has no doubt been towed, so we'll take a cab. Come along."

Still on the steps, Hana balked. "Ernie, I'm sorry right down to my toes that you got caught up in all this—"

"Best fun I've had in years."

"But you have absolutely no right to boss me around. I'm not your student anymore."

"Uh-huh, you've done such a good job staying out of trouble with-out me."

"With you, don't you mean? I think you also agreed to our strategy of breaking into the transit agency vault."

He took her elbow to escort her down the stairs. "Let's not argue at least until we're a few feet from police headquarters."

When they were a block away from possible surveillance cameras, Ernie flagged a cab. As it pulled to the curb he said, "I think you need to stay in my spare room until all this is over. It's not safe for you alone in that hotel room."

As they sat in the backseat of the cab, she eyed his calm face suspiciously. "What do you have planned, Ernie?"

He lowered his voice. "Did they offer you immunity?"

She took her copy of the agreement from her jeans pocket and offered it to him. He read it quickly and gave it back. "So you think you can find the place?"

She hesitated a moment too long.

"I thought so. Your agreement is contingent on finding the damn compound. You would have said anything to get out because you're so worried about Takeo." He sighed heavily. "So am I. There is an alternative." He lowered his voice even further, now whispering in her ear, so even the cabdriver, a possible police informant, couldn't hear.

He said softly, "Ms. Doyle—man, I can't wait until I ruffle those armored feathers—agreed to approach the brass with making me the informant instead of you. And if I accept Kai's offer to tutor his men, I can say I need the money, which is true. I'll have a natural entry point."

Hana sat back, her face drawn. At first she shook her head. "I can't ask you to put yourself in any more danger than you already have."

"This isn't your decision, Hana. It's mine. I love Takeo too. He needs you. All you have to do is help me find the place. Have a little faith in me... when the time comes, I'll see he's protected."

Still gnawing at her lip, Hana nodded reluctantly.

In a small conference room in John's office complex, Zach sat across from his father, Ross, and Abigail.

"So what did you think, Zach?" asked John Travis. "Was she telling the truth? Can she really find this compound?"

Zach shrugged. "Maybe. But there's still something she's not telling us."

"You think she's involved somehow in the murders?"

This time Zach's shake of the head was certain. "No. Gutting someone asleep in their bed is not her style. She's probably not above skewering someone if she feels justified—I think we could all see that in her ease with the katana. But she'd do it face-to-face in a fair fight, not against a prisoner or an unarmed man."

Wryly, Ross shook his head. "You talk like you admire her, Zach."

"I do. I've faced her hand-to-hand twice and she got away both times. I probably outweigh her by a hundred pounds."

"Ability does not equate with innocence, Zachary," pointed out Abigail. "Usually quite the opposite."

Zach shrugged again. "You asked my opinion. I gave it. As to the extent of her involvement with Kai and his ilk, on that I feel less certain. We took a risk letting her go. Could be she's still involved with him and will warn him we're close."

Abigail nodded. "Your instincts are good." She shoved over her own interrogation notes from her meeting with Ernie. "It took some persuading, but Mr. Thibodeaux can be quite... voluble when he chooses."

Abigail's face took on a quizzical expression as she contemplated their other suspect's picture atop her second file. But her face cleared to its usual calm professionalism when she looked at John, Ross, and Zach in turn. "I believe Mr. Thibodeaux's long relationship as something of a mentor to Ms. Nakatomi has made him quite protective of her. He was much more forthcoming when he realized it was quite possible they could both get out on immunity agreements. Apparently, he also tutored Kai when he was a young man. Kai recently asked him to train his men. Mr. Thibodeaux refused, but he's proposing that he give a belated acceptance and use it to infiltrate the compound."

The three men exchanged a look. Zach looked relieved, but John was hesitant. "How can we trust him?"

"Dad, you just said you don't trust Hana, either," Zach reminded him. "It sounds like this guy is a better choice than Hana, especially with his mob ties."

John was noncommittal. He nodded at Abigail to go on. "What else did you learn?"

Abby continued: "I have a long history now of Ms. Nakatomi's relationship with Kai. It's far more complex than she let on. If the facts are true as Mr. Thibodeaux described, our case against Ms. Nakatomi for felony breaking and entering is unlikely to lead to a conviction. Another good reason to use Mr. Thibodeaux as informant. He has unsettled priors that give us leverage."

John frowned. "Why do you say we can't convict Ms. Nakatomi?"

Zach's hands gripped the underside of the table. Through lowered lashes, John watched Zach's expression as Abigail finished. "The gist of his statement is that Ms. Nakatomi's feeling that Kai would not trust her because of past acrimony is probably both accurate and justified. She broke it off with him about a year into their relationship, five years ago, apparently partly because he left her dangling when she was arrested as his drug mule."

Zach pounced. "Partly?"

Abigail hesitated. "The other more pertinent reason is that she had his child. A son."

All three men were taken aback, but Zach's hands clutched the underside of the table so hard that the legs scraped against the floor. Ross looked at Zach, and then saw the way Travis furtively watched his son. Frowning, he looked back at Abigail.

Abigail was also aware of the byplay, but she doggedly finished. "The boy's name is Takeo. He's five. Kai has apparently kidnapped their son to use him as leverage. The real reason Ms. Nakatomi risked her freedom to steal the sword? Her grandfather, true, but the overriding reason was her son. On the day she gives the katana to Kai, he's promised to hand Takeo back to her. Then she intends to disappear so he'll never influence Takeo again."

It was her turn to look at each man in turn. "Quite aside from the fact that she is undoubtedly the last Nakatomi heir, with a moral if not a legal claim to the katana, how can any jury—or for that matter, prosecutor—convict her for trying to protect her only child?"

That night, shortly after sunset, Zach wandered the grounds of his home. He'd been unable to eat much at dinner, causing his mother concern, but John had only shaken his head at his wife. John kept trying to get his son alone and Zach kept avoiding him. No one had to tell him John was worried his son's feelings toward Hana were not objective.

He was absolutely right, Zach admitted in the disquiet of his own thoughts. Now that he understood the reasons for the desperation he'd sensed in Hana, he realized he'd never been objective even when he was having her cuffed. The truth was, something in this wild child of mixed heritage and mixed motives drew him as no woman ever had.

As he moved around the spacious grounds, nodding at the occasional guard leading a *Malanois*, he replayed Hana's interrogation in his head. He always returned to the same remark, one of the last she'd made: "There are innocents there . . ."

Now they all knew what she meant, and why she'd been reluctant at first to admit she could help them find the compound. She was worried Takeo would be hurt in the raid. And he also recalled his father's flippant response that even Rangers had finesse.

Although that was no doubt true, Zach also knew that anything and everything could go wrong during a raid. The key to smooth operations was meticulous reconnaissance. And they couldn't monitor a place they couldn't find . . . unless they delayed everything, risking more murders, to give them time to insert themselves in the compound after Hana found it.

At the end of their session, John had agreed to try out Ernie Thibodeaux as informant, to Zach's great relief. But his task would be very dangerous, not to mention time-consuming. If another murder occurred, they wouldn't be able to wait for proper intel. And Hana would never sit by and watch if her son was in danger.

How the hell could he come up with a way to protect her and Takeo and still do his duty?

As soon as Hana showered and changed, they secured another vehicle so they'd both have one to drive. "I have to go see Jiji before I do anything else," Hana informed Ernie.

He nodded. "Do you want me to come?"

Hana shook her head glumly. "No, I'd love for you to be there if I can ever show him the katana, but since that seems unlikely . . ." She trailed off, biting her lip. As worried as she was about Takeo, it ate at her that she couldn't offer the slightest solace to her grandfather during his passing.

"OK, kiddo, take the little heap. I have something I need to do too. We'll meet back here to plan, say, around nine p.m."

She arched an inquiring eyebrow, but Ernie had already turned away.

Grabbing up a newspaper she could read to her grandfather, Hana dismissed Ernie's erratic motivations and went to the little economy car he'd loaned her. The next night she'd agreed to try to find the compound, so she only had the rest of today to see Jiji. She knew it was a forlorn hope, but maybe, just maybe, his condition had improved.

* * *

Back at the balcony again, Zach paused and touched the wrought iron, visualizing that long, lithe, superbly fit female form climbing up the ornate rails to reach his open window. If he'd known that night that she'd replace his tortured dreams with more pleasurable ones, he might have turned around when she'd snatched his wrap away.

His little smile faded as he recalled the tears in her eyes when she touched the Nakatomi katana. At a visceral level that surpassed his own deeply engraved morals, he knew she had more right to the blade than a business consortium intent on displaying a private family heirloom to the world. For education or not.

Going into the study, he keyed the digital code into a keypad hidden behind a boring set of encyclopedias. Part of the bookcase swung forward, revealing a full-length safe. He keyed in the second code and the full-sized door popped open with a *hiss*. He went inside and lifted the katana off its stand.

Taking it back with him into the study, he tried using it as Hana had, two-handed, but her sheer speed and fluidity of movement was beyond him, for they were moves he'd never practiced. He felt awkward whether he tried with one hand or two. He recalled a segment he'd seen on TV of a mock battle between an armored samurai and an armored Viking warrior. Despite being smaller and physically weaker, the samurai had won the sword fight due to superior weaponry, training, and tactical ability.

As he tested the blade until it whistled in the air as if hungry for flesh, even Zach—a novice in samurai ways—felt the pure lethal beauty of the sword. This blade was designed for one purpose: to cut human flesh. Yet he also felt its majesty as he recalled once again its power in the hands of the last Nakatomi heir. Even bound by leg irons, Hana seemed free of earthly constraints to achieve a mythical warrior ethos he'd heard of many times, but had never seen so vividly on display. It was as if the sword elevated her, not vice versa, infusing her with the same nobility of spirit as her samurai ancestors. Duty, honor, courage, fealty to an ideal even if it meant death.

For the first time, he began to understand—a little, at least—the obsession the Japanese had for these ancestral legacies. They truly were more than swords.

When he put the katana back in the sheath, he knew what he had to do. To capture Kai, and keep Hana and her son safe, he had to win her trust. This blade had brought her into his life. It was only fair that it ease the passage of the person she most loved, its last rightful owner, as he left hers.

Putting the sword back into the safe, he went in search of his father.

Chapter 8

His decision made, Zach strode to the living room, where he found his father sitting with a file on his lap, making notes while his mother crocheted. It was a couples' ritual during which they discussed the issues of the day, and he seldom intruded, but this couldn't wait. Knocking lightly on the double-wide open doors, he entered. He kissed his mother's cheek and admired her new afghan, hoping inwardly she wasn't giving him another one, as he already had four in his storage unit. Besides, he knew she'd tried to take up domesticity to please his father, but her heart wasn't in it. The pattern, meant to be a series of neat squares, looked more like isosceles triangles.

But that wasn't why he'd come. He looked at his father. "Can I talk to you in the study for a moment?"

"About damn time." John set aside his file. "Back in a bit, honey."

Mary looked between them uncertainly. "Zach—"

"I promise not to pull out the dueling pistols, Mom," Zach joked. "Though we may end up fighting over the katana."

John gave him a sharp look, but led the way to the study. He sat down at his desk and turned on the desk lamp.

Zach frowned at the open shade over the window. "Dad, I've told you over and over you shouldn't have that shade up, especially at night when you're working with a desk light."

"And I've told you over and over I won't be a prisoner in my own home. Besides, with all the guards outside, what is there to fear? Now, quit stalling and tell me what the hell's going on in that scrambled brain of yours about this ninja chick?"

Sprawling before his father in the wing chair, Zach almost laughed to hear his conservative, stodgy father use a slangy term that could have come from a Quentin Tarantino film. "I think she's more trained as a Shotokan karate expert than a 'ninja chick,' though there is admittedly a lot of crossover in the skill sets."

"Yeah, well, I don't trust her not to greet us with one of those blow-dart doohickies if we stand between her and her son. It's time we had this out in the open, anyway."

Zach braced himself, but he knew this script so well he could almost quote his father before he said a word.

Sure enough: "I can see you're very attracted to her, but she's dangerous, Zach. That's the simple truth. And, of course, totally inappropriate as an alliance for the last direct male descendant of—"

Zach sat bolt upright, his glare so fierce his father stopped midsentence. "So help me God, if you lecture me one more time about my rights and responsibilities, I'll resign from my new position and take the oil-rig job instead."

With a heavy sigh, John subsided. But his erect posture looked a bit wilted. "Your mother has introduced you to so many nice girls—"

Zach made an impatient wave of his hand to cut him off. "Precisely. Does it occur to you I'm not interested in nice girls? Like someone else we know, perhaps?"

When his father remained glumly silent, Zach relented. He measured his words carefully because he had to have his father's approval of his plan. "I've thought this through. I think the best way to find the compound and get enough evidence to put this Kai bastard away for life is to let Ms. Nakatomi borrow the sword."

John's mouth dropped open but he was, for once, speechless.

Zach hurried on: "Look, she won't sell the blade, that's for sure. And if it's true that Kai wants it, it gives her leverage and a degree of safety while she goes in to get her son out of there before we pull the trigger on our raid."

"Good God, are you saying you don't trust us to avoid collateral damage when we go in? We always have to consider that."

"Yes, I know, but this is not a standard op. And even the best ones almost always require adjustments at the last minute. When the time comes, I'd like your permission to lead the raid as head of the security detail."

John frowned fiercely. "This is not standard, you know that. The Ranger reconnaissance team—"

"Can be reallocated as you see fit. And as good as they are, they haven't faced the kind of firepower I faced in Afghanistan or led as many covert ops."

John was still reluctant. "This will be extremely dangerous. I don't—"

"Are you saying you won't allow it because I'm your son?"

John was stubbornly silent.

Zach changed tactics. "This is premature now anyway, but I just want you to think about letting me lead when the time comes. First we have to find the damn hideout, and to do that we need to gain Ms. Nakatomi's trust."

"Uh, I think you have that backwards. Why should we trust anything she says? Much less trust her with a priceless artifact that I don't own?"

"Dad, I know y'all have plenty of insurance on the blade. Even if something happens to it, the partners will be reimbursed."

"Yeah, but I can't authorize you to give it away. Are you nuts? I have the other members of the LLC to answer to."

"If you tell them it's a key piece of evidence in the murders that we have to use as bait, they'll hand it over to you gladly." When his father still looked appalled, Zach spread his hands wide as if his next point were self-evident. "It's hardly going to reflect well on either the Texas Rangers or your LLC if Hana and her son are killed because we wouldn't let her use the best leverage we have."

After a long moment of looking for a hole in that argument and not finding one, John shook his head. "Who the hell taught you to argue?"

Zach laughed. "A stubborn son of a bitch I used to think was an idiot."

The stubborn son of a bitch-cum-former idiot threw up his hands. "I infer from that I've finally made it up to average intelligence." Zach grinned, his dimples showing beneath amazing azure eyes that matched those peering back at him. "Oh, you're way past that. This conversation is something in the way of a Mensa exam."

John had to give a reluctant smile. "All right, all right, it's for sure you got that charm from your mother, not me. Okay, let me make some calls."

Happy that he'd at least convinced his father to let Hana have the blade for now, Zach did something he hadn't done in years: He rounded the desk and kissed the top of his father's head. "Thanks, Dad."

Zach hurried to the door, but he turned on the sill. "Think about what I said..." He trailed off. Something clogged his throat, and it wasn't allergies. In the bright glow of the desk lamp, he saw tears in his father's eyes and they brought a moisture to his own that embarrassed him. Only then did he realize it had been years since he'd given his father such a heartfelt, spontaneous gesture of affection.

"I'm sorry, Dad," he said again. This time they exchanged a long look that traveled down many years of good memories. "I'm... enjoying working so closely with you."

Feeling as awkward at that moment as he had when his dad hugged him among all his classmates after he graduated from boot camp, Zach turned toward the front door. Time to review the watch logs and set his mind at ease that no snipers had been sighted. But he also vowed to be more affectionate with the man who was, after all, the most important in the world to him.

Hana sat next to Jiji's bed, her hand clasped in his, trying to come to terms with losing him forever. He was awake, sort of. His eyes opened when she leaned over him. It had only been a couple of days since she'd visited him, but it felt like a lifetime. He'd been pale then, but now he was the color of his sheets. He stirred when she tightened her grip. His skin was hot and dry, and as fragile as the origami he'd tried so patiently to teach the young, impatient Hana.

"Jiji, I'm here. I've missed you. I've been... busy with Takeo. I'm sorry I didn't come yesterday. I have a paper to read to you." When he feebly clasped her hand and asked to sit up, she used the bed control to raise his head slightly. She'd never told him Takeo had been taken. There was no need to upset him at this point.

Stifling her grief at the knowledge that soon he'd be gone too, she settled next to the bed and opened the paper.

But with extreme effort, he raised a trembling hand and traced the shadows under her eyes. "What is hurting you, Hana?"

This time she couldn't hold back the tears. "I wasn't able to get the sword, Jiji. I tried, really hard...." She bit her lip. "These Travises, they care for nothing but their own wealth and power."

This time his hand covered her lips. "What have I always told you, granddaughter? My favorite Buddha saying?" He began, *"Holding on to anger . . ."*

His hand still against her lips like a blessing, Hana finished, *"is like drinking poison and expecting the other person to die."*

His hand fell away and he sank against his pillow again, as if even that movement exhausted him, but he managed a tiny nod of approval. "Live your life by letting go of anger, Hana, if not for yourself, for Takeo." He closed his eyes. "Now, read."

Hana dashed her tears off on her sleeve and began reading. First the headlines, then the opinion page, and so on. She read the paper in order, the way he liked it with his organized mind. That, thank God, he'd never lost even as his body failed him. She was about two hours in and had reached the business pages when she felt a presence at the half-open door.

She looked up. Zachary Travis stood there, half in, half outside the room, staring at her. He looked . . . surprised? Enthralled? She couldn't quite peg his expression, but he'd obviously stood there for a long moment listening to her read.

When she put the paper down, staring toward the door, Jiji turned his head slightly, with obvious effort. His old eyes, sunken and dark, flickered in surprise as a very tall, handsome young man entered the room. But it wasn't Zach's chinos and dress shirt Jiji or Hana noticed.

It was the red silk-wrapped katana in his hand.

A long, rambling Texas farmhouse-style home glistened in the rays of sunlight fingering through protective oak trees. The house had shutters and a rambling, covered porch that wrapped around three sides. The metal roof caught the sunlight too. Even in the shade, the architectural style seemed made for laughter and family gatherings. The house sat high on a limestone cliff at the end of a long caliche road. The caliche road met another caliche road, each fronted with only a cattle guard to pen in the Black Angus cattle dotting the rolling landscape.

The acre around the house, however, was enclosed by high wrought-iron fencing that crackled with electricity as a stray leaf caught on it. An acute observer might have noticed the many surveillance cameras situated at strategic points all the way around the parcel, eyes glowing red even in the sunlight.

A black Land Rover roared up the drive, pausing at the electric gate. The driver punched in a ten-digit code, waiting for the gate to open sideways. When it did, he drove inside, not moving again until the gate was completely shut behind them.

The Land Rover stopped on the half-circle drive in front of the house. The same two muscular men who'd invaded the Taylors' home, still dressed in black, went to the rear and opened the tailgate, pulling someone out. Ernie's tall form, still in his habitual Hawaiian shirt and shorts, straightened as if he felt stiff. His head was hooded. They pushed him between the shoulder blades. "Move."

Ernie froze. "Take off this blasted hood. I haven't the slightest idea where I am or how far we came. Falling on my ass is no way for me to start teaching your men. You want me to look ridiculous?"

The two men exchanged a look. The older one jerked off the hood. "Up the steps. Kai is waiting."

Ernie paused a moment to put both hands behind the small of his back and stretch, but his eyes carefully appraised every inch of his surroundings. In three seconds flat, which was all they allowed him, he saw the guards stationed in trees, wearing camouflage, one with their surroundings as only someone trained in ninja tactics could be.

He saw an extremely sophisticated security system and more electronic equipment in various arrays on the roof.

He saw solar panels covering the western exposure on the roof.

He saw several lazily turning wind turbines some distance away in a cleared pasture with more cattle grazing at the bases. He saw chickens in an open pen to one side of the house and a tall stock tank brimming with dripping well water along with a windmill, blades whirring, between the chickens and the cattle.

And he heard a quiet *purr* he recognized: a huge generator around the side of the house.

When they pushed him up the steps, keying in another complicated code beside the door, his expression was blank, but inwardly he was appalled.

No wonder they'd never been able to get a read on Kai's compound. It was totally off the grid. He'd wager even Kai's computer systems were in a secure room proofed against electronic interference. He was equally sure Kai used only the Dark Web for his Internet access and probably had rotating IP encryption on every computer.

The cops would never track this place without some help. He also understood why Hana had never tried to sneak in and spirit Takeo away. It would be suicide. By the looks of the precautions against such an incursion, even a task force combined of Texas Rangers, DEA, and local Travis County SWAT would have a hard time breaking in. Kai had the best security limitless drug money could buy.

Inside, the house was cool and dark. Ernie realized the windows weren't just shaded; they had metal electronic panels. One of the men who escorted him removed a tiny remote from his pocket and pressed a button. The metal panels raised enough, receding into the attic space, for him to see a coldly modern living room totally at odds with the house's cozy architecture. Low furniture, Japanese screens, even a niche with a Buddha and an unlit incense burner. Ernie had to swallow a scoff at the pretention. What could one say of a man who'd savagely butcher another human being as easily as he displayed reverence for a religion built on peace and harmony?

But he merely gave Kai a respectful half nod, half bow, as he entered. Kai wore his usual black attire, with a katana in the sheath on his back and the shorter blade, the *tanto*, in his belt. "Welcome," Kai said in Japanese, slightly bowing in return. He swept a hand at the low couch, but Ernie folded his long form before the long, low coffee table, sitting on a cushion, as he knew Kai would sit across from him. He didn't want to tower any more over the shorter man than he already did.

Quite literally bad form. Ernie began: "Kai, I appreciate your faith in me, but I haven't been an official sensei for many years."

Kai shrugged. "Practice first. It will come back to you. I would not be the swordsman I am today without your tutelage." Suddenly, he leaned forward very intently. "It isn't just my men I want you to teach. It's Takeo. He's at the perfect age to start the discipline. I've tried to teach him, but . . ." He waved a frustrated hand. "He's more interested in painting. And he already knows you and likes you."

Ernie accepted the heated cup of sake Kai offered and sipped slowly, searching for the right words. He said slowly, "But I understood that he'd be going back to his mother soon."

Kai slammed his sake cup down so hard a bit of liquid sloshed on his wrist. "Hana told you this?"

Ernie nodded.

"Takeo will stay with me. He's my son and needs a firm hand."

"You know they arrested us both when we broke into the transit company safe?"

Kai nodded shortly. "This is why my men were so cautious and searched you for a wire. But your loyalties to Hana will have no bearing on your role here, because you will not see her until I am satisfied with Takeo's progress and my... business negotiations are complete. You will be my guest. For an extended stay."

Silvery eyes met black across the low table. Ernie didn't miss the slightly menacing gesture as Kai's hand lowered to the hilt of his *tanto*. This, he had not expected. He'd been instructed by his DEA handler to make note of every ingress and egress, the security, the number of guards, any signs of an escape tunnel, the timing of the watch shifts, and so on. But they hadn't dared put a wire on him, for which he was now grateful. How the hell was he to contact them from this fortress?

He tried a feeble protest. "But I don't have any spare clothes, no razor, no—"

Rising, Kai clapped his hands sharply. A diminutive girl of mixed Asian heritage entered the room, her eyes downcast. "She will take you to your room. I'll allow you to get settled and I'll have you escorted into the ring in an hour. You'll find proper attire in your room."

Ernie also rose. "As you wish." But as he followed the girl to the door under Kai's watchful gaze, Ernie couldn't avoid his own subtle warning. He turned and said slowly, "Hana won't give up on the sword, Kai. Surely you know that. What happens if she brings it to you? Will you honor your bargain with her?"

Kai shrugged. "I won't have to. Now they know she's after it, she'd have to get past the mighty Texas Rangers and one of the most respected and wealthy families in Texas to steal the sword. She'll never touch it. Takeo is mine."

Inside Jiji's hospital room, Zach sat on an institutional vinyl chair with the katana across his knees. Slowly, he offered it to Hana across the small gap between their two chairs. "My father and his group have agreed to loan it to you for a short time. Until we secure your son's release. I don't need to remind you how important it is you keep it safe."

"It will not leave my side, even when I sleep. I swear it."

Their hands touched when she reached for the sword. They both flinched slightly at the electrical current that flashed from him to her and back. But when she at last held the sword in her lap, her eyes misted. "I have you to thank for this, don't I?"

Zach merely smiled. "I was watching you go through the samurai stations while you were being questioned. It's vividly apparent this sword is part of your blood. I can't imagine anyone else using it with such grace and skill. It almost . . . cleaves to you."

"And I to it." Hana rose and carefully unwrapped the blade. She unsheathed it, holding it out to her grandfather on her extended arms. She bowed deeply. "Jiji, as I promised, here is the Nakatomi katana Masamune made for our ancestor. With my eternal gratitude and devotion."

Jiji struggled to sit up. Hana pushed the bed remote to raise the bed, but Zach gently caught the frail old man and lifted him until he could prop pillows behind his back.

Jiji's hands trembled as he lovingly followed with his finger the long groove running the length of the slightly curved blade. He traced the diamond pattern on the hilt, following the pattern to the guard, which still showed a bit of the original gilding. Finally, he turned it slightly, with obvious effort, to look at his own reflection in the shining steel. He whispered something in Japanese.

When Hana had to turn away, obviously moved, Zach asked, "What did he say?"

Hana said shakily, "He said, 'You brought me the soul of my ancestors. I will forever be in your debt. The memory of it will guard me as I travel on my final journey.'"

Zach had to swallow a lump in his throat too. He recalled reading a favorite Japanese saying: *The sword is the soul of the samurai.*

Jiji did something very strange, then. Turning the blade with obvious effort, he touched his forefinger quite deliberately on the razor-sharp edge and pressed hard enough to draw blood.

Zach moved forward to stop him, but Hana caught his arm and shook her head. "Let him do this," she mouthed.

Zach froze. As he watched, Jiji ran his bloody finger down the entire length of the blade, leaving a trail of red. Then, with a contented sigh, he subsided against his pillows. Hana snatched a Kleenex from the bedside and wrapped it around Jiji's small cut.

Zach was still mystified and Jiji must have sensed his confusion. The old man whispered, "Now my blood marks it too. It is the only thing of value I can give in honor of my ancestors."

Now Zach understood.

"Young man," Jiji said even more softly.

Zach moved close.

"I know our sword has much value. But it belongs with my heirs. Hana. Takeo. Find a way to keep it with her, in honor of your own ancestors. It may save your life one day...." Jiji's voice grew softer and softer.

His eyes fluttered, and he went inert against the pillows as if his last store of energy had been exhausted. The sword slipped down on the covers, leaving a little trail of red, but he still held the hilt as if he couldn't bear to let it go. In a moment, his breathing evened. Exhausted, he slept. The blade sagged down to his lap, almost falling to the floor. Hana picked it up and used a paper towel, dampened in Jiji's sink, to wipe the blade until it gleamed again. Still holding it in one hand, she leaned over and kissed his brow.

"He's exhausted."

"What do the doctors say?"

Hana shook her head. "They can only treat his pain. The cancer has spread."

Slowly, very reluctantly, she wrapped the sword again and offered it to him. "Thank you. From the bottom of my heart." Her eyes widened when he refused to take the sword.

"I got my father and his partners to agree to let you keep it until... until..." He took a deep breath. "For Takeo. If Kai wants it so badly, it should give you some leverage. We'll recover it during the raid."

Hana was so shocked that she was, for once, speechless.

Then she did something that left him equally speechless.

She kissed him.

Chapter 9

As kisses went, it didn't quite cause an earthquake, but it shook both of them in a far more fundamental way: their preconceptions. Hana had only intended to give him a quick buss of gratitude, but the touch of his lips—warm, surprisingly soft—tempted her to linger. Curious at first, she only slid her lips gently from side to side, but since he was utterly still, she had free reign.

That knowledge made her exploration all the more pleasurable. What was this tough, arrogant heir to a dynastic Texas family, the same man who was responsible for arresting her, doing trusting her with something so precious? Why had he come, really, with a deadly sword as a peace offering?

In the taste of his lips, she found no answers, only more delicious questions.

What would all that smooth skin lightly dusted with hair feel like against hers?

Would he be as athletic and powerful in bed as he was in hand-to-hand combat?

Would he be that ultimate paradox every woman pined for? Strong enough for true gentleness, with nothing to prove but pleasure given and returned?

She had to know . . . she opened her mouth to him in invitation.

The next thing she knew, she felt him closing the half-open door. He lockstepped her to the wall beside it, as he'd lockstepped her once before an eon ago in his father's study when he planned to call the police. But this time, his posture wasn't angry.

Still, his intent was more dangerous to her than a mere arrest: He meant to pleasure her into surrender. Tilting her head back with a gentle tug on her hair, he wrapped his other arm about her slim form and settled against her so she could feel every inch of him. So different, yet so complementary. She'd almost forgotten. How long now had it been? Three years; no, almost four . . .

And then recollections were beyond her, for he'd tired of her light, teasing, side-to-side kiss using only her lips. He slanted his head sideways to fuse his mouth with hers. Warm, no longer gentle, demanding she give in to the sexual tension that had been brewing between them since the moment they'd met. His touch matched the deepening contact of his mouth, exploring, stroking the curve of her waist down to her hips. As if he needed to know her in every sense too. His hand lightly skimmed the underside of her breast.

When she gasped, he caught it with a soft little laugh. He nudged her lips wider, pressing deeper still, and then she felt the sting of his teeth pulling at her lower lip. But he didn't thrust his tongue inside. He knew what she wanted, but he only moved his lips in a gentle suckle, his clean breath mingling with hers, at the same time caressing her side. Fire licked his path, as if she were the tinder; he, the flint. Her breathing quickened. No, this wasn't enough. She wrapped her arms around his waist, trying to get closer still. She felt his ultimate male response, hard at her abdomen, but he wasn't so crass as to grind into her. He left the next moves up to her.

When she squirmed slightly, he moved back immediately, and on some level she wouldn't understand until later, she knew he'd read her fear of confinement. That he would never use his superior strength to hurt her, as Kai had.

The last of her fear faded away, leaving only the moment.

She drew her mouth away long enough to manage a garbled, "Let me . . ."

He leaned back from the waist to give her room, still leaving her lower body tangled with his. His right leg was thrust forward, his booted foot planted between hers to leave her slightly off balance on the ugly green hospital linoleum.

Strange. She was his prisoner, trapped between his hard form and the wall, but she didn't feel threatened.

His voice was more of a purr, and it sent shivers down her spine. "What do you want, Hana? Tell me."

Hana looked over at her sleeping grandfather. The opposite bed was still empty because the other occupant was in physical therapy. She looked back up at the handsome face looming above her. For a long moment of pure promise in a place where people died, their gazes locked. The depth of feeling they'd shared by kiss and touch was affirmed in that exchange of glances.

Straightening to her full height, her shining ebony gaze plumbing his, Hana said simply, "This is what I want."

She caught that beautiful face between her hands and pulled his head down to her level. Tilting her head sideways until his shoulder and throat were bathed in the silky warmth of her long hair, she kissed him. No hesitation, no shyness. Full bore.

She was no longer a girl grown up too soon.

He'd tempted her to become a woman who knew what she wanted.

She dipped her tongue between his lips, urging them wider. This time it was she who swallowed his little exhalation as he helplessly opened to her need. She explored his perfect teeth, running the tip of her tongue along the rim, then tasting the vulnerable skin lining his mouth, circling around in a touch so dainty she wondered if he felt it. God, he tasted good. . . .

He felt it. With a groan, he caught her so tightly into his embrace that she had to go on the tips of her toes. Pulling her away from the wall, he bent her back over his arms until her hair almost brushed the floor. Then he consumed her. No other word fit his insatiable hunger. Now that she'd finally invited him in, he took full liberty. He thrust into her mouth in the little duel that presaged a greater intimacy, male and female no longer opposing, but moving together in one joyful leap and retreat, leap and retreat.

The little muscle of his tongue did to her mouth what the larger muscle below promised, erect and pulsing against her abdomen. And as she reveled in the most moving, intimate kiss of her life, she used all she had, all she longed to be, in response. She kissed him back deeply; tongue, lips, teeth. For the first time in years, she felt that warm feminine moisture lubricating his way. His throbbing called to her own, and if he'd pressed her down on the vacant hospital bed, she would have opened to him, craving to be sundered, to revel in her femininity as he filled her to brimming.

A slight cough.

They didn't hear it at first because Zach was indeed half walking, half carrying her, to the bed. Then a firm, "Excuse me, it's time to bathe Mr. Nakatomi."

With a shuddering sigh, Zach raised his drugging mouth. It still took a couple of seconds for Hana's senses to clear. Then Zach pushed her away. She stumbled, her knees literally weak in a way totally foreign to her, and he had to catch her shoulders to support her.

At the disapproving look of the portly, middle-aged nurse, Hana blushed. She looked between Zach and the nurse, her teeth biting her lip. She winced, only then realizing her lips were sore and a bit puffy.

"Uh, sorry." Grabbing up the sword, she managed, "I'll keep it safe," and fled, not once looking at Zach.

But he watched her leave, his eyes midnight blue with promise.

A few hours later, in Kai's cavernous basement-cave beneath the house, Ernie climbed out of the practice ring. From the time he'd investigated his spartan quarters to this moment, he'd been watched. While he'd carefully observed the rooms lining the huge cavern as he made his way into the ring, he'd seen nothing resembling a communications room or computers that would allow him to contact Ms. Doyle and tell her he was being held. Kai had watched him for a bit, then left when he was summoned by his men.

Still, the Rangers would know soon enough when he didn't keep his prearranged intel meeting tomorrow. For now, he concentrated on impressing his captors with his karate skills. First alone, then with a punching bag, he went smoothly from the various *tsuki-waza* punching moves to the *geri* or kicking, moves, and so on. While he hadn't trained anyone in years, he still regularly practiced in his own small ring, so honing skills perfected since his twenties was not difficult. The various stations were second nature to him.

When he kicked the bag with the side of his foot in the *yoko geri* move, his long form making an L shape, the thump echoed throughout the cavern. The heavy bag went almost perpendicular. Panting slightly, he looked out at the two men sitting quietly, watching him.

Watching him with AK-47s held at the ready.

One of them gave him a head nod in salutation. Ernie put his hands together and bowed deeply in return. Then he tightened his obi a bit as he climbed out of the ring, using a towel to wipe away his sweat. He approached the man who seemed to be head guard. "Kai said I could see Takeo when I was finished."

The man jerked his head back toward the circular staircase. "Back into the house. You are to have dinner with him."

Ernie climbed back up the stairs, well aware that he was tailed with a machine gun, not quite pointed at his back but at the ready at the slightest provocation. Ernie scowled, hating his helplessness, but he couldn't even protest.

Suck it up, stay subservient. Right now, Takeo was the priority.

Ernie was allowed to shower and change, and then he was escorted into a dining room with oak floors, ogee molding, and a sleek inlaid Japanese table centered on a gorgeous silk Oriental rug. Two places were set, smaller dishes and chopsticks at the head of the table. Takeo was to sit in the place of authority. Ernie wondered if the boy would even know what that meant. Or care. He hoped not, but if Kai had the raising of him, he'd soon enough have the same sense of privilege and superiority as his father.

Takeo came into the room, wearing thonged clogs, white socks, loose trousers, and a shirt tucked into an intricately tied cloth belt. He seemed a bit awkward in the clogs, but when he saw Ernie he ran forward easily enough.

His round little face lit up. "Uncle Ernie!"

A catch in his throat, Ernie bent to Takeo's level and hugged the stocky little figure. "How you doing, bud? Your mom misses you."

"When is she coming? My papa says I'll be seeing her soon."

Ernie helped get Takeo situated on a couple of cushions before taking his own seat, set at Takeo's right. He knew the same two guards were both watching and listening, so he had to be very careful what he said. "So do you take your other lessons, Takeo, reading and writing?"

Takeo nodded, manipulating his chopsticks expertly to bring bits of rice and steak to his mouth. His mouth full, he said, "My papa trains me. I rise, have breakfast, exercise, study, practice my kanji characters, have lunch, go into the ring with my papa, bathe, read, and after supper I learn about my samurai ancestors. Sometimes Papa reads to me before I sleep."

Inwardly cursing Kai's strict regimen, Ernie said gently, "When do you get to have fun?"

Takeo tilted his head as if he'd not thought lately of the concept. "I don't have any friends here, but sometimes my papa lets me play with the dogs." He finished his food, wiping his mouth politely. For the first time, he looked sad. "But I miss Mama."

"She misses you too, bud. Tons." Ernie hesitated, wondering if he could get in a whispered comment that his mother would be coming for him, but he felt their hovering company and repressed the urge. He was glad of that because in the next moment Kai entered with his usual leashed power and silence.

Ernie wondered when Kai would start training Takeo in the darkest ninja arts. That would probably be next.

Kai looked between them, his face unreadable as he asked, "Takeo, are you happy to see your new teacher?"

Takeo looked curiously at his "uncle." "I've seen Mama practice with Uncle Ernie. She told me it was too soon for me to take such lessons. She wanted me to concentrate on my painting and reading and writing."

Kai waved a dismissive hand. "You are a much bigger boy than she thought. I was in the ring at three."

Yeah, and look how that turned out, Ernie wanted to butt in, but held his tongue.

Kai bestowed a rare smile on his son. His severity relaxed, making his face very handsome, almost as if, before he perfected the art of killing, he'd been a charming young man of fitting temperament for Hana. "You have worked hard, Takeo. Your uncle Ernie will train you, as he trained me, and you will be a fitting leader of men to take my place when I am gone."

Takeo frowned. "Are you going somewhere, *Otosan?*"

Kai shook his head, his smile fading. "Don't be obtuse. Do as you are told and tomorrow, I may let you have an hour with your Legos."

Takeo beamed. When his father gave him a perfunctory hug, he clung to Kai's neck. Kai patted his back awkwardly, but Ernie saw the look on his face.

How was it possible to be so tough on a child you obviously loved as Kai loved Takeo? Ernie knew the answer: when you're the rebellious only son of a Yakuza boss. In Kai's twisted logic, he wasn't warping his son. He was teaching him to be strong.

Resolving to do all he could to keep the boy away from his father, Ernie wiped his mouth to hide his disgust as Kai lifted his head to smile his pride at his old teacher.

The next afternoon, when Ernie didn't make his meeting with Abigail, she waited a full hour in the dusty stacks of the Perry-

Casteñeda Library at the University of Texas. He'd suggested the meeting place because he knew it was a locale neither Kai nor his men ever frequented.

For the umpteenth time, she checked both texts and e-mails on her encrypted smart phone, looking for a message from him. Of course, he could have skipped. They hadn't dared to put an ankle tracker on him since he was becoming a confidential informant. But on some level she didn't want to acknowledge, she knew Ernie wouldn't desert Hana and Takeo. His love for both had shined through too brightly in the interrogation to be a lie.

She waited a few more moments, then—her long face drawn with concern—she rose and sought out the elevator. Tonight had been planned to duplicate Hana's transport to Kai's compound, right down to a similar van and blindfold. But if Ernie was missing, the mission had changed. Locate the compound, yes, but should they also raid it? Or delay?

She pulled out her phone and requested an urgent meeting with John Travis. A few minutes later, she was driving toward Tarrytown.

After the gate guards checked her ID and noted a text from John allowing her entry, she parked in front of the mansion. For the first time, she saw that John Travis, as she'd heard, had plenty of money. He really was a dedicated lawman by choice.

She'd barely rung the doorbell before a portly woman, short and smelling of flour and onions, let her in. She smiled, her pudgy cheeks dented with dimples. "Señora Doyle, I have heard much about you. Come in, come in."

Abby was clueless, but soon enough Zach came into the foyer from a side door, obviously having heard Abby's voice. He hugged the little woman. "Consuela, what are we having for dinner tonight? Something delicious, as usual." He winked at Abby over her head. "Can you stay for dinner? We're eating at six tonight. I have to leave by eight, as you know, so I can be in the van when—" He broke off at Abby's expression.

Consuela looked between the two, her merry expression falling, and left them without another word.

Abby said simply, "We may have to delay the mission. Ernie Thibodeaux missed our meeting and I haven't heard a word from him."

Zach showed her into the study.

They found John at his desk trying to dent his pile of ever-growing paperwork. Abby sat in the chair before his desk. Zach remained standing, watching uneasily as his father clicked on the desk light, illuminating him against the dark wallpaper.

John divided his time between the desk phone he propped on his shoulder so he could talk, and the requisition list his men had given him for the planned incursion into Kai's stronghold. After listening, John said calmly, "I know, Jimmy, I don't like having the sword out of our control either, but without this girl we'd have even more operational holes to plug. You know I can't give you details, but it could also offer greater security to both my men and my informants to allow her to borrow the blade, and that's all it is. A loan. Remember, we have plenty of insurance to cover the value."

He listened again, watching Zach go to the window shade. But when he reached to pull it down, John glared at him so fiercely that Zach's hand fell. He took to pacing.

Abigail watched this byplay; then she looked sympathetically at poor Zachary William Barrett Travis, the chief of executive Ranger security. Guarding John Travis would not be an easy task. Especially if you were his son.

"Look, I have to go for now," John finished. "I promise you, we'll get the blade back when the operation is over. Worst case, I'll make good on any balance myself to cover the full cost if it goes missing. Good enough?"

When he got the answer he wanted, John put the phone down, making a mock swipe of his brow. "A disgruntled LLC member, the only one of the five that voted no on letting the girl borrow the blade. But I think I convinced him to wait rather than sue me." He smiled at Abby. "You said you needed to see me right away?"

Abby said without embroidering, "I think Kai has probably imprisoned Ernie Thibodeaux."

John scowled. "How do you know he didn't skip?"

"I don't know for sure, but I think Ernie really cares about Hana. I don't believe he'd desert her. After all, he's the one who offered to take her place."

Zach stopped pacing long enough to say, "For what it's worth, Dad, I agree."

John frowned for a moment longer, then said, "Okay, if he's being held, we have to be even more careful. What if they torture him? I'm sure they know we arrested him, and they also know we often recruit informers. If he talks, even Takeo could be in danger."

The three exchanged an uncertain look.

But Zach's expression cleared as he said, "I know one person who can help us figure out what's happening. I'm going to pick up Ms. Nakatomi."

"I don't want her brought here," John said sternly.

"Under the circumstances, we need to regroup before we start planning the op," Zach argued. "She's expecting us to pick her up anyway to do the van reenactment, but I think we should wait a night or two on that. We need to reassess. This changes everything. Instead of reliable intel on what we're getting into, we have another hostage."

John groused, "You can question her at headquarters if you want, not here."

Zach argued, "But she's been here before. I think she'll be more open if we question her here."

John made an impatient gesture, but when he did, the stack of invoices he was initialing fluttered to the floor. As he bent down to pick it up, a slight *ping!* sounded and then a bullet embedded itself in the wall behind where his head had been a second before.

Chapter 10

John had been around firearms all his life and he knew what a silenced long-range weapon sounded like. He went flat on the floor behind his desk.

Zach swept Abby out of her chair. "Stay down!" Then to his father, "You okay, Dad?" Zach's heart was racing so fast, he heard his own breathless tone. Good God, he knew the guys behind the murders had to be bold, but this went beyond bold to crazy. Still, time enough to put together all the whys later.

Even the imperturbable John sounded a bit shaken. "Yes, son of a bitch, I can't believe they took a potshot at me in my own study!"

"Both of you stay put!" Zach crawled to the window, stood to the side and pulled the shade down. "Where's the radio?" he demanded.

"On the desk. To reach it I'll have to sit up."

"Don't move!"

"Why the hell haven't the guards reacted outside?"

"I don't think they heard anything. Can you reach the desk light without sitting up?" Zach inquired.

John fumbled with one long arm, but managed to reach the light and yank the little brass chain. As he did so, another shot pinged, going through windowpane, shade—and John's hand if he'd been one inch to the left. John shied away, going totally flat on the floor. But the light was out and the room was almost pitch-dark except for the dim light from a wall sconce.

"Holy shit, they must have some kind of imaging equipment," Zach warned. "Stay there until I get the window covered."

Still keeping to the side wall, Zach pulled a decorative escritoire out from the paneling. It had long, slender legs and a tall pediment of solid wood that would cover most of the window. Without ceremony,

Zach dumped everything in it, including some of his mother's prized Steuben glass vases and Lladró figurines, onto the floor, oblivious to the shattering of thousands of dollars' worth of décor. Then he picked the heavy mahogany escritoire up and heaved it against the window. It teetered but stabilized.

"We should be shielded now." Zach felt secure enough to dash for the radio. With no time for niceties, he muttered, "Take Abigail to the pantry off the kitchen. Wait for me. Get Mom and Consuela too. Take your piece."

For once, John Travis obeyed someone else's order.

Running into the hallway to check the door, Zach growled into the radio at their very expensive security detail, "What the hell is wrong with you guys? Don't you know what a long-range silenced rifle sounds like? They just took two shots at us. Get to the trees outside the wall now. That's the only place they could be. *Now*, dammit, before they get away!" Zach went from room to room to check that all was secure, but he didn't find any broken windows or smashed door locks.

As he passed the pantry on his way to the back door, he rapped on the heavy portal. "Y'all okay in there?"

"Yes. We're fine," his father groused. "I don't like hiding here like a coward, Zach. I want to come out and help catch these bastards."

"Yes, well, as chief of executive Ranger security I'm telling you to stay put until I get a site rep from the guards. I radioed them to check the trees and I've confirmed we're secure on ingress and egress in the house for now, but I'd rather y'all stay there until I know more. Just a few more minutes."

Without waiting for his father's response—for he knew he wouldn't like it—Zach raced out the door, his own pistol at the ready.

Inside Ernie's kitchen, trying to calm herself with peppermint tea, Hana checked her watch for the umpteenth time. Ernie should have been back before now. He'd intended to go with Hana on the route, having just gone through the same routine with the hood and van, except his journey was in daylight. Surely, between the two of them they could find the compound. But it was only an hour before they were supposed to be picked up by the security guys and Ernie still wasn't back from his earlier meeting with Kai.

To distract herself, Hana pulled the sword out from the secret cupboard where she'd hidden it. Being an expert safecracker gave Ernie unusual perspective on how to secure his most valued possessions. He'd showed her the stash spot when he'd asked her to stay with him. She'd been touched then at his trust of her, but when she pushed and pulled the succession of levers and handles that swung out a side cupboard, she'd found it empty.

She'd looked at him strangely. "I don't own anything worth going through all these maneuvers."

Ernie had smiled. "Just in case."

Now, in his practice ring, as she went through the old moves that were as natural to her as breathing, she wondered if somehow—with that amazing sixth sense of his that made him such an expert sensei—he'd hoped they'd let her borrow the sword.

Both arms raised high above her head, she exhaled on "hai!" simultaneously bringing the sword down. The move was designed to cleave the enemy, clavicle to hip, in a downward left diagonal. As she moved into the upward opposite diagonal, Hana for the first time began to understand why the ancient samurai called exquisite weapons like this five body blades. Merely practicing the moves with Masamune's masterpiece made her wonder what it would be like to use it on its intended target: human flesh. Would it slice through flesh and bone as cleanly as it had Ernie's straw target?

The sword sang in her hands as it whistled through the air, and then a thought came to her that so upset her, she froze mid-move. Dear heaven, if she felt this way wielding this deadly weapon, how would Kai react? Did she dare let him have the blade, even briefly, as a ploy to get her inside the compound? What if the raid failed and he kept the blade?

She still struggled against the pit-of-her-stomach certainty he was behind the grisly killings. But she also knew if he'd committed such mayhem with an ordinary katana, he'd feel like a shogun with complete dominance once he held this weapon.

She was so upset at that thought that she didn't hear the first knock. The second one came as a bang, really. At the door.

She wasn't sure what to do with the sword and finally stuck it in the sheath strapped to her back. It was safest with her because she'd die protecting it.

She unlocked all the heavy door locks and swung the huge hunk of metal open. On the stoop she found two uniformed DPS troopers. Immediately her hackles rose. "Yes?" Just in case this was an unannounced visit, as her immunity agreement stated they could perform until she'd located the compound, she held up her ankle. The blinking light was vivid against her black nylon jumpsuit. She'd put it on to practice while she awaited Ernie.

The older trooper, who looked much more seasoned than his younger partner, said curtly, "Very good, but that's not why we're here, ma'am. If you'll come with us for questioning."

Hana scowled. Now what? "Why? That's not part of my immunity agreement."

"There have been . . . recent developments. I've been tasked with bringing you to Deputy Director John Travis at the direct request of his chief of security."

That was Zachary Travis, Hana knew. Sighing, she stuffed her driver's license, some cash, and a credit card into an inside zippered compartment in her form-fitting tuck-in blouse. Locking Ernie's door and pocketing the key he'd given her, she meekly followed the deputies to the cruiser waiting for her, lights blinking. "But the security detail was going to pick me up in about thirty minutes—"

"We've been instructed to tell you that has been delayed until further notice."

Totally mystified, and now becoming concerned, for her immunity agreement was tied to finding the compound, she got into the back of the cruiser. As they drove, she looked yet again at her phone, hoping she'd missed the *ding* of a text from Ernie.

Her screen was blank.

At the formerly peaceful Travis mansion, chaos ruled. Flashing police cruisers blocked both ends of the street. Wearing a bright orange jacket that glowed in the occasional headlight, a police officer waved approaching vehicles to turn around. Yellow tape was strung all around the huge trees fronting the street, as well as the mansion's heavy wrought-iron fence.

Various forensic personnel, including Abigail Doyle, wore gloves as, under very bright lights set up in the street, they carefully examined every inch of the grass. Their trained eyes knew what to look for, but from their resigned expressions, even they seemed to think seeking the minutest hair strand or clothing lint in the dark was foolish. They'd hoped for a casing, but Zach knew they wouldn't be that lucky. Whoever took the shots no doubt had picked up his spent shells before he left.

Pissed they'd been caught napping, Zach grilled each and every member of the security detail for the third time. In between, he glanced occasionally at Ms. Doyle. She was very systematic, working in a grid system around the trees, making copious screen shots of every angle with her iPad. That compilation would later help with the ballistics.

Another man dusted with high-tech powder, trying to pick up fingerprint samples from the trees themselves. Yet a third had climbed the big oak, his thin form totally hidden in the thick foliage. Really, it was no wonder they'd not spotted the shooter, but now Zach second-guessed himself. Why the hell hadn't he insisted the trees be pruned down to the trunk?

The guy in the tree yelled, "Here it is! There's a homemade rifle rest!"

They all waited while he took measurements and careful pictures. Finally he half shimmied, half jumped down, two pieces of wood nailed together in a rough V in his free gloved hand. After the print forensics analyst dusted for prints, he offered it to Zach. Zach, also gloved, turned the crossed pieces of wood in his hands, noting the slightly darkened ends where the fresh cuts in the wood had been exposed to a recent rain. It appeared as if it had been constructed out of short pieces of two-by-fours and nailed into a V of the tree—directly opposite the study window.

Zach and Abby exchanged a grim look.

She said with concern, "From the weathered look of the wood, this was planned, not opportunistic."

"Could be they put it there before we even hired our security detail. Which means they must have been scoping us out for days...." Zach's voice trailed away, but Abby finished his thought.

"Since Ms. Nakatomi first went for the sword." They exchanged an even grimmer look.

Zach couldn't voice the suspicion that dried his saliva, but Abby had no such compunction.

She said slowly, "Do you think she's been lying to us? That she's really been working with Kai all along? Is it possible we think we're trying to turn her into an informant, but she's already one for him?"

Zach shook his head adamantly. "I don't care what the time frame is, I don't believe she'd ever endanger her son and her friend by working with that monster, especially after he left her in jail when she was pregnant."

Abby reminded him, "Yes, but if Mr. Thibodeaux is correct, Kai didn't know she was pregnant."

Zach ignored that. He carefully bagged the tree rest. "Besides, just because the rest has been there for several days, it doesn't mean someone has been hidden there all that time. Why would they risk exposure until they were ready to fire? Not good tactics."

Abby nodded a bit uncertainly at that logic, but she was obviously still bothered by the matching time frame.

They were still working when a cruiser came up and Hana Nakatomi, the katana strapped to her back, got out of the backseat, shunning the trooper's helping hand. She stood very still for a moment, watching all the activity. Zach and Abby went to meet her. They both watched her expressions and mannerisms closely, but she displayed neither shock nor satisfaction, only a curious fatalism. She shifted the sword slightly, as if it felt burdensome.

She looked at Zach's cold expression. Something vulnerable flickered in her eyes under the bright lights, but then she lifted her chin and stepped up to him until they were toe to toe. "There's obviously been another attack, but I'll save us both an interrogation. I was at Ernie's place all day, practicing in his ring while I waited for your men to arrive for our trip to the compound. I had the security system on and I'm sure they can verify that I didn't shut it off until thirty minutes ago when the troopers picked me up."

"Easy enough for someone with your skill set to circumvent," Zach pointed out.

"Easy enough for you to pull Ernie's video footage too." She stared up at him with an unflinching gaze. She proffered the key Ernie had given her. "I'll wait." She held up her ankle bracelet by raising her foot. "But then, you always know where I am anyway, don't you? All you have to do is make one phone call to confirm."

Zach relaxed slightly, but he accepted the key and gave it to the same senior trooper who'd brought her. The trooper turned back to his cruiser without another word.

"I was told your father wanted to see me?" Hana asked, not even watching him go.

Zach glanced at Abby, but she waved him toward the house. "I can finish here."

And so, a few minutes later, Hana and John Travis stared at one another across his wide desk. Hana seemed too fidgety to sit, so she paced in front of his desk, totally unaware of the leashed athleticism and sensuality she displayed in her tight clothing as she strode up and down. But Zach was all too aware. With the katana sheathed to her back, her long black hair flowing like luminous, liquid silk around her shoulders, she was the sexy ninja chick of every male fantasy. Zach shifted uncomfortably, crossing his legs, but since that only proved her effect on him, he rested both his feet flat on the floor and hoped neither his father nor Hana looked in his direction.

Luckily, they were far too intent on their battle of wits and wills to pay him any heed. On one of her trips toward the windows, Hana tested the bullet holes in the window with her gloved fingertip. Even more restive, she stalked from one side of the study to the other, answering John's rapid-fire questions all the while.

"No, I'm not a good shot with a long-range rifle—"

"Yes, I'm dressed this way because I've been in Ernie's ring most of the day practicing."

And: "No, I had no idea your house was under surveillance the night I broke in. I've already told you my source was a maid fired from your service. I assure you Kai and I have not been sharing information."

She paused long enough to hear Zach's explanation about the likely weathering of the tree rest they'd found that possibly matched the date of her visit. She said curtly, "Kai knew I was coming for the blade, so it's possible he sent someone to keep an eye on me. But I used that tree to climb over your wall and there was no one there that night. That I'm sure of."

"Who in Kai's organization has the skill to use a sniper rifle like that?" John demanded.

Hana shrugged. "They all train with weapons of every type, including pistols and rifles. Ninja stars, blowing darts, everything. I've also seen them use night-vision technology." She looked at the holes in the heavy leaded glass windows and then back. "I'd suggest you cover your windows with shutters and rearrange your furniture so your desk is away from any possible surveillance with heat-sensing goggles."

Finally, John's stiff posture began to relax. He said, "Of course. We've thought of that. He won't get another chance."

Hana looked at him as if he were crazy. "You really don't understand what you're dealing with, do you?"

John scowled. "A particularly vicious drug dealer. We nail them all the time."

Hana stopped her pacing directly in front of his desk. She shook her head in an almost pitying manner, her hair flying like a black warning flag. "No. He's much worse than that. Kai believes he's the last of the samurai, but his only fealty is to himself. The fact that he wasn't born to that lineage makes him much more dangerous. He feels all the allure of the power and triumph over enemies, but very little of the counterbalance of honor. This is why he wants our sword so badly. It legitimizes him, not just in his own eyes, but it will frighten his rivals because they will know what he wants to do with it and its long legacy of bloodletting." She pulled it from its sheath and held it so it caught the dim light.

Even in the illumination of the single wall sconce, the polished steel edge gleamed as she turned the blade from side to side. "Do you remember all the tales of Excalibur? How the legend said that removing it from the stone gave Arthur the throne? Well, amp that legend up by about ten and you come close to understanding the significance of a Masamune blade to the Japanese. The annals of Japan are much bloodier than the mists of Avalon, with decapitated heads our measurement of valor, and seppuku the ultimate choice between death or dishonor. And while modern Japan is much too civilized to practice such things, Kai was brought up in the Yakuza. When he came here, he decided to create his own near-religion by combining the cultures of the samurai, the ninja, and El Chapo."

Even John paled a bit at that analogy. He looked at his son. Zach saw his father remembering Abby and Ross's slide show warning about this very mix and its influence on the illicit drug trade in central Texas.

Zach said quietly, "You sound like you were almost a convert yourself."

She turned on him. She bit her lip savagely, leaving it red. He suddenly longed to kiss her again, not passionately as he had in the hospital, but gently, sweetly, like the champion she so sorely needed—whether she knew it or not.

She had to swallow hard to master her emotions, but the glitter of tears was hidden when she shuttered her eyes with long, dark lashes. She began haltingly, but her voice grew stronger with every word. "Yes. I was. I was an impressionable sixteen-year-old. My father had just died and he was my anchor. My mother left me to return to Japan when I would not conform to her notions of a marriageable young woman." She looked back at each man in turn, her face now composed. "I won't make any excuses for that. I wouldn't have Takeo otherwise. But yes, I lived firsthand under the power of Kai's twisted ideals. He is very charismatic. So please heed my warning not to take him lightly. And there's one more thing." She braced herself, as if she knew they wouldn't like her next remark.

"It would not surprise me if he has an informant somewhere in your division."

John started a protest but Hana interrupted him. "I suggest you quietly start checking on that. The last thing we need is for Kai to know the date and time of our incursion." Again, she looked between both men. "Just be aware as you plan your raid that Kai will use any tactic of his three religions that will help him win his territory against rival gangs, and—"

She brought the sword straight up before her face in a salute "—against the Texas Rangers. Including implicating me in murders I didn't commit and acts of violence I'd never countenance." She cradled the sword over her bent arm, as if for comfort, as she added, "Kai wants my son for his heir. Probably even now he's indoctrinating Takeo, or trying." For the first time, she smiled and such love transformed her face that Zach's breath caught in his throat. She looked over John's head at the wallpaper, but she was obviously seeing her son.

At that moment, Zach knew he'd been kidding himself ever since the strange night they'd met. Even when he was having her arrested, he was in lust with this woman. And if she proved to be as honest and reformed as Ernie claimed, he knew he'd fall deeply in love with her too. Family approval would then be immaterial to him.

At that moment, he also vowed to see that expression again, except with a very adult, female focus. Of one thing he was certain: Since that passionate kiss, she lusted for him too.

Hana's next comment brought him back to the present. This time, his thoughts had made his predicament quite hard, literally, and he had to take a magazine from his dad's desk and hold it on his lap. He pretended to leaf through it to distract himself.

Hana gave him a curious look at his seeming inattention, but finished: "But my son is quite perceptive for a five-year-old. He's also very intelligent. I believe he's smart enough to see the vicious inconsistencies in his father's teachings. So . . . we have a few days to prepare, anyway." A long pause, then she added, "There's something else you must know."

She waited until both men had fixed their worried gazes on her. John had been recording her the entire time, and Zach knew from his expression that his father was deliberately letting her talk. John Travis knew from many interrogations that when persons of interest spoke, it was best to let them ramble, because that's usually when the most useful information surfaced. Zach gave his father a look. John didn't even glance his way.

Hana said quietly, "No matter what happens during the raid, once we get Takeo and hopefully Ernie out of danger, I'm expendable. Use me however you will, but don't let Kai get away with this sword. He'll believe himself invincible then. If I have to fight him hand-to-hand to protect it, I will, but he's practiced much more than I have over the last few years—"

Zach surged to his feet, the magazine falling to the floor. "No! You're just an informant, not a—not a—" He was relieved when Hana's gaze switched to his face. He also felt his father's stare at the wrong place, but he'd have to deal with that later.

Hana was obviously too offended to notice or care about his other feelings. For the first time, she showed a tinge of anger. "Samurai? You think females in Japan didn't act as samurai? You'd be wrong. Many women died in battle, protecting their lands and loved ones. I have that right too." Without asking, she grabbed a pen off John's desk and scribbled a name.

John read out loud, "Nakano Takeko?" He stumbled a bit over the pronunciation.

"I suggest you both look up her history. She was one of many valiant samurai women who fought against the emperor's men in the 1860s. She took to the field of battle, leading women from her household to protect their lands because their men were away. She fought so fiercely that one of the soldiers fighting for the emperor was afraid to engage her hand-to-hand. He resorted to shooting her from a distance. When she lay dying on the battlefield, she begged her sister to cut off her head rather than leave it as a trophy for the enemy. Her sister did so and today her head is interred in a place of honor beneath a Japanese shrine."

While both men digested this, she stepped back, admiring her family blade again. "There are worse deaths than dying beneath an enemy's blade."

Over their silence, after a slight bow, Hana shoved the sword back in its sheath. With the sound of steel brushing against steel ringing in the air, she added softly, "Our goals are aligned, Mr. Travis. We both want to stop Kai. We both want to protect my son and the sword."

She smiled sadly at Zach. "Did you not consider when you convinced your father to let me borrow the blade that I'm the only one who knows how to use it?"

Chapter 11

Hours later, with dawn finally tingeing the sky orange, Hana signed the affidavit recording her third interrogation. The trooper returned with the video footage showing her practicing in Ernie's ring for hours, confirmed both by the GPS tracking data emitted by her ankle bracelet and the video time stamp. They told her she was free to go.

She didn't need to be told twice. They'd rearranged her trip to find the compound for the following night and still hadn't heard from Ernie. She was making a beeline for the front door when she found her path blocked. The short, rotund woman in an apron had a full, winsome face that looked as if it had not been constructed for such a severe expression.

Hana almost laughed at the assessing scowl in those dark eyes made for laughing.

She looked Hana up and down and then moved two steps to block the door. "You come with me. The mistress wishes to meet you." She crossed her arms over her generous bosom. "We have coffee and biscuits on the patio."

The twinkle in Hana's eyes went out. She'd been bossed around enough by these people, and now the housekeeper too? "Thank you, but no. I accept the fact that I'm not welcome here, and I don't feel comfortable. It's best for all concerned if I just go."

She moved aside a few steps, but the woman closed the gap by likewise stepping sideways.

"No. Just a moment, please."

Hana opened her mouth to refuse again, but before their confrontation could escalate, Zach entered the foyer from the study. He caught his housekeeper from behind to give her a bear hug. "*Numero dos mamacita, qué pasó?*"

With the familiarity of a second mother indeed, she whacked his hands away. "*Basta!* Tell this impert—impur—"

"Impertinent," he corrected her gently. Then he looked back at Hana. "She is that. And much more..."

The way that blue gaze ran over her, head to heels, heated away the last of her cold desolation along with her willpower. How much more fun it had been to let him lead in Jiji's hospital room. But such thoughts brought pink to her cheeks, so she pretended to study the art-filled niches lining the foyer.

"Please stay long enough for a cup of coffee," he asked Hana. Nicely. Like a true Southern gentleman instead of a Texas Ranger who suspected her of gruesome murders.

How could she say no after that? For once he wasn't being lord of the Travis dynasty. His expression put his dimples on display, and his eyes were such a sunny blue she found herself nodding.

With old-fashioned courtliness, he offered his arm. "Shall we? I promise if you let me lead, you won't regret it."

Sensing but ignoring his double entendre, she rested her gloved fingertips very lightly on his arm and followed him through the kitchen to a back exterior patio. It was screened in and had shutters for warm or cold days, but the sun was rising above the horizon and the shutters were raised.

A very pretty, middle-aged woman sat at the head of the table. The minute she heard their steps, she poured them each a cup of coffee from the stainless-steel carafe at her elbow. "Good morning, son," she said cheerfully, as if she were used to all the commotion out on her front lawn.

She cocked her head to the side as she appraised their peculiar guest. But if she disapproved of Hana's strange garb and even stranger choice of cutting implement, she didn't show it. She waved a gracious hand at the empty chair to her right.

Inwardly, Hana groaned. One interrogation had been enough for this day. She was still smarting from the Travises' obvious suspicion she'd been aiding Kai all along, so being grilled by Zach's mother was enough to send her temper, never mild at the best of times, soaring.

She took a sip of coffee, using the excuse to hide her expression in her snowy linen napkin. Her eyes met Zach's over the fabric. His mellow expression had hardened to a warning.

Do not upset my mother, he said clearly without saying a word.

Incongruously, his protectiveness soothed her wrath. This evidence of his love for his mother brought a lump to her throat. For the first time in a long time, she admitted how badly she missed her own. Except for the occasional duty phone call on holidays or Mother's Day, she seldom even spoke to her mother, who had happily remarried to a very wealthy, traditional Japanese businessman after her return to her homeland.

She hadn't seen her mom in almost six years. Hana took another fortifying gulp of coffee.

Mary Travis gave her son a look. He scowled, but obediently rose. With a curt nod to Hana, he exited, closing the double French doors behind him, leaving the two women alone.

"There, now we can have a comfortable chat," Mary Travis said, offering a plate of biscuits. "The men in our family can be so intimidating, don't you agree, dear?"

Hana concentrated on buttering her biscuit, but managed a sincere nod.

"I'm sorry if John was a bit... insistent, but that's one reason he's very good at his job. And quite frankly, financially he could have retired many years ago, but the oath he took so long ago as a Texas Ranger means a lot to him. And to me, and to Zach, by extension."

Hana added a bit of prickly-pear jam to her biscuit, on one level admiring the gorgeous rosy color, but on another wishing herself back pacing before John's desk. That brand of torture was less excruciating than this one. She'd never been good at cotillions, proms, or fancy breakfasts. She especially resented the fact that this tea, scones, and ersatz sympathy was designed to elicit intimate confessions from her. She was tempted to spring up and bolt like the intruder they obviously still considered her, but she couldn't bring herself to be that rude.

Mary eyed her with unsettling blue eyes. "You miss your mother, don't you?"

Hana froze with the last half of the biscuit partially buttered. For the first time, she looked at her hostess. Really looked at her. There was more to her than met the eye. Hana saw a sweet woman, happily married for many years to a very conservative, traditional man, but Mary Travis also relished her place as mistress of the household. And her timeless elegance despite the early hour, her graying blond hair secured on the top of her head, crisp white-lace blouse and sleek black skirt, reminded Hana of Grace Kelly. She was a woman who might seem fragile and biddable, but Hana had seen the immaculate house, the manicured gardens, and she knew who was responsible for that order. She suspected John Travis had no idea of who really ruled this household. However, Hana had no wish to be managed too.

Meeting those not-so baby blues dead-on, Hana said stiffly, "I'm sorry to be the fly in your ointment, ma'am. I know when I'm not welcome. I tried to leave, but Zach and your housekeeper insisted I stay for coffee."

"Of course they did. I asked them to. I seldom make demands, but when I do they are always obeyed, even by Zach." Mary gave a little trill of laughter that made her lovely face crease with laugh lines that, instead of aging her, somehow brought back to life the girl she'd once been. "Even John obeys, for the most part."

After one polite bite of biscuit, Hana shoved her plate back. "Very well, then. Why did you ask for this meeting? How do I fit into your neat household?"

With a mirthless smile, Mary folded her napkin beside her plate. "You don't."

For an instant, mutual hostility fed the almost electrical spark between black eyes and blue. But then Mary sighed and patted Hana's gloved hand. "You do, however, seem to fit my son's notions quite exquisitely. So I made it my business to check into you."

At Hana's lifted chin, Mary shook her head sadly. "You're all alone, aren't you? I'm sorry for that, my dear, and I understand how you feel more than you know."

Hana's eyes narrowed. "If you want to psychoanalyze me, at least quote me a going rate. Three or four hundred an hour?"

Mary, with the next remark, shocked Hana into silence and made her regret her cutting remark.

"You shouldn't treat your possible future mother-in-law with such impertinence, my dear."

When Hana's mouth dropped open, Mary gently used her fingertip to close Hana's mouth, teasing, "Just listen for a moment, please, and all will be clear."

Mary rose and began to pace the small area. Her slim skirt flared slightly at the knee, allowing her strides to be long and restless. A prickling at the back of Hana's neck put her on edge, as her senses warned of danger. She looked around at the peaceful yard and patrolling guards and dogs. Why was she suddenly so antsy? The urge to run became more acute, and she had to twist the napkin in her lap into a knot to make herself be still. Why couldn't she pinpoint the source of her unease?

Then Mary stopped and seemed to peer into her head again with those strangely piercing blue eyes. "John and I have introduced Zach, at one time or another, to most of the eligible debutantes in our immediate circle. But he didn't want any of them. As he told his father, he isn't attracted to 'nice' girls."

Then she said something very strange: "Like father, like son, I suppose."

Hana was still trying to decipher that when Mary walked up to her on almost soundless feet. "And he is very much like his father in another way: He will love once, and forever. He hasn't been so interested in a woman since a disastrous college fling."

Using that imperious finger, she tilted Hana's chin up until she could read every curve and line of her face. "So I made it my business to get to know you. I know you had Takeo when you were very young. I know you adore your grandfather and worked two jobs to try to help him save his house from foreclosure. I know you're very bright and very brave. And very rebellious of anything or anyone trying to restrict you. And most of all, I know that—adversaries or not—you are very drawn to my son, as he is to you."

"How could you possibly know all that? We haven't even met before today."

"John never hides anything about our son from me. We both adore Zach and we both want only the best for him. He's seen the way the two of you react to one another. He doesn't like it. Whereas I . . ."

Hana surged to her feet. "In that case, I'll wish you 'good day' because I am definitively not good for him, nor is he good for me."

Nimbly, Mary moved in front of her to block her exit. "Sit back down, please. This won't take much longer."

Short of making a scene, Hana could do nothing else but sit. But her mouth was set in that mulish slant her grandfather would have winced to see. "Mrs. Travis, what did your husband tell you about Kai?"

"That he's a drug lord with a peculiar set of skills."

Hana had not been able to get through to either Zach or John Travis the dangers they were facing, so she decided to try with Mary Travis. She also, perversely, wanted to prove she was not a good match for the brilliant, handsome, rich, and powerful Zachary William Barrett Travis. To think she might be a fitting wife for him led her down a dangerous path she dared not follow, especially when Takeo was in so much danger.

"Kai had a very strange upbringing, as did I. *Ya ku za...*" she said quietly. "Do you know what it means phonetically?"

Mary shook her head.

"There's an ancient card game that's been played for countless years in Japan called *oicho-kabu*. The sum of eight, nine, and three is twenty, which is the worst possible hand. The phonetic sound of eight, nine, and three is *ya ku za*, meaning 'worthless.' However, the more subtle modern meaning is a societal misfit."

Mary had to laugh at that. "Then both of us, my dear, are *ya ku za*."

Hana bristled. "While I admit that might have fit me in my rebellious teens, I've spent the last five years trying to do what's right."

Mary raised a questioning eyebrow, and Hana had the grace to flush at what the other woman was obviously thinking.

"In the final analysis, I have more right to that sword than a rich family with no Japanese heritage that wants to flaunt its power to the world."

At Mary's unyielding stare, Hana exhaled slowly to tamp down her rising temper. "You're not Japanese. You don't understand. Kai is very dangerous because he doesn't recognize societal norms. No justice, no mercy, no fear, no compassion. He will act only in his own best interests, including practicing the eight cuts on living flesh." Hana rose. "His goal all along has been to implicate me in these murders and attempted murders. I'm the one who has to face him, not your son. He will not stop, he will not rest, he will not halt his campaign of violence until he's dead. Even then, his men will probably carry on his work if they're not arrested."

Mary frowned, reading between the lines. "You can't possibly mean to face him alone."

Hana evaded with the biggest truth she knew. "Since I can't get Zach to understand, perhaps you will. This sword is both a gift and an obligation. The blood of my ancestors obliges me to fight for my own honor, and the honor of my son, and his descendants."

Mary was not deterred. Her hand rested on the top of Hana's shining hair as if she almost hoped she could impart some of her own hard-earned wisdom into Hana's head. "I know that you will do anything, risk your own life, to save your son from this man, this Kai person. Again, I respect you for that. But you don't have to do it alone."

Mary sat back down, resting her hands in her lap, looking every inch the lady to the manor born. "Thank you for your honesty. I will give you the same: My reason for this meeting, and my question to you is quite simple: If you succeed, what then?"

"I—I don't know what you mean, ma'am."

Mary gave an impatient little shake of her head. "I detest that term. I'm not in my dotage yet." She leaned forward. "I mean, my dear rebellious Ms. Nakatomi—After this is all over, do you want my son enough to change your ways and conform to what will be required of you to be a Travis?"

Outside Austin, in the farmhouse on the limestone cliffs, Hana's offspring faced his sensei with a similar mulish expression.

Takeo, sweat ringing the arm pits of his *gi*, stood in the corner of the ring, his *bo* on the floor before him, his arms crossed over his stalwart little chest. "I'm tired, Uncle Ernie. I want to paint."

Ernie picked up the *bo* and offered it to his pupil. "I know, Takeo. Just thirty minutes more and then we'll break for breakfast." Since he'd arrived, Ernie had worked his new student relentlessly. Takeo thought it was so Kai would approve of him, but Ernie had a far simpler motivation: to keep him away from Kai as much as he could. Kai had approved of the tough regimen, even allowing them extra time over other lessons.

When he wasn't training Takeo, he was training Kai's men. And his diligence was paying off in another key way: The watchful gaze of his captors was becoming less vigilant. They were beginning to believe he'd come here just to train them, that he had no other motivation other than his fat briefcase full of cash.

However, Ernie never made the trek down the circular stairs without noting which rooms were lit and occupied at what hours. Occasionally, he even saw people enter or exit, so he knew all the rooms were controlled by electronic keypad codes. He'd still seen no sign of a control room or computers, so even if he could get away long enough to do a frantic e-mail, he had no access. Instead, he concentrated on Takeo and creating a new schedule for him, so he'd know where the boy was any time of the day or night.

He and Takeo were sitting at breakfast, eating rice and smoked fish, when a commotion sounded outside: Shouting, a piercing, long scream. Then silence. Automatically, Ernie rose to close the heavy dining-room doors. Then he moved to stand protectively behind Takeo's chair. Takeo tried to rise, but Ernie held him still.

"No. This is your father's affair, not yours." Ernie had heard the sounds of torture often enough to recognize them.

"But—" Before Takeo could finish his sentence, the doors opened and Kai's trusted lieutenant entered.

"Come. Both of you. Kai wants you to see this."

Ernie hesitated, but when hard, dark eyes narrowed on him, he picked Takeo up and carried him into the living room, as the man indicated, then through a side door into the enclosed garage. It was the first time he'd been inside the garage, and even in the stress of the moment, Ernie noted another door led off a side wall. It not only had a keypad, it had a heavy, vault-like metal door. No window and no sound, but Ernie realized he'd just glimpsed the entrance to the control room.

However, it was the scene in the middle of the garage that riveted him and Takeo. A man, his bare chest imprinted with various Edo Shihan tattoos, was suspended by his wrists from hooks in the ceiling. His head was bent down on his chest, but he groaned again as Kai, standing before him, whacked him with a short stick on his upper arms. Ernie realized the tattoos looked so vivid partly because the man was covered with bruises. The curling dragon covering his entire chest looked untouched.

Kai, bare-chested, revealing a similar tattoo in the same colors on his own prominent pecs, stood before his prisoner. He took a *tanto* from his belt and poised it over the snarling dragon tattoo on the man's chest. "Takeo, I want you to see this. He will no longer wear my colors. He's a traitor. He knew the consequences of betrayal."

Takeo quit squirming in Ernie's arms and went very still. For a long moment, Takeo stared at his father. Then, like the little boy he still was, he hid his face in Ernie's shoulder and began to cry.

When Kai lifted the knife again, Ernie spit out, "He's five, Kai. Allow him to grow up a little before you turn him into your miniature!" He held the back of Takeo's head so the boy couldn't look. But Takeo was limp in his arms, and Ernie knew he was too scared to peek.

"He has to know how to deal with enemies," Kai snapped. "This traitor has been feeding information about my operation to the Green Gang." Kai belted the *tanto* and strode up to Ernie. "Give him to me."

Ernie took two steps back. "No."

When Kai angrily reached for his son, Ernie said rapidly, "You know his entire training is dependent on learning to clear his mind. Do you really want him to be seeing this as the endgame every time he spars in the ring? He has to learn peace before he can know the glories of war."

A long, tense silence. Then Kai's hands dropped. He jerked his head at the door and looked at his lieutenant. "Get them out of here. He's seen enough. For now."

Without further prompting, Ernie carried Takeo back to the dining room, but when he set him gently into his chair, Takeo ignored his half-full plate.

Ernie waited and when the lieutenant closed the door and left them alone, he turned Takeo's chair around and knelt before him, smoothing his hands down over Takeo's knees in his baggy trousers. "It's okay, bud. Your father would never hurt you that way. And that man—well, he wasn't a good man, either."

Takeo dashed the last of his tears on his sleeve. "But he'd do it to you, wouldn't he, Uncle Ernie? And anyone else who doesn't obey him."

Ernie looked away. How could he tell a son that his father was a horrible man?

But Takeo learned very quickly, just as Hana had foretold. He said slowly, "My daddy is mean. He wants to make me mean too."

A lump in his throat, Ernie could only nod.

And then Takeo asked the next exquisitely logical question: "Uncle

Ernie, what will my papa do to Mama if she comes and fights with him to get me away?"

In the more genteel confines of Tarrytown, Hana stared across the table at Zach's mother. "If your son is interested in me as more than a possible suspect, he hasn't conveyed that." When Mary gave her a skeptical look, Hana nervously arranged and rearranged her silverware to avoid meeting her eyes. Surely Mary didn't know about that passionate kiss, or Zach's obvious response to it. But that was only sex . . . a far step from that to the altar.

Mary sighed. "Very well, then. We'll table this for now, but I think we both know the subject will likely arise again. Please do me the courtesy of seriously thinking over what we've discussed. I assure you I've never had this talk with any of Zach's other . . . ah, dates. But I know my son very well."

Nodding, Hana stood quickly, taking long strides toward the patio door. Lord, she'd rather be in chains again than to suffer through another interrogation like this one! Her hand was on the door lever when Mary interrupted, her tone very matter-of-fact.

"Ms. Nakatomi, one last thing, please." When Hana reluctantly turned to face her, Mary shoved back her own untouched plate. She took a bracing sip of coffee, then looked at Hana again, that trace of mischief back in her eyes. "Before you go, wouldn't you like to know how John and I met?"

No. Not really. But Hana could only nod, the etiquette her mother had drilled into her not forgotten.

Mary wiped her mouth and rose. "Why, he arrested me. On drug charges." She smiled broadly at the utter shock on Hana's face.

Her laugh lines on display again in a way that added character, not years, to her face, she finished succinctly: "You and I are more alike than you know. You see, I was a rebellious debutante, the youngest of my very proper older sisters. I had my tattoos removed when I wed John, who even then was a very conservative DPS trooper. As I said, like father, like son. You might think of that too as you contemplate a possible future with Zach. All I ask is that you keep an open mind. None of us are ever what we seem only on the surface, are we? We'll talk again after all of this is over."

Hana fled, totally confused. Was the woman giving her blessing or offering a word of caution? She absolutely didn't know.

She'd look forward to another chat, all right.
Not.

Still pondering the strange Travis family, Hana had barely started the small car and turned toward Ernie's place before her cell phone beeped shrilly. She'd set an alarm to go off whenever she heard from Jiji's doctor. The clarion ring tone she'd selected instantly terrified her because she knew what it meant. At a light, she looked down at her screen.

The message said only: *Come immediately.* It was signed by Jiji's cancer specialist.

Inside the Tarrytown mansion, Zach sat across from his mother. "What did you say to her? She lit out of here like a scalded cat."

"You know your father is opposed to this girl as a . . . date for you?"

Zach shrugged. "Yeah."

"Well, I wanted to get to know her a bit. She's quite . . . formidable."

"If she held her own with you, I agree," Zach said with a half laugh. "But you didn't have to scare the bejesus out of her."

"Did you know she plans to face this Kai person alone?"

Zach scowled. "Luckily, it's not her decision. She's an informant, not a crusader."

"Zach, don't you understand that when you gave her the sword, you also bestowed on her—in her mind, at least—a sacred obligation to protect both her son and her family name? This man has betrayed her and tried to frame her for horrendous crimes she didn't commit. What do you expect her to do in response?"

Zach leaped to his feet, appalled. Dear God, he'd not thought this far. . . .

"Zachary," his mother began, and at the sound of his full name, Zach knew he wouldn't like what she was about to say.

He was relieved when his phone interrupted with a *beep.* Excusing himself to a quiet corner of the lawn, he took the call from Abigail. "Yes?"

"You know we tapped Hana's cell phone?" she asked without preamble.

"Dad told me, yes."

"She just got a text from her grandfather's cancer doctor. He told her to come immediately. I thought you'd want to know." Abby hung up.

With only a quick, "Later," to his mother, Zach rushed into the garage. Hana hadn't asked for moral support, but Zach knew only that she needed it, and he needed to offer it. He took his bike, because it was fastest.

Hana reached Jiji's hospital room in record time because she didn't bother with the eight-story parking garage; she left the economy car in the emergency short-term lot. She ran the distance to his room, fighting back tears and praying too. She'd so hoped to let him hold Takeo one more time.

Hana burst into Jiji's hospital room to find a team of doctors tending to him. They adjusted his drip, consulting the chart displayed on his TV screen. Quietly, they all conferred over the list of drugs they were giving him. Two nurses, meanwhile, tended to Jiji, removing soiled bedding and gently turning his frail form over so he wouldn't get bedsores.

Hana just stood there, knowing what this gathering meant. Knowing this would be the last time she saw him alive. She was frozen a step into the room, still in the doorway, between the past he'd made bearable and the empty future without him. The supervising cancer doctor looked up and saw her. At the tears she couldn't hide, he waved everyone else away until the room was quiet except for the sound of Jiji breathing into his respirator.

The doctor came over to her and said quietly, "We've done all we can. I don't... believe he even wants to fight any longer."

Hana's voice was thick with tears. "He's wanted to go for a long time."

The doctor nodded. "I'm going to leave you both alone. His great-grandson Takeo. He's asked for him multiple times. Is it possible to get him here?"

Hana could only shake her head, and her hatred of Kai was acid in her veins.

The doctor went to the door. "Please try not to upset him." Then he was gone.

Hana crept to the bed and took her grandfather's hand. It was cold. She pulled his covers up, panicking for a second because his chest didn't seem to be moving, but then Jiji took a deep breath and his eyes fluttered open.

Weakly, he tried to clasp her hand, but she barely felt it.

Hana wanted to be strong.

She wanted to offer him a last, loving smile.

She wanted to take to heart and soul every lesson he'd tried to teach her.

She knew he was in pain and it was selfish of her to want him to stay.

But she only had strength enough to fall to her knees beside him.

She tried a wavering smile, but it dissolved into sobs. She buried her face in his covers so he wouldn't see.

Something gave him strength enough to smooth down her hair. He struggled to remove the breathing mask, and she lifted her head long enough to slip it down so he could speak.

"Shhh... our ancestors will watch over you, Hana," he said, wheezing between every word, his words so labored she had to strain to hear. "Teach Takeo what I've taught you." He fell back, exhausted. He tried to touch the sword on the sheath attached to her back, but he was too weak.

Knowing what he wanted, Hana removed the sword and laid it across his chest. With a deeper, contented breath, he clutched it, but he was so weak it began to fall, and she had to help support it. He seemed happier knowing it was there, and the pain on his face eased to a peace that was so final she knew it would be his last expression. Then his breathing grew so ragged she had to put the mask over his mouth again.

His breaths were painful now, and she compulsively watched the slower and slower rise and fall of his chest. When the movement stopped, a second passed, and then all the monitors sounded shrill alarms.

When doctors and nurses burst back into the room, she stepped back, the sword still in her hand. Tears fell hotly on the shining blade, but she didn't notice. The doctors made a cursory effort to revive Jiji, but then they disappeared one by one. Only the cancer doctor was left. He looked from Hana's ravaged face to the blade in her hand, and then he exited again to give her privacy.

This time, Hana felt no movement at all when she knelt and rested her cheek on Jiji's form. He was still warm, but Hana felt the loss of his spirit and goodness so acutely that the sword pricked her hand as it slithered off her lap to the floor, clattering.

Then she was sobbing, so loud she didn't even feel another presence until a tender hand stroked down over her hair.

"Sweet Hana, I'm so sorry," said a deep, husky voice.

She looked up and Zach was there. She didn't question how or why. She knew only that she needed the comfort of his arms and his strength. She stood and took that tiny step to bridge the last gap between them, unabashed and unafraid in her weakness.

And he was there, arms wide and welcoming.

She buried her face against him and cried, the sword for once forgotten at their feet.

Chapter 12

An hour later, when they came for Jiji's body, Zach looped his arm in Hana's and led her to the door. She found her car missing and realized she'd probably been towed because she'd been there too long for the short-term lot.

Her senses were so dull that she didn't care. While Zach got the information on where to get the car out of impound, she stood near the entrance, feeling chilled despite the growing warmth of the day. So many plans to make . . . Jiji had a small life-insurance policy he'd taken out years ago, enough to bury him. And Takeo? How could she get word to him? She couldn't, because she had to be there to tell him herself.

Zach came back astride his motorcycle and put his spare helmet over her head, latching it securely. "Where do you want to go, Hana?"

Her eyes swollen with tears, she said huskily, "Ernie's. I want a bath in his big tub." Once she was astride his powerful Harley, though, and he'd easily maneuvered them through heavy traffic toward the freeway, she added in his ear, "The long way around."

And so Zach drove them along Route 360 through Austin's colorful hills, popping out now in April with mantles of blue, yellow, and red. Gorgeous native wildflowers, bluebonnet, Indian paintbrush, and sunflowers, decorated major highways throughout Texas, a legacy of Lady Bird Johnson's 1965 beautification project.

Zach seemed to sense her need for speed and they roared across the 360 bridge. He stopped at a scenic overlook that displayed the downtown skyline. They sat there idling, and slowly the sights and sounds softened Hana's grief to melancholy. She wrapped her arms tightly around Zach's waist and rested her cheek, as best she could in the helmet, against his back. "Thank you," she whispered.

He made to turn, but she caught him more tightly. "Take me to Ernie's. Will you stay with me?"

"Of course." She felt as much as heard his murmur vibrate in his strong back.

Not since Kai had Hana trusted a man's strength, because it could so often be turned against her. But somehow she knew that Zachary Travis would never hurt her. She gave herself into his hands, not watching the road, just moving as he moved for the short trip to Ernie's.

When they arrived, he looked around curiously at the oddly elegant structure, but inside he only opened cabinet doors until he found a can of chicken-noodle soup. "Consuela's would be better, but this will do in a pinch," he said. "Go take your bath and I'll have this waiting for you."

She felt his gaze follow her as she went into Ernie's luxurious master bath with its sunken, jetted tub. But as she put in foaming bath salts and made the water as hot as she could stand, she thought of Zach, the sweet caring in his eyes and touch, and the last of her bitter, self-imposed shackles fell away.

She would never be a fitting match for the rich and powerful Travis family. She had not put her heart in the care and keeping of any man but Kai, and his betrayal had hurt so much it had warped her perception of men for too long. Zachary had grown up privileged in a way she couldn't even imagine, and she'd seen firsthand the love his entire family bestowed on him. Yet he seemed unspoiled, independent, with a wild streak that relished life in a way she fully understood. As she scrubbed her flesh until it was pink, she peered inward at a nakedness more revealing than her nudity. It was as if a veil had been lifted from her eyes by his kindness toward a person who'd entered his life as a prime suspect of heinous acts.

He'd risked a lot to help her: His father's respect, his job, even his standing in the elite circles he traveled if he chose her for a mate. She began to see not their differences of stature and wealth, but their similarities in temperament and ambition. To protect hearth and home, most especially those they loved. To stay strong and independent, to follow their own path whether it was sloped uphill or down.

As she stroked a soft brush over her breasts and waist, she remembered their kiss. And she knew he'd felt then what she was feeling now: a lust more than carnal, a need to take and give in equal measure. As she drained the scented water, she watched it whirl away, faster and faster, and with it went the last of her inhibitions.

She didn't know what the future held, she reflected as she dried herself in the soft, oversized towel. She didn't know if she'd kill her former lover or he'd kill her, though she was pretty sure one of those fates awaited her. But she could take Jiji's training to heart and make the most of every day she had until then. Jiji would approve of her choice.

Hana stepped out of the tub and went in search of the short silk robe Ernie had loaned her.

In the kitchen, Zach puttered around, trying to ignore the sounds of splashing he could just hear through the thin walls. His heart had begun that tappety-tap, like a drummer calling soldiers to battle. No matter how he told himself to can it, now wasn't the time, his erection grew full and needful as he imagined Hana in the bath. He so longed to go to her and tend her, not for sex, but to smooth soap into her silken skin, to massage her, to comfort her.

But he had no right for that degree of intimacy, especially when she'd just lost the man who meant the most to her. So he cut a couple of wildflowers off Ernie's patio and put them in a crystal bud vase he'd found. He set out an embroidered place mat and even found one of those napkin thingamajigs to wrap around the matching linen napkin. He opened a good bottle of white wine and had to pour a glass to be sure it was OK. The longer her bath took, the more he decided he'd better test the vintage one more time. And once more, until he saw with surprise there was only one glass left. He put that back in the fridge to chill for Hana.

Since he hadn't eaten all day, the wine felt a bit warm all the way to his fingertips. When he heard a sound at the door between the kitchen and what he assumed was the master suite, he was embarrassed to feel his cheeks turning red. He wasn't usually so free with alcohol, but holy hell, this indomitable woman made him nervous.

When he saw her, standing there in a brilliant-blue silk robe that barely reached her knees, her nipples thrusting against the damp silk over her bosom, he inhaled sharply and took a huge, compulsive stride forward before he reined in his urges. Composing himself and feeling like a randy teenager confronted with the prom queen, he only managed a brusque nod. He fled to the stove to pour out her steaming soup, glad to have an excuse to turn around.

Her movements were quiet even in shoes; in her bare feet she might have glided, rather than walked over the floor. He didn't hear a thing over the ring of utensils as he stirred the soup. The next he knew, she'd clasped her arms about his waist and snugged her torso against his back.

He'd reached for the pot handle to pour the soup, and he froze for such a long moment that his hand began to burn. He released the handle, very carefully setting the pot back down, at the same time as he managed a garbled, "Soup's on—let me pour it for you."

"I'm hungry," she said softly, with a purr in her voice he'd never heard, only fantasized about. "But not for soup."

What would he do now? If he turned around she'd feel his hard-on. If he stayed turned away like this, she'd think he wasn't interested. He compromised by pulling her arms closer around his waist: "Hana, I didn't come here for that," he said sincerely. "I'm here for emotional support. I didn't know him well at all, but it's obvious your grandfather was your rock and I'd never take advantage of your grief—"

"I know that," she interrupted huskily. "This is my choice, isn't it? Besides, Jiji would be the first one to tell me to celebrate his passing with joy, not sorrow." She lifted slightly on her toes to reach the back of his neck. She kissed her way from one throbbing pulse on the side of his neck to the other.

Every hair in his body stood on end. Between kisses, she murmured into his skin so softly that he had to strain to hear, "Love me, Zach. I know we don't have tomorrow, because your father will never accept me. But Ernie and Jiji both would be thrilled to know I've finally learned to appreciate what I have today."

Unable to resist any longer, Zach whirled and engulfed her in a bear hug so hard she gasped. He caught the breath with his kiss, but the minute he felt her sweet lips, his desperation eased to tenderness. He relaxed his hold, pushing his hips into her abdomen so she'd feel what she did to him. He was half-afraid she'd bolt, but instead, she pushed back, moving her abdomen from side to side to show her response.

With one supple twist, she opened her robe and let it fall to the floor. "I want you. For now, that's enough."

His gaze ran over her compulsively. She was so fit that she didn't have any fat, only muscle. Her arms, her legs, her flat stomach testified to a workout schedule he suspected must be even more rigorous than his own. No wonder she moved so fluidly and quietly. No wonder she'd twice escaped him in hand-to-hand fighting.

And then the analytical part of his brain that admired her physique was subsumed by a rush of pure, primitive need. He knew only one goal: to touch her, to feel her skin against his. Everywhere.

The roaring in his ears made him clumsy, but when he pulled off his shirt, her adept hands were there to assist. When he unzipped his trousers, she helped with the stubborn button. When he'd kicked them off and reached for his white jockey shorts, she'd already tucked her fingers in his waistband and pulled them down. He kicked them off, clasping her wrist to pull her toward the bedroom, but she pulled back. "No, here. The chair. I want to see your eyes."

His need flared hotter as she led him to the large, overstuffed chair in Ernie's living room. She had presence of mind enough to spread an afghan over the leather. Then she stepped back from him several paces, put her hands on her hips, spread her legs, and cocked her head to the side as she examined him, head to toe.

It took all his dwindling control to stand there and let her look, for while she appraised him, he absorbed every sexy inch. Her damp hair shielded and then bared her small, pert breasts with every movement. The black thatch at the apex of her legs hid but could not disguise her own arousal, for he saw it in her dilated eyes and hard-tipped nipples. Her skin was white, untouched by the sun, and if it was as soft as it looked, he wondered if he'd finish too soon. It felt like he'd been fantasizing about his ninja chick forever.

He was so busy absorbing every inch of her that he didn't realize how much he aroused her too, until she launched herself at him, wrapping her arms to pull him close so she could rub every silken inch against him. This time, she could reach his mouth, and she took full advantage, kissing him with tongue and teeth, not a rebellious young woman, not even his sexy ninja chick.

She was a woman grown who knew exactly what she wanted.

And when she caught his hand to bring it to the V of her body, he could no longer doubt how very badly she wanted him too. With her other hand, she caught his erection, gently moving her palm up and down. He felt the floodgates rising and clasped her hand to pull it away. His eyes were literally unfocussed now, his 20-10 vision blurry and filled with one image: Hana's face.

Her mouth was half open with her quick breaths. Her nostrils flared as she inhaled his scent. Her tongue, pink and enticing, rimmed the mouth already reddened from their passionate kisses. And her eyes— never had he seen them so huge and velvety black. He could not tell where her irises ended and her pupils began. He felt himself falling into them and wishing himself well lost.

Here he belonged, he knew instinctively. For a long moment, their gazes met and held, his own that azure color of the Mediterranean at its sunniest, hers black as mink, and equally soft and warm. He knew then why his reactions to her had been so extreme. They were a match in every way: physically, mentally, emotionally. By her own choice, no matter what followed, she'd chosen to bend her indomitable spirit to his. She offered herself to him to mold and to cherish. To open to him in that way of all women that made her vulnerable, yet simultaneously the most powerful force on earth. For the first time in his life he knew what the Bible meant when it bade a man to cleave to his mate. He wanted to pull her into himself, to possess her utterly. Then they'd be as they truly were: With no physical boundaries of man and woman, but instead love personified, both carnal and sublime, one powerful force, in the best way that few couples ever find.

Tears came to his eyes and he buried his face in the scented hollow of her neck, kissing it softly, with a tenderness he'd never felt, nor showed, to another woman. His throat was so tight with emotion that he couldn't speak. He pulled her back with him, groping for the edge of the chair. Finally, he felt it pressing against the backs of his knees. He fell into it with none of his usual athleticism, his desire so acute he was clumsy with it.

Then she was straddling him, touching him, torso to torso, her hair caressing every inch of him as she bent her head to suck one of his erect nipples into her mouth. The hot moisture at his chest allied with the silken warmth of her hair tickling him from his shoulders to his testicles, scattered the last of his tenuous control.

With a sigh that was part torment and part her name, he lifted her until he felt the moist gate of her body opening to his need. That first touch made his eyes flutter closed, so divine was the warm, snug welcome. He tried to push her down, but she was poised on her knees beside his hips, and she resisted.

"No," she said, her voice so deep and shaky he scarcely recognized it. "Let me."

Zach had always been masterful in bed, but his eyes fluttered open at her demand. He had to blink to focus, and when he saw the utter sensuality in her face, the need she suppressed by biting her lip, his hands at her waist became caressing rather than demanding. By letting her set the pace, his mastery became hers, but in capitulating, he won her total fealty.

Somehow he knew she had never trusted a man with such total intimacy. He was further humbled and intrigued. In return, he ceded himself to her as he never had to any woman, letting her do what she would with his powerful body.

Smiling, her expression soft, she lowered herself a tiny bit at a time, relishing the long slide to unity. The immersion, slow inch by inch, was the most sexually humbling experience of his life, for Hana remained real to him, more than a feminine sheath designed to give him pleasure. She was his choice, he was hers, and the full intimacy of what they did would leave them both forever marked. Together they reached, so entwined they had no beginning and no end. Then he was finally master of her body, deep inside her, while she luxuriated in his power, cradling him inside to the tip of her pulsing womb. For a long moment, with him engulfed all the way, she stayed still. She rested her cheek against his chest, listening to the throb of his heart, feeling the same pulse in the throbbing muscle inside.

Again, she spoke, saying simply, "Look at me, Zach."

Totally bewitched, he opened his eyes. Her little smile all the more sensual because she licked her lips, she held his eyes and tightened her inner muscles upon his length. Then he couldn't see her at all because his eyes fluttered closed at the powerful sensations. Once, twice, again, and then he could stand no more.

His instincts took over. He lifted her away, ignoring her protests, needing leverage, and bent her forward over the wide arm of the plush chair. Immediately, he buried himself in one fierce lunge. He heard her groan, but he knew it wasn't with pain. He withdrew slowly, letting her feel each inch, then immersed himself again in a famished lunge so hard the chair scraped against the floor.

He didn't even hear it. The next time, he caught her hips to tip her up slightly to better fit inside. The next thrust sent him as deep as he could go, but it still wasn't enough. He withdrew and pushed back, harder, again, again. At the same time, he reached around her to touch the turgid nubbin designed to welcome him. He heard her groans become pants. He thrust in one last time with all the power of his lower body, his feet planted to give him strength. He felt her body bow in his arms to take it. With joy, with celebration in his power, she pushed back, opening, opening. He felt her hips squirm to take more of him, her pants becoming a keening, primal need. With equal savage instinct, he knew he'd found his match, in bed and out of it. This time, exultation shattered the last of his control.

The floodgates crashed open, the tide rushing in with every surge, higher and higher. And then... cataclysm. He burst, and she screamed, her womanhood pulsing around his ejaculation. Man, woman, neither apart, but complete, a shared little death in the conquest of life.

Both of them shivering, the dying pulsations slowly leaving them weak, they fell into the chair. He lifted her onto his lap, cradling her into his arms. She listened to the beat of his heart; he held his hand over her breast, cupping the gift of her in his palm.

Like that, totally relaxed and entwined, they slept. As he drifted off, Zach clutched her close, knowing that no matter what happened, he'd find a way to protect her from the battle to come, and to win her for his own ever after.

The second time, in the bed, was longer and much more tender, but when Zach finally stirred himself to go, Hana had to restrain her urge to clutch at him. She saw the look on his face as he glanced at his watch. She knew it was almost time for the van to pick them up for the trip to find the compound. She'd known she was only delaying, not ending, the reckoning awaiting her in Kai's lair, but somehow the passion she'd just experienced made her stronger for the ordeal.

He gave her a quick kiss, promising he'd be back with the others in the van. Then he was gone, leaving her not bereft, but resolved. The pleasure he'd given her in his savage taking brought pink to her cheeks as she looked at herself in the mirror. A love bite on her neck was turning blue and she knew she'd have to wear her primmest turtleneck. Hana knew, no matter what his mother thought, that she could never be an appropriate love match for Zachary. But for now, knowing he'd chosen her because he both wanted and needed her desperately, was enough.

However, as she took a quick shower and dressed in her black spandex, she gained another certainty. Kai already hated all law enforcement, especially Texas Rangers. He'd taken a shot at Zach's father. If he saw her and Zach together, no matter how indifferent she tried to be, he'd know she'd fallen in love with the man who'd caught and arrested her.

She had to avoid that at all costs, because Zach was inherently an honorable man. He had no idea how ruthless Kai could really be. If Zach confronted Kai in his lair, Kai would be as dangerous as a wounded grizzly. He'd not fight fair.

Therefore, both to protect Takeo and to avert a disastrous confrontation between Zach and Kai, she had to find a way to enter the compound before the raid.

Alone . . . perhaps then, using the sword as bait, she could find a way to at least partially neutralize Kai. If she knew Ernie, he'd been snooping from the day he arrived and would already know how to cut Kai's surveillance system.

When a couple of hours later, Zach came to fetch her for the ordeal of trying to find the compound, Hana had won back most of her composure. As much as she wanted it for protection, just in case, she secreted the sword in Ernie's hidden safe room. If they somehow got caught, she wouldn't dare risk Kai seizing the blade from her as an interloper. She only had leverage if she walked boldly to the front gate to complete their bargain. Then she typed a quick text.

A few minutes later, she had to hide a smile when she saw Zach's face, blackened in a way that somehow only accented his symmetrical bone structure. He, like the two DPS troopers across from him, wore camouflage. Hana knew they didn't intend to waste any time. If they successfully found the compound, job one was to reconnoiter and test the security points for any weakness—now, tonight. So they'd dressed accordingly.

As she shunned Zach's assistance to get into the back of the paneled van, she wondered if he knew his mother had vetted her as if she were a prize mare about to be presented to the stable's best stud. But the slight soreness between her legs was a badge of honor, proof of his interest in her as more than an informant.

If he knew her thoughts, his manner wasn't any different. Brisk, professional, he only touched her to put the hood over her head and bind her hands loosely in front.

They'd duplicated as closely as they could her prior trip: enclosed van, the same time of night, around midnight, hood and bindings, starting from the same place. And now as then, because she couldn't support herself and tell when the turns were coming, they were easier for her to read because of the way her body swayed as the van took corners.

Their point of origin, Hana's former day hotel, lay directly off Interstate 35, so the first leg of the trip was easy for Hana to re-create. "We made a left onto the entrance ramp; I could feel it in the turn of the vehicle," Hana said. "So we went south down thirty-five."

The driver turned as she indicated.

"Can you estimate how far before the next turn?" Zach asked softly, hoping not to interrupt her concentration.

She shook her hooded head and continued her counting out loud. When she reached 2007 she said, "There should be an exit in the next few seconds."

They took the next exit. But here they had to pause because Hana was listening closely. "I heard some kind of loud music before, like a honky-tonk country bar. We turned past it, to the right, I think. The road was bumpy and full of potholes. It curved and it felt narrow, from the movement of the van."

Past the access-road stop sign, they looked around and finally spotted a little dive bar, its lights off, the gravel parking lot empty. It was a Sunday night.

"OK," Zach said, his voice a bit tense. "We see the bar. We made a right. Now what?"

Hana was counting again. When she reached 966 she said, "There's a sharp turn to the left off this road onto something rougher, like gravel or caliche. I heard and felt the stuff hitting our undercarriage and the surface crunched, so it definitely was not asphalt."

They had to back up because they missed the turn at first in the dark. It was nothing more than an opening in a barbed-wire fence. The rough road led over a cattle guard. They shone the lights on it.

"Was there a cattle guard?" Zach asked.

"Yes. And another one further down a few minutes, if we're on the right road."

They turned as she indicated.

Zach leaned toward the driver. "We'd better turn off the lights and go very slow. If this is the right road, we don't want them to hear us or see us, obviously."

The driver did as Zach suggested. He paused a minute after the turn to put on a pair of night-vision goggles, and then he drove on with more surety.

This time, her count was only 201 before she said sharply, "Turn to the left."

Again, they missed the turn and had to back up. After they crossed the second cattle guard, this caliche road was even more narrow and full of potholes, as if it were deliberately not maintained.

"Stop for a second, please, and let me get my bearings."

The driver stopped immediately. Hana tilted her head, as if listening. "I heard cattle lowing that night. Do you see any?"

Zach climbed out of the van and shone a powerful xenon flashlight through the trees. He saw numerous Black Angus lying in the grassy clearing. His light also hit something else in the broad meadow: windmills. At least a dozen of them, the tall kind with the single propeller.

Snapping off the light, he got back in the van. "This must be it. There's a ton of those windmills that produce power. They cost a fortune. Your typical rancher wouldn't need that much power. He's staying off the grid. That's why we never found him."

"If this is the right turn," Hana continued, "you'll come to a very long asphalt driveway. At the end is an electric gate. I heard it hum as it was opened. We went down that driveway for about fifty seconds before we stopped and they let me out, leading me up steps into a house. It had wooden floorboards and felt like a porch."

Zach looked at his colleagues. "What do you think? On foot from here?"

The other two troopers nodded.

When Hana heard the van door swing wide again, she yanked off the hood. "I'm coming."

Zach paused, half in, half out the door. "Like hell you are."

Her mouth set in that mulish scowl, she only looked at him, holding her bound wrists out to be cut. They locked gazes, this battle of wills even fiercer than their former tussles.

"I know Kai's tactics," Hana said calmly. "He'll have guards posted in the trees. I promise to only observe."

When Zach shook his head, her voice turned soft and pleading. "Please. I might see Takeo. It worries me we haven't heard from Ernie. I have to know they're both okay."

Sighing heavily, Zach unsheathed the Ka-Bar from the holster in the middle of his back and used it to cut her bonds. She bounded up and outside the van, looking around, her long black hair tied in a ponytail at her nape.

Zach was busy giving orders. He looked at the driver. "Take the van back up the road to the first turn. Try to pull it off and hide it in a clearing if you can. Drive back here to pick us up in thirty minutes." Zach looked at his watch and said, "We all need to synchronize. If we get separated we meet back here at oh-one hundred. Sharp. That gives us thirty minutes."

They all synchronized their watches. After they'd put on their night-vision goggles, Hana pulled on her hood with the inset lenses.

She warned them, "They'll be in camo too. Watch every possible hiding place, including trees and brush. They'll have night-vision also and they're very stealthy."

Zach ordered, "Keep to cover as much as possible so they can't see your body heat."

"What if we're spotted?" one of the troopers asked. "Do we engage?"

Zach hesitated.

Hana didn't. "I realize there are rules for this type of thing in law enforcement, but I can tell you this much: If Kai's men find us snooping around and successfully capture us, we're all dead."

"Use your discretion," Zach said finally. "Take them captive if you can so we can get intel, but if your life is at risk, defend yourself however necessary."

They scattered, each in a different direction.

"You stay with me," Zach said curtly to Hana.

Hana tossed him an irritated look that said he wasn't the boss of her, but she followed him nonetheless. Soon enough, her heart was beating hard at her ribs, and not from the short hike. She knew Takeo was probably in bed, but something in her felt she'd finally glimpse him herself. This close to him, she had to try. Maybe then she could sleep and quit having nightmares that something had happened to him.

Inside the compound, all was quiet. At this late hour, even Kai was in bed. However, guards both inside and outside were still vigilant.

Ernie tossed off his covers and pulled his baggy *gi* over his nakedness. There was no safe time to do this, so he had to think of a distraction. He knew no one slept on Kai's watch: Partly because of their incessant training, but mostly because of the severe punishment if anything went down on their guard duty. Kai had written his own manifesto of sorts. Every one of his converts had to memorize it, for it laid out both rewards and punishments. Ernie had been given his own copy.

The first offense of sleeping on the job was only a loss of the tip of one pinkie. A second infraction led to the loss of two fingers, and so on. Kai had embraced this barbaric part of the Yakuza tradition of cutting off appendages as a means of discipline. Only two of Kai's men in his entire complement of forty or so were partially missing a pinkie. After he read the manifesto, Ernie had started watching all the men who paraded in and out of his ring. He suspected he knew why only two of the gang members were missing pinkies—and none, so far as he could tell, were missing actual fingers.

They never survived long enough to suffer the indignity of a loss of fingers.

And so, when Ernie snuck out of his room supposedly from hunger, on his trip to the kitchen—which, conveniently enough, was adjacent to the garage—he knew he was risking his life. But he felt he had little choice. After he'd seen the rigor and cruelty to which Kai had subjected his son, he knew all Hana's fears about getting Takeo away as soon as possible were totally justified.

The Rangers had to have some idea of Kai's infrastructure or their raid would be a disaster. Particularly how to disable the security system. Assuming he ever got out long enough to share the intel. . . .

He fingered the little black book in his pocket. He'd taken to keeping the manifesto close, just in case.

Wouldn't the Texas Rangers love to get a copy of this little black book? Talk about MO right there in black and white.

Ernie took his sandwich and chips with him. He nodded at the guard stationed in the front hall and stopped before the one stationed at the garage door. "I need to get in to fix Takeo's bike. I promised him I'd fix it when I get a moment and I'm so busy training you all, I never have time. Couldn't sleep, so might as well do it now. Kai approved it."

Kai had approved it, but not at 1:00 a.m.

With those magical words, the guard used his code to open the garage door that led off the hallway. Ernie offered him half his sandwich. Looking a bit guilty, he took it and ripped away half of it in one large bite.

He didn't know Ernie had crushed two Xanax, which he'd filched from the infirmary area when he'd been binding up a wounded fighter, into the spicy mustard he'd spread on the French bread. If the man lost a finger . . . well, Ernie would feel guilty, but he knew the sort of boss he'd sworn loyalty to, and he knew Kai wouldn't hesitate to kill any of them.

Ernie tossed the other half, untouched, into a refuse bin. True to his promise, he got to work on the bike, using his acute sense of internal timing—since he didn't have a watch—to gauge thirty minutes, which was about how long he expected the Xanax to fully work its way into the guard's bloodstream.

Meanwhile, outside, Zach and Hana had zigzagged through trees and brush as much as they could to reach a corner of the exterior wrought-iron fencing that wasn't lined by trees. Zach tossed a twig at the fence and heard an electrical fizz, so he knew the entire perimeter must be wired. Using a tiny pocket flashlight he held close to the ground, he walked the fence perimeter, looking for a sign of buried cable so they could disable the source of the electricity when the time came.

He was so intent on what he was doing that it took him a second to realize Hana hadn't followed him. Cursing under his breath, he moved to retrace his steps, but he knew with a sinking feeling in the pit of his stomach that he was too late.

Sure enough, as he regained the relative safety of a thick clump of bushes, he saw a light come on at the gate, which in the moonlight he could see some distance away. Guards dropped from trees at the far corners, and grouped around the tall, slim intruder.

In the light, Hana was visible, her hands in the air as she was searched.

Chapter 13

Oblivious to danger, Ernie put the second part of his plan into action. He attached the small but powerful Hewlett-Packard calculator Kai had given him to keep track of his students' match points to the keypad beside the door. He attached two improvised cables. He couldn't afford any wounds on his hands, so he used a sharp screwdriver to pierce his own wrist, near his artery but just missing it. However, he pressed the small wound, hard, to make more blood come out until it dripped on the garage floor. He moved to the calculator, groaning as if in agony, loud enough for the men inside the control room to hear him, but not loud enough to escape the garage's soundproofed walls.

After a minute or two of his groaning, he heard the control-room interior alarm system ring with a series of beeps as a code was entered into a keypad. To his relief, his improvised encryption device worked. He saw a long series of numbers flash across the calculator screen. Hitting the memory button on the small device, he disengaged it, put it in his pocket, and moved back just as the door opened. Cradling his dripping wrist as if agonized, Ernie swayed slightly as a man he'd never seen before, who looked more like a Goth than a drug dealer, poked his head outside.

"What the hell?"

The man saw the blood and Ernie swaying, his eyes closed as if he were about to faint. Irritably, he looked toward the garage door leading into the house, but when no one came, he carefully closed the door behind him and approached. "What happened?"

Ernie blubbered, "I cut myself. Bad. I need a first-aid kit. You got one?"

The man looked at the blood on the end of the screwdriver on the floor. "You the martial-arts guy?"

"Yes, but if I don't get this patched up I won't be able to work." And as if in sudden panic: "Dear God, Kai will kill me." He looked at the man. "Please, get me a kit. I need QuikClot. I'd go to the infirmary myself, but..." And then Ernie toppled to the floor, as if out cold.

Looking mightily irritated, the man hurried outside, the door into the hallway slamming behind him.

Ernie figured he had about three minutes and he didn't waste a second.

Reading off the security code on the small calculator memory pad, he punched the code into the keypad, praying they kept a skeleton crew of only one this late at night on the inside of the control room. Otherwise his ruse was for naught and he was probably dead.

At the gate, the senior guard on duty apparently recognized Hana. "What are you doing here?"

"I had a deal with Kai and I've come to begin our exchange."

"How did you find us? You were blindfolded when we brought you here."

Hana shrugged. "I have a good sense of direction."

He still looked at her with narrowed eyes. "Where's your vehicle?"

"A dirt bike. I stashed it in the trees. Are you going to tell Kai I'm here? I demand to see Takeo before I give him the sword."

Looking a bit pale with dread even in the moonlight, the man snatched the radio at his belt and pressed the *talk* button. "Wake up Kai."

Hidden behind the heavy shrubs, Zach was still close enough to hear the exchange. He saw more guards pouring into the glade where Hana stood, and he realized the sentries had all been called from their posts. They were clear, at least for a few minutes, to search. Ignoring the gut-wrenching fear binding his rib cage, he used the time she'd purchased for them by darting along the fence line until he found a transformer post on one corner. Shooting the exact location with his GPS range finder, he hurried back to see what was happening at the gate.

When he saw the guard push his face into Hana's, trying to intimidate her, he automatically reached for the pistol butt at his holster.

Hana stood her ground, and he heard her say, "You can threaten me all you want, but this is Kai's decision."

The guard gave a disgusted grunt, but then he punched a long code into the security-pad stand beside the road leading through the gate. The gate opened and Hana was shoved up the drive, her hands bound before her.

Helpless to do anything but grind his teeth in frustration, Zach swore he'd beat her himself once he got her alone. The woman was a menace, dangerous just as his father warned. But she'd obviously planned this, and short of storming the gate, there was nothing he could do but wait.

And pray . . .

Then, checking his watch, he zigzagged back the way he'd come to meet his men at the van at the appointed time.

About the time Hana entered the gate, Ernie was ready to exit the control room, glad he'd put together this elaborate scheme that had, so far at least, worked flawlessly. The control room was empty, just as he'd hoped. He hadn't touched anything, and since Kai had confiscated his cell phone, he had no way to take pictures. However, he understood surveillance systems about as well as safes, and he realized this was a monster.

Monitors lined two walls. He counted rapidly: twenty. They had twenty different angles all over the perimeter. With a glance, he saw not one, but two backup systems. A main feed, a secondary one, and a last one, apparently wireless. He saw a satellite icon on the main control hub, a huge flat-screen display with an ergonomic chair in front of it. He realized that here was the master control center. Anyone who sat here controlled the entire compound's circuitry.

Ernie knew his time was about up, so as much as he longed to keep investigating, he had to get the hell out of here. He was turning for the door when movement on the gate monitor caught his eye. He glanced that way and then froze, two steps from the door.

Hana—oh my God. Walking with that lithe, easy stride as if she hadn't a care in the world, she let herself be shoved up the drive toward the house.

Instantly, Ernie knew she'd risked her life to check on him and Takeo. She'd been able to re-create her prior journey on her own, without his help, which didn't surprise him. But she wasn't wearing a sword... what the hell was she thinking? Without the katana to bargain with, what kind of leverage did she have?

But he also knew he had little time to spare. He took a quick look around, trying to commit as much as he could to memory, keyed in the code on the pad beside the door, and exited. Once outside, with the door secure, he broke open his closing wound again, spreading blood on his *gi*. He staggered to the door and looked outside at the guard he'd drugged. He was still, inert against the wall, snoring peacefully. Ernie felt so guilty at what would happen to him that he held a gasoline-soaked rag under the man's nostrils. He coughed, stirred, and sat up.

"You'd better get back on your feet or you'll be in big trouble," Ernie warned. "You sick or something?" He held up his wound, cradling it with his free hand. "I yelled for help, but you didn't hear me."

The guy looked at the few bread crumbs left from his sandwich, and back at Ernie. Ernie pretended not to notice the suspicion directed at him as he nursed his sore wrist.

He'd retreated back inside the garage to sit weakly against the wall when Kai's lieutenant entered. He bit back obviously harsh words and waved forward the guard who'd left the control room to get the first-aid kit. He eyed Ernie narrowly, pulling his wrist close without ceremony and turning it from side to side. He looked down at the sharp-edged screwdriver tipped with blood, sprawled next to the bike, then relaxed slightly.

Glad he'd made the wound deep enough to look real, Ernie said weakly, "Thanks," and tried to open the QuikClot kit with shaky hands. This time, it wasn't an act. His heart was pounding so hard in fear for Hana and Takeo that his hands really were shaky. He was listening for Kai's voice, because he knew Kai's men wouldn't act against Hana without direction.

The lieutenant brushed Ernie's hands away and applied the QuikClot for him. He gave it a quick, rough bandage and then he said, "Come with me. Kai has directed us to meet in the dining room. Hana Nakatomi has tried to break in to take back her son."

Wonderful. Ernie knew exactly why Kai wanted him there.

This was a loyalty test.

Kai would threaten Hana and see how her old friend would react.

Genuinely a bit green about the gills this time, Ernie did as he was told.

* * *

Back at the van, one of the troopers was already there. With a prize. He had a short man, sporting gang tattoos on his neck, bound and gagged on the floor of the van. He was clad in camo. Zach was thrilled despite his fear for Hana. He gave his fellow law-enforcement pal a high five. "Good work!"

"He jumped me from that big oak down the fence line. Almost slit my throat, but I'm bigger." His grin showed white teeth as he looked down at his captive, who glared back. "And meaner."

The other trooper returned, holding what appeared to be a surveillance camera. "I figure the lab can pull this apart and tell us what we're up against."

Again, Zach was impressed. He felt a bit guilty for the former opinion he'd voiced to his dad that Texas troopers were in general less impressive than active-duty personnel. "Brilliant."

They all looked at him expectantly, then inside the van and around the clearing.

Zach's smile faded. "She's been captured. Or I should say, she surrendered."

They looked pissed. "So she is a plant for this asshole," one of them griped.

Zach searched the van and found her ankle bracelet, the backup battery steady red, sliced neatly and shoved under the backseat. "I don't think so. Why would she have brought us straight here? She would have pretended she couldn't find it. Besides, if she was conning us as a double, then Kai would know she was playing informant and he'd expect a tracker." Zach's voice went very quiet. "She removed this because she went in there hoping to see her son. You need to go back to HQ immediately and question this guy. And I mean put the screws to him, whatever you have to do to see if we can get some idea of the interior layout. Tell John Travis and Ross Sinclair I'm staying behind to observe. Send someone trained in stealth ops back to help me."

"How many?" the lead trooper asked.

"Oh, just a few. Like . . . everyone." Zach added somberly, "If we're lucky, Kai will taunt her a bit and let her go. We just need to have transport for her when she gets out. And I'm not budging until I see her."

The troopers were not happy to leave him alone, he could tell that, but he was leading the op. And for the first time, Zach saw an advantage in being John Travis's son. He suspected his colleagues cut him a bit more slack just because of who he was. He looked at the driver. "Can you re-create the trip and bring them back as quickly as possible?"

The driver made an A-OK sign. "I've locked in the GPS."

Zach took one of the AR-15s from the weapons stash, along with several extra magazines and an armament belt to hold everything. He double-checked both his pistols, each fully loaded, and reached back to adjust his knife to the perfect throwing angle. Then he grinned, feeling alive for only the second time since he got back to Austin and gentility.

The first time was his life-altering night with Hana....

He stepped back, closed the van door, and tapped it with his palm in the universal military sign of "good luck and safe journey."

Then, alone again, he turned back toward the place in the fence where an oak, ancient and sturdy, grew at the fence line. It had been previously occupied by the guard his trooper had captured, so Zach took his spot and used the elevation and his night-vision goggles to watch the entrances and exits.

He'd barely positioned himself before he heard a radio crackle. He shimmied back down, following the sound to a pile of brush. He moved leaves and bramble aside, hearing a harsh spate of garbled Japanese. The radio had obviously been lost in the struggle. When no response came, the same words, more urgently, were repeated. Then silence. Zach picked up the long range, expensive two-way radio, both thrilled and dismayed.

Thrilled because he could eavesdrop on what was happening inside. Anything in English, anyway.

Dismayed because when the guard didn't report in, they'd come looking for him.

Zach melted quietly into the trees away from the fence, taking the radio with him.

Inside the dining room, Hana paced, waiting for Kai. She was too smart not to be scared, but also too smart to show it. She whirled toward the door when it opened. Kai's right-hand man entered with Ernie close behind.

Hana gasped at the blood spattered on him, but behind Kai's man he gave her a broad wink and she relaxed. If anyone could make rattlesnake boots while in a den of vipers, it was Ernie. She felt such a rush of affection for him that she gave him a luminous smile. She was so happy he was OK. For now, at least... Kai's lieutenant saw her reaction and turned toward Ernie suspiciously, but Ernie only fumbled for a chair and fell into it, nursing his bandaged wrist on the table before him.

A second guard came in and whispered something to the lieutenant. He frowned and exited, reaching for the radio at his belt. "All posts, report in," Hana heard him say in Japanese.

When the door opened shortly after, Hana felt electricity in the air. She knew before she saw him that the great man had arrived. With his quiet power, Kai strode into the dining room. Kai was not tall, but he dominated almost any setting. As she lifted her chin, meeting his eyes directly, she wondered who'd win the power-of-persuasion battle if he ever competed with Zach. But she'd evaded Zach partly to avoid that eventuality, whether he understood it or not. Instinctively, she knew if these two met, a battle to the death would likely result.

All these thoughts ran through the back of her mind as she stood still and let Kai study her with those flat, dark eyes.

"Why are you here?" he finally asked, a hint of menace in his tone. "How did you find me without an escort? And where is the katana?"

Hana smiled a smile that wasn't mirthful. It was meant to taunt him right back. She saw from the flexing of his jaw that it worked. "One, I want to see my son to confirm he's okay. Two, I've retained a goodly amount of my Zen training even if you haven't. The eyes often betray you, so don't use them to the exclusion of all else. Three, the katana is in my custody now. In a safe place. Did you really think I'd bring it to you without confirming Takeo is all right?"

She watched for the play of emotions behind his wall, but found none. Time was when she knew every flicker of eyelash and twitch at his mouth. But now? It was over three months since she'd seen Kai. Was it her imagination, or were there a few lines in that handsome forehead? Kai wasn't even thirty yet, but his lifestyle—to put it mildly—was very stressful, chosen or not. And his eyes, once alive with mirth, were dead and flat, like a shark's. Or a snake's.

The charming young man who'd wooed and won her was dead. In

his place was a murderous drug dealer, a monster who'd chosen for himself the apt symbol of a snarling dragon. Cold-blooded, rapacious, merciless.

Takeo's father.

The irony didn't escape her, and her own emotions were so heightened she had to force herself to listen to his response.

"I don't believe you have it. It wouldn't be the first time you've lied to me."

"Or you to me." Hana had expected this. She pulled her cell phone from a hidden pocket in her bra they'd missed when they searched her. She showed Kai the time stamp on the close-up pictures she'd taken of the blade. The last one displayed the *mon*, or heraldic symbol of her family, the hawk in a circle, engraved on the haft of the blade. "The Travis family had it refurbished. It is . . . gorgeous."

She handed the phone to Kai when he held out his hand. He avidly paged through the photos, then stuck the phone in his own pocket.

Undeterred, Hana finished: "And it will remain hidden until I see my son. If you refuse to allow me to leave safely, you'll never see it, for no one but I knows where it is." She glanced at Ernie, who made a good pretense of weakness as he leaned his head back against his chair.

But she knew he'd absorbed every word and that he understood her subtle signal that she'd left the sword in his safe room. "We can do an exchange in a few days. I'd prefer to do it in public, somewhere in Austin, not here." Hana's heartbeat had accelerated as she steadily met Kai's eyes. If he was to be captured and defanged, it would need to be here, not in public where he could use any number of escape methods and innocents as hostages. Not to mention that her immunity agreement hinged on his safe capture and enough evidence to put him away for life, which also meant they had to take him in his lair. But she knew him well enough to taunt him to overrule her, just so he could display his power.

Sure enough, he scowled. "No. Here. Ten p.m. Three days."

She held her breath. "And Takeo?"

"I'll have him ready for you and if the blade is all you say, you may take him with you." He ground the words out as if they were unfamiliar, like disgusting medicine he'd never expected he'd need.

Hana gave him a bigger dose. "And Ernie. I want him to come with me too."

Kai glanced at Ernie, who seemed to almost be dozing. "That's his decision. He was hired to do a job for me, and he's not finished."

Ernie roused, his eyelids still half closed. "Sorry, they gave me a painkiller and it's made me sleepy." Ernie used his uninjured hand to lift his other wrist. It had begun to swell and turn purple. "I just wanted to surprise Takeo with his fixed bike, but I guess I was more tired than I thought. Sorry, Kai, but I may be out of commission for a bit anyway. However, once the exchange is finished, you have my word I'll return to finish the training."

Kai's smile didn't change his flat, black eyes. "The timing was quite odd, don't you think? For such an adroit man to injure himself like this, so clumsily, just as Hana barges in to negotiate with me?"

Ernie's cheeks flushed with color. He leaned forward to enunciate: "The screwdriver slipped. It happens. I couldn't sleep and I made your son a promise I was keeping. You also gave me permission to fix the bike. You took my cell phone. I had no way of contacting her, or anyone else."

At the steady beam of those luminous quicksilver eyes, even Kai had to look away. He conceded, "Whether you go or stay is your decision. My men can wait a few days until you heal."

Hana knew Kai was testing Ernie's loyalty. She looked at her mentor, holding her breath.

Ernie never even glanced at her. He stood, swaying slightly, his uninjured hand on the chair back to support himself. "I don't like to leave a job half-finished. I'll stay. For now, I'll fetch Takeo. Okay?" He looked at Kai for permission.

"It's late," Kai growled. "He'll be too tired to finish all his lessons if we wake him."

Hana said simply, "Then take me to him."

Outside, hidden in a grouping of brush, Zach cooled his heels as best he could, but he couldn't say the same for his temper. He checked his watch for the umpteenth time. She'd been in there for over thirty minutes now. An eternity in dangerous situations like this. He was tempted to say to hell with it and use that huge oak's overhanging branch to drop down inside the electrical fence, but he knew that would be suicide. They'd have no way of getting back out without the gate code. So he ground his teeth together and stayed put.

He'd seen several guards, wearing night-vision goggles, approach the oak tree and look for any signs of a struggle or why their sentry was missing. He'd stayed low, totally hidden by the brush, and finally they conferred and then went back inside the gate.

He'd listened to the little he could make out of their conversation, hoping he'd at least hear Hana's name mentioned, but he didn't understand a word. Now what? They'd be very suspicious of her with a missing sentry, so she was in more danger than she realized. He knew her well enough by now to hope and pray that she'd gone in there with a plan. Probably to open negotiations on the exchange: her son for the katana. But why hadn't she shared her intent with him? Had he not proved he trusted her just by letting her borrow the blade?

That trust was obviously not reciprocated. His frustration level rising, Zach shifted position and forced himself to wait. But his movement had made the dry leaves rustle slightly. He froze. The next thing he knew, a guard was upon him, rifle raised to use it as a cudgel.

Zach had only half turned over before the rifle butt came down, but he managed to use his free leg to sweep the guard's feet from under him. Then they were fighting, hand-to-hand, the rifle useless in such close combat. The guard tossed it aside and engaged him with wrestling moves.

In college, Zach had made the wrestling team, so he knew many of the choke holds and ways to evade being immobilized. But this guy... he was much smaller, but Zach couldn't get a decent grip on him. Every time he almost grabbed an arm, a leg, or jabbed with an elbow, he barely grazed skin because the guard had read his moves and adjusted his position accordingly.

What was he, a pocket sumo?

Zach had struggled hand-to-hand with many different types of combatants, but this gang member had preternatural timing. When Zach grabbed the sentry's wrist, the man foiled his handhold with a twist and jab. When Zach tried to clutch his longer legs around the man's ankles to hold him still in a choke hold, the guy shifted his weight, braced, and whirled them around. Now Zach was on top and had no defense when his opponent's legs came up in a vise around his waist.

However, the guard was obviously not used to battling men of Zach's skill set, either, because from his position of better leverage Zach rammed both his elbows into the sentry's abdomen, winding him. Zach twisted free and jerked off the man's hood. Then he wrenched the man's arms behind his back, finally immobilizing him. He saw panic flare in the dark eyes. The man opened his mouth and Zach knew he was about to call for help. Zach pressed his strong forearm into his throat. The Asian made a garbled sound, but Zach pressed harder. He only intended to wind him, but then he felt something sharp at his rib cage. He pressed down in one motion with all his strength and felt the blade penetration stop. At the same time, he heard the man's neck snap.

His opponent went limp. Breathing heavily, Zach pulled away and tugged up his shirt. A gash between two of his ribs welled with blood and it hurt, but Zach knew it was just a scratch. He unsnapped a pocket in his camo pants and applied a bit of QuikClot and a bandage. Then he looked down to see what he'd been stabbed with.

To his utter consternation, he saw his own Ka-Bar, only the very tip gleaming with blood in the moonlight, lying on the ground next to them. Holy shit—as they grappled, the man had lifted the blade so stealthily from his back sheath that he hadn't felt a thing. Zach shivered a bit, not from the wound, but from comprehension of what they faced. In his experience, sentries were trained well, but they were on the lower echelon of any military group's pecking order. If this man had almost skewered an Army Ranger who'd killed his fair share of special-ops soldiers in hand-to-hand combat, what would Kai and his upper rank be like to face?

And Hana was in there alone.

Zach was climbing the tree—to hell with the consequences—when he heard the quiet purr of a muffled motor. He jumped back the short distance to the ground. He was astonished to see two familiar faces: His father and Ross Sinclair led the way out of a jeep outfitted with huge tires and special mufflers.

Kai hesitated, then nodded. "He's been asking to see you," he admitted grudgingly. He moved aside and indicated she precede him out the door.

She'd only taken a few steps into the living area when his most trusted lieutenant hurried in and whispered in his ear. Kai lifted a hand to indicate she halt, but Hana pretended not to see, continuing toward the hallway door and the presumed location of the bedrooms.

Her thoughts were now only on her son, to hold him and reassure him.

Kai's hand caught her arm so harshly she winced.

He swung her to face him. "Another of my men is missing. One coincidence of timing I might overlook, but two? What the hell do you think you're doing? Who's helping you, you traitorous bitch?"

Poised between the door to Takeo's room and the exit, Hana faced Kai. She knew it would do no good to lie. "My lover. He's in security."

Kai's sneer sounded like a hissing dragon's. "You mean Zachary Travis."

"However, he didn't know I was going to try to... to... communicate with you. But he's probably still outside waiting to hear from me. Given who he is, do you want the Texas Rangers, DEA, and everyone else he can contact to show up?" This time, her smile was genuine and one he'd helped teach her, because it was reckless too. "Did you really expect me to come here without backup?"

Kai glared at his lieutenant. "Call in all the sentries. Barricade everything. Go to total lockdown." The lieutenant disappeared.

While Kai was conferring quietly with his subordinate, Ernie jerked his head at the garage door and made typing motions in the air. Hana knew immediately that central command must be behind that door.

They were both glum and motionless when Kai turned back to them. The lieutenant was busy keying in a code in the exterior panel. Hana lifted her chin and stared Kai down. "If you let me go, I promise to hold them off. You have my word."

"For how long?" Kai scoffed.

"I can manage three days, for sure. Until I bring you the sword. You'll have time to fortify—or run." Her own smile turned nasty.

He slapped her so hard her head flipped to the side. With her cheek bearing his hand imprint, Hana only composed herself and looked at him again. "Pity that. You used to have more finesse."

"You used to be trustworthy, *kono baita*," he flung back.

"If I'm a whore, you made me one!" Hana retaliated, finally stung.

This time, he almost wrenched her arm from its socket. His free hand caressed the *tanto* stuck in his belt.

Hana knew he was debating whether to kill her or force her to his dungeon.

Suddenly alert, Ernie tensed on the balls of his feet.

Outside, as two SWAT guys hauled the dead man into a van and did a quick clean of the site to disguise signs of their struggle, John Travis eyed his son severely. "Where the hell do you think you're going? You didn't have the OK to invade the compound, only to find it."

Zach nodded. "True enough."

"If you think being my son allows you to disobey direct orders—"

"Hana is in danger," Zach said simply. "If you want me to resign, I will. But if she doesn't show up in the next five minutes, with or without help I'm going in after her. You in? Or out?"

In the hallway inside the house, a new arrival came in yawning, his hair standing straight up. Takeo looked at his mother. All his sleepiness gone, he ran to her. She caught him up in her arms, hugging him so hard he winced.

"You're okay, Takeo?"

He nodded reluctantly, tracing the outline of the hand on her cheek. "*Otosan* did this, didn't he?" He turned his head to glare at his father.

Kai's anger slipped behind a charming smile that didn't move anyone, including Takeo. "She lied to me, Takeo. And two of my men are missing."

The ugly silence was more resounding than the former argument.

Chapter 14

Outside, Zach unsnapped the Velcro pocket where he kept his badge. "Look, I didn't set this agenda. Dad, you know I never wanted to be a Ranger. I did it to keep you safe. I know we're a few days early. I know we haven't had time to properly plan. But a lot of our usual raid protocols won't work anyway, because this Kai SOB obviously has backup to his backup. But if we can catch them now, when they're not prepared, we'll have plenty of evidence and finally they'll be neutralized." He punctuated his plea by offering his badge to his father.

John glared and ignored the gesture. "You can't quit now. Especially because of a—a—"

"Female? Woman? Inappropriate match for the scion of the Travis family?" Zach stepped up to his father and put his badge in his dad's jacket pocket. "I think your best term for her is *ninja chick*. They all fit, but they don't go deep enough." He stepped back again. "But now's not the time for this." With a reckless grin reminiscent of Hana's, Zach looked at Ross and the seven troopers around him. "So, you with me, or agin' me?"

In unison, all eight men, Ross included, looked at John Travis.

Blowing a bitter breath between his teeth, he nodded. He used his radio. "All available units, converge on . . ." and he gave the GPS coordinates. "When you arrive, if I'm not here, wait for instructions from Captain Ross Sinclair." He clicked off and looked at his men. "Okay, we have all of about fifteen minutes to plan our op before reinforcements arrive. First, weapons assessment."

While the troopers checked their weapons and extra ammunition, he looked at his son. "Do you know where the main power line comes in? At least we can force him to his first backup and perhaps get past the fence before he can rearm it."

Ross looked around. "And how do we know they're not watching us right this minute? I see a helluva lot of surveillance equipment."

Zach responded, "We're in a black zone; that's why I chose this post. My guys took the closest camera back to the lab. But Kai knows we're here because of his missing men. All the more reason to act fast."

Per his father's instruction, Zach led John to the transformer he'd found on a corner post. While they were apart from the others and out of earshot, John held out Zach's badge. When Zach hesitated, John said evenly, "Resignation declined. No badge, you're a private citizen. Then I can't allow you to be involved. Your choice."

Zach stuck the badge back in his pocket. Using a metal spike he'd found, he finished the digging he'd started earlier, revealing a large, buried cable.

Inside the house, Kai broke the silence by the simple means of snatching Takeo from his mother's arms. For a moment Hana resisted, but rather than have Takeo be hurt in a tug-of-war, she was forced to let Kai take him.

Takeo cried, but Kai merely looked at the three men he'd summoned by radio and said, "Guard them." He carried Takeo back to his room, set him down inside it, ignoring his son's pleas to stay with his mother. One of his guards went into the room at Kai's gesture.

"Protect him with your life, but don't let him leave with anyone but me. You know where the hatch is." Kai locked them in with a key he took from his pocket.

Hatch? Ernie and Hana exchanged a quick glance.

Kai was back in command again. "Nothing on any of the cameras?"

The man shook his head. "Control says a motion sensor was tripped, but the camera in that section has blown."

"Check it manually," Kai ordered. "And send the drone with night-vision equipment to that segment so we have fresh eyes. And bring me the UV flashlight."

Hana and Ernie were both mystified at this last order, but the lieutenant soon appeared again with a heavy UV flashlight. He handed it to Kai.

Then Kai tilted his head to the side and eyed Ernie, up and down, and back again. "I still think it odd that such a gifted athlete could wound himself so clumsily," Kai said softly. At his look, the lieutenant caught Ernie's unwounded arm, shoved back Ernie's sleeve, and held his hand palm up.

Every muscle in Hana's body went rigid as Kai flicked on the flashlight. Bright half moons appeared on the fingertips of Ernie's right hand. Kai clicked off the flashlight, hefted it in his hand, and without changing tone or expression, clubbed Ernie on the side of the head.

Ernie didn't have to pretend to stagger this time, but he straightened quickly. When he looked back at Kai with a rueful smile, he had a bump and a growing bruise on his cheekbone.

Since they didn't have time to task a satellite or drone to get up-to-date imagery, John Travis was relegated to using Google Earth to try to get their bearings on where best to station his forces to maximize their attack and cut off potential retreat. They were all gathered around his laptop, which he'd set up on a tree stump, viewing the house's metal roof from above, when they heard a slight buzzing. Several of the troopers looked puzzled, but Zach knew instantly what it was. They'd used many of them in his special-ops missions.

Grabbing a machine pistol from a surprised trooper, Zach waited until the drone cleared the trees and sprayed it with gunfire. He missed because it zipped sideways. The red eye beamed down on them intrusively.

Inside the house, Kai appeared genuinely disappointed this time as he looked at his old sensei. "Just a little precaution of mine. I routinely have the inside control-room keypad dusted with an invisible power that only shows up under UV light. It clings to everything." He lifted the flashlight again like a club, but Hana caught his arm.

"Please. Don't. He only came here to protect Takeo. You'd fault him for that?"

"My son needs no protection from me, only his lunatic mother." Kai tossed the flashlight back to one of his men and gathered control around himself again as he tightened the black belt that held his *tanto*. He wore his night garb, as if expecting trouble.

Then he bit off, "We'll settle this later. What I have in mind will take too much time." Kai shoved Hana between the shoulder blades. "Move. You know the way. Down to the basement."

"But Takeo..." Hana protested.

"He'll be fine. One of my men is watching out for him." Kai shoved her harder, so hard she stumbled. "You? Not so much."

She glared at him. "If you'd let me go, they wouldn't have acted. I only wanted to set up our exchange—"

"You have. I like this better anyway. I'd rather take it from them than you. Let's see how much your rich pretty boy loves you. You for the sword. I'm itching to try out the katana on a real body, anyway. I've seen him. Six feet plus. He'll make a great target."

Hana's heart flip-flopped as her worst fears seemed to be coming true. She knew what Kai was doing. If the sword was delivered while she was in custody, he'd have no reason to let Takeo go . . . and he wanted to kill Zach as gruesomely as he had the Taylors.

"But they don't know where I hid it . . ." was the only protest she could think of.

"I'll let you use your phone for one text. Easy."

After that, she couldn't think of any more excuses or delaying tactics.

Opening the heavy metal door leading below, Kai jerked his head at Ernie to follow. With a worried glance at Takeo's door, Ernie obeyed, the lump on his cheek beginning to turn blue.

Hana's hands were clenched so hard her knuckles were white as she listened to her son's crying, but then they were climbing down the circular metal stairs into darkness lit only by dim fluorescents, The slam of the heavy metal door muffled all sound from above. Kai heaved a very heavy metal slide over the door. It would take a battering ram to break it, Hana reflected grimly. And so far as she knew, this was the only way into the cavern.

Then she remembered: What had Kai meant when he mentioned a hatch?

Zach's second burst of fire smashed the drone into smithereens. Grimly, he handed the machine pistol back. "So much for the element of surprise. I'm sure they got a good view."

Ross smiled. "Yeah, of ten men."

As he spoke, an armored van pulled up. Heavily fortified officers, some from the Ranger reconnaissance team, others wearing Travis County Sheriff's Department uniforms, spilled from the side door.

Ross smiled more widely, his white teeth gleaming as the earliest shimmers of dawn illuminated the horizon. "Make that thirty."

The entire team gathered around as the hasty plan Zach, Ross, and John had hashed out a few minutes prior was relayed. As directed, the first order of the day was simple: Get rid of the surveillance as much as possible. Several men went in opposite directions around the fencing, systematically shooting out every camera they spotted.

Down below in the cavern, Kai had a wireless receiver attached to his head as he bent over a laptop one of his tech guys had open on a folding table. For now, he ignored Hana and Ernie, but since AK-47s were pressed against their backs as they were marched down the corridor by two different gang members, they could only obey orders. As instructed, they climbed into the martial-arts ring.

Hana strained to hear Kai's muttered imprecations as she passed and she caught the technician saying, "Every one of them. Out. The drone too. We're blind."

Then she was past them and could hear no more. The entire cavern bustled with activity. Boxes and equipment were being ferried out of the chemical room down a long dark corridor. The workers inside followed close behind.

Black bags went onto carts from another alcove, but this one had a heavy vaulted door. They too were wheeled down the same corridor.

Kai's stash of cash? Hana wondered.

That's all Hana had time to see before she and Ernie were handcuffed, back-to-back, and shoved down in the center of the martial-arts ring. Lights illuminated them from every corner, leaving shadows on the edges of the cavern, where Kai's men lurked. Hana knew why they were put on such public display: They were staked out like bait to draw a tiger. Anyone coming into the cavern from any angle would see them first.

Inside the martial-arts ring, while Kai was conferring, Hana muttered to Ernie, "Okay, ragin' Cajun, what now?"

"Kiddo, I'm fresh out of ideas. Unless you have a knife they missed or something, and even then we might as well be on Broadway with all these lights."

Hana whispered, "Just in case, I brought a pick with me. They didn't find it because it's in the sole of my boot. Like you taught me, teach."

"Be sure you send your brilliant teacher a shiny, gorgeous apple when we get out of here."

"OK, new MacBook Pro my treat, but we have to take Takeo with us."

"Deal," Ernie shot back.

"Problem is, with my hands behind me I can't reach it. If I can turn sideways a bit, do you think you can reach my boot? The heel snaps off."

Ernie glanced into the shadows. "Sure. But they'll see."

Indeed, Hana's skin crawled from the feel of the scopes sighted on them from so many different quarters. She gnawed so hard at her lip that she drew blood. For the first time, she wished she'd taken a moment to confer with Zach about what she was doing. She'd confirmed Takeo was okay, and whether Zach realized it or not, she'd also tried to abort the very raid that was about to happen because she feared what Kai would do to him. But at what cost? Ernie would have been discovered eventually anyway, but Kai had been better organized than she'd expected.

If the Rangers didn't come soon, there wouldn't be any evidence left.

Even worse, Hana suspected the minute Kai heard any sounds of a raid, she and Ernie were dead.

Outside, each man had an assigned task. They'd come fully armed, including a cutting torch. The man who wielded it was standing over the exposed main power line while Zach assisted. His phone rang when they were about to cut the main power line. He almost jumped out of his skin because he'd turned off every call but Hana's.

John, standing next to him, saw his reaction and raised his hand to indicate a halt. The man with the torch shut it off. Every tense eye fixated on Zach's face, dimly lit in the growing dawn.

"Hana. Why the—" Zach choked back his question, his expression going cold and fixed. "How nice to chat with you too, Kai. Why don't you simplify things and put out the welcome mat? We won't stay ... long." Zach put his phone on speaker so they could all hear.

On the other end, Kai's very slightly accented voice said, "I usually don't invite breakfast guests who have armored trucks and automatic weapons... but in your case I might make an exception. Still, twenty to thirty men are a lot to feed."

John and Ross exchanged a grim look. So much for the element of surprise.

Kai continued as casually as if he really were inviting them to breakfast. "Just know the price of entry: If you force your way in, Hana and Ernie will be the first casualties. Bring me the sword, Zachary, and I'll let you, and you alone, in." *Click.*

Zach's gaze was unfocused with rage when he rammed the phone back in his pocket.

John asked, "Did Hana tell you where she left the blade?"

Zach was shaking his head when, a minute or so later, a text buzzed in his phone. He pulled it out and read the message aloud: "Hana's phone again. She says: *katana in Ernie's secret safe room at his place, a false panel in his living room bookcase opens.*" He read off the combination. "That's it."

Zach sliced his finger across the phone as if he wished it were Kai's throat, shutting off the text. "If we delay long enough to get the sword, he'll be long gone," he said grimly.

"Bull," Ross protested. "We have every entrance and exit under observation. Even if we have to delay the assault, they'll never be able to shut down an operation this complex without leaving something behind." He added morosely, "Besides, we don't have a choice but to get it because now he knows where it is."

John nodded agreement and reached for the radio at his belt. "One of my guys still has the key Hana gave him. I'll tell him to bring it to us."

Unable to be still, Zach had taken to pacing. He was on the edge of the clearing when his father spoke quietly into the radio, so he saw the small jeep first. Driving it was Abigail Doyle, her tall, slim figure imposing even in jeans and T-shirt. And when she got out of the car, she carried with her a long, red silk-wrapped object: the katana.

Inside the cavern, Hana could only watch as Kai had lifted her cell phone to his ear. She knew from his expression he was taunting Zach. When Kai climbed into the ring, he'd shoved the cell phone in her face. "Tell me where the sword is."

It was her only leverage, and she used it. "Uncuff me. How do I type?"

"You can talk, can't you?"

Hana had only looked up at him, mute. When he'd drawn his hand back as if to strike her, she never broke her gaze from his: Fearless and unafraid—ironically, because he'd helped her mature. She'd gone to him an unfocussed, undisciplined, and impetuous teenager. By the time she had Takeo and they split, she was sober, resolved, and systematic in proving to him and everyone else that she was both a worthy Nakatomi heir and a good mother.

Something had flickered in his eyes and she'd realized he was remembering too. His hand fell. He'd taken a key from his pocket and uncuffed her, pulling her to her feet and handing her the phone. She'd typed rapidly, revealing the location of the katana. Kai looked over her shoulder to read. When she was done, he'd snatched the phone back and typed something she couldn't see, then stuck it in his pocket.

He lifted the cuffs, indicating that she turn around, but she said, "Lock me in with Takeo. At least allow me to protect my son."

"You'll take him the first chance you get."

He walked around her and roughly looped her wrists together.

"I won't," Hana lied.

But he snapped the handcuffs back in place, hands behind her back. He shoved her roughly down next to Ernie, but at least they weren't back-to-back this time.

He was climbing out of the ring when Hana's phone rang. Kai looked at the name, smiling in satisfaction as he answered. "You are timely." He listened. "Very well, you'll be met at the door. And escorted to me. Do as you're told or Hana won't live to see your shining face." He hung up. "They had the sword all along. Your lover is bringing it to me, just as I predicted."

Hana stared over his head into space, not allowing him the satisfaction of reacting.

Kai shook his head, but there was an angry look about his mouth when he mocked, "The poor sucker really loves you, doesn't he? Daddy must be upset to know his son loves a woman wanted for murder. He's about to discover just how dangerous you really are." He ducked out of the ring and hurried back to his logistics.

Hana took advantage of his departure, knowing his men would be watching him for any new orders, and stomped her right heel into the mat, as if frustrated. Her heel came off. Immediately, she went still. Ernie shifted, as if uncomfortable with his hands behind his back. He managed to move sideways enough that he could reach her heel. He fumbled behind his back while Hana did her best to shield him with her body.

His satisfied little grunt told her he'd found the pick. Swinging around, they went back-to-back again, but this time Hana felt Ernie inserting the pick into her handcuffs. Shielded from view by their position, his hands were not visible at any angle.

Inside his room, Takeo had dried his tears on his sleeve, but his face was sullen. When his mother left, the house grew uncannily silent and Takeo knew his mother must be in the cavern. The man tasked to guard him obviously didn't like his job because he paced up and down, occasionally glaring at his charge. Takeo scooted off his bed. The man caught his arm, but Takeo only glared back at the man's face far above him.

"I need to pee," he said bluntly.

The man moved aside, allowing Takeo into the bathroom. Takeo locked the door and without missing a beat, he climbed on top of the bathroom vanity, on tiptoes to reach for the tiny window above the bathtub-shower combo. The half window was meant for ventilation and had been designed too small for a man to breach, so it wasn't covered by a heavy metal shutter.

It wasn't designed to stop a child.

Takeo reached and reached, but he had to move his feet to the very corner of the vanity to bridge the short gap. If he stood on the tub he wouldn't be tall enough. His wooden clogs were slippery, so he kicked them off. They hit the floor with a clatter.

Immediately there was a bang on the door and a query from the guard in Japanese.

Takeo's chubby little right hand reached the small ledge beneath the window as the first blow came at the door.

Using the new upper-body strength his training had bestowed on him, he dangled from the ledge on one hand until he could plant his feet against the wall and brace himself. He levered himself up enough on a precarious knee to support his weight so he could open the window.

The window latch was new and it opened smoothly. Takeo pushed the screen out and scooted out, back-end first. He heard the door crunch as it was forced from its hinges. For an instant he was stuck, but he inhaled deeply and wriggled, and then he was falling for what felt like forever, to the ground.

His teeth jarred in his mouth, biting his lip as he landed, but he'd taken enough falls in the ring to know to land with his knees bent. The scrubby ground was hurtful, but then he was up and running, ignoring the jabs of pain on the tender pads of his feet.

If something bad was happening, Takeo instinctively knew his mother was in the thick of it. He was pretty sure his daddy was really mad at his mother and he'd seen how his daddy acted when he was in a temper. Takeo also instinctively understood that his presence acted like a brake on his father's worst inclinations. If he could make his way into the cavern, his father would not hurt his mother in front of him.

Besides, he didn't like it here anymore anyway. He wanted to go home. He wanted to see Jiji.

But it would be difficult to reach his mother if he tried going through the house. There were too many guards for him to slip into the cavern unseen.

However, his father had shown him his greatest secret one day when he was pleased with his son's performance: the secret entrance and exit from the basement.

To reach his mother in the cavern, Takeo knew he had to go up to go down.

Chapter 15

In the makeshift base of operations John had set up outside the fence perimeter, Abby hefted the wrapped katana. John Travis looked at her in amazement, accepting it. "I knew you were good, but not this good. How the hell did you know to bring it to us?"

"Hana texted me hours ago and asked me to. She told me where to find it. The office gave me your GPS coordinates and I came straight here."

"What time did she text you?" Zach demanded.

She glanced at her phone and gave him the exact time. Right around the time they'd entered the van for their trip, he realized. Her body was still warm with his lovemaking when she'd decided he was too weak to face Kai. . . .

Zach's drawn look went positively grim. She'd planned this, just like she'd told his mother. She was going to risk her life against Kai, both to protect the blade and her son. And, Zach knew in a deep part of himself that he refused to acknowledge, to protect him too.

Fury at her lack of faith in him made his hands shake as he snatched the sword from his father. "I'm going in."

John bit off, "Negative. That's exactly what the bastard wants."

"Give me thirty minutes and blow the power," Zach said as if his father hadn't spoken. "I'm taking some flash bangs and tear gas with me. I'll deploy them at the appointed time, so wear your masks." Sticking the sword into the side strap of the knife harness on his back, Zach turned to shimmy up the big oak tree so he could drop down into the pasture past the fence.

His father stepped in front of him. "I forbid you to do this. It's suicide."

"I won't let Hana fight him alone. You can fire me for insubordination if I live long enough." Zach moved to step around his father, but John only sidestepped too, still blocking him.

In the glow of the rising dawn, two remarkably similar faces squared off in the exact same posture: mouths set with resolution, cleft chins stubbornly slanted. In that moment, father and son uncannily resembled one another.

Inside the martial-arts ring, Hana felt her cuffs go slack with a very slight *click*. All she had to do was twist her wrists to be free, and the knowledge that Zach was coming gave her even more urgency. She had to be free before Kai saw him. She knew his tactics: He'd be sure Zach saw her staked out like a prized goat, then Kai's little war of words would escalate to global violence. . . .

Takeo? Locked in his room, guarded, he should be safe enough from all the turmoil. He certainly had nothing to fear from the Rangers and it was obvious all the action would take place down here. If she could get him free, Ernie could protect Takeo.

However, no matter how she fumbled, Hana didn't have Ernie's skills with the pick. She looked around furtively, trying to spot Kai, but he wasn't hunkered over the laptop anymore. She also noted that several of their guards had disappeared. She suspected someone still watched them, but didn't know from which quarter. However, she was out of options.

Ernie sensed her frustration. "Go on. Arm yourself. You and Takeo get the hell away."

"I'm not leaving you, Ernie. Takeo should be fine upstairs; Zach knows about the subbasement and the fight will happen here. But I can't . . ." Her frustrated whisper trailed off as she dropped the pick. "I'll get the key somehow and come back."

Flicking the cuffs off her wrists, Hana stood and ducked out of the ring. She held her breath as she did so, but no one stopped her. She heard voices coming down a corridor she'd never ventured into and realized Kai was probably deploying his forces. No doubt he'd called everyone to a meeting to plan the next hour.

Her urgency and fear for Zach increased. She searched the perimeter of the main cavern.

Hana found a nylon jacket over a chair, but it didn't have a key in the pocket as she hoped. Her frantic gaze settled on the clean room where Kai's worker bees made his wonder drug. She ducked inside the gaping door. She was glad to see it had been cleared of all personnel, so at least no workers would be hurt. However, all the proof of his operation was gone too.

Except for a few bottles of various chemicals that... her blood went cold. She didn't know a thing about bomb making, but she knew the universal signs for poison and danger. Several large bottles with hazardous labels of obviously volatile chemicals had been wired together. An attached counter showed descending red numbers: *57:30. 29, 28...*

Dear God, Kai had rigged up a bomb. Hana looked at the complicated wiring but she saw it was all connected to a central black box with a tiny meter. She was afraid to try to disconnect it. It appeared to have some type of tampering trigger, but she needed Ernie to look at it. She'd turned toward the door when a shadow darkened it. It was Ernie.

"I realized they weren't watching us and just left..." he said. His words trailed off as he too saw the bomb. He bit off a nasty curse she'd seldom heard him use even in extreme moments.

Her heart sank. As if the circumstances weren't dangerous enough, now they had a very strict clock for the entire operation. Kai had let her keep her watch, at least. Automatically, she synchronized her stopwatch dial to the time on the counter.

"Can you disarm it?" she asked Ernie as she set her watch.

He shook his head. "I don't have the proper tools and I'm not a bomb expert. But I'm pretty sure that meter is an electrical-charge monitor. See how everything is wired into it? If you don't cut the wires in the proper sequence, it will read the change in ohms and detonate. Besides..." He tried to shrug, indicating his hands were still cuffed behind his back.

Hana searched every drawer in the empty cabinets, hoping to find a key. In a lower, heavy metal drawer, she found another hazardous bottle and this name she recognized: "hydrochloric acid."

Ernie saw it too. He looked down at the big glass dropper left with some other paraphernalia, including a pair of heavy rubber gloves. He turned around. "Do it."

"But... your hands."

"Wrap some of that gauze around them and try to use the acid sparingly."

When she still hesitated, he snapped, "Now, Hana. We don't have time to argue."

Reluctantly, Hana pulled on the right-hand glove and opened the bottle.

Takeo saw that it was growing light outside. He wondered if the guard inside could see him if he looked out the window, and that made him run even faster because he knew the guard would alert his father that he'd gotten away. Takeo finally reached the windmill, which was still spinning. He easily ducked beneath the legs and saw the hatch his father had showed him before. It was embedded in the dirt and couldn't be seen from the outside, or that the spinning windmill wasn't attached to a pump.

But when Takeo tried to turn the big flywheel, it wouldn't budge.

Meanwhile, Ross and Zach had jumped down from the tree and started across the pasture when, in the bright rim growing on the horizon, they saw the lazily spinning windmill beautifully silhouetted in the light. They both would have missed the small figure almost hidden in the depression beneath the structure, if not for several frustrated cries that reached them on the soft breeze.

Warily, wondering if he was entering a trap, Zach approached the windmill so he could see more clearly. Nothing except... his eyes narrowed on the very top of a small person's head and what appeared to be tousled black hair.

Holding up his hand to indicate *halt* to Ross, Zach eased closer still. Either the depression was very deep or the person standing there was very small. Zach crept nearer until he could look down inside the dug-out hole where he'd expect the piping to be. He froze, blinking in shock, but knew instantly who it was.

"Takeo?" he called softly.

His face streaked with tears, Takeo turned toward him. He backed away from Zach's blackened face and heavily armed figure. He turned to run, but Zach added, "I'm here to help your mother. She knows me."

With those magical words, Takeo's fear subsided. He looked way up at the tall man as Zach dropped down into the depression with him, almost crowding him out. "What are you doing, little guy? Why are you out here by yourself?"

Takeo gave the flywheel an angry look. "My daddy showed me

this way into the cavern. Inside, they guard me. I want to get to my mama because I think—I think—" He swallowed back his words.

Zach was both amazed and touched, for he realized instantly Takeo was afraid his mother would be hurt by his father. "That's why I'm here. To protect her."

Takeo nodded eagerly. "I will help too."

"You already have. They won't see us coming if we go in this way." Zach picked the little boy up and, ignoring his protests that he could walk and he wanted to come too, lifted the slight weight up toward Ross's welcoming arms.

Takeo shrank away from Ross, and thinking he was afraid, Ross said, "It's okay, little guy, I'm just going to take you to a safe place while we go find your mother."

When Ross took him, instead of subsiding, Takeo squirmed and kicked. Ross wouldn't let him go and started toward the fence line, trying to restrain him without hurting him.

When Ross didn't release him, Takeo bent his head and bit him in the wrist.

Inside the clean room, Hana had to use the dropper three times in ever greater quantities, holding her breath each time she opened the bottle to avoid the nasty fumes. She heard Ernie's sharply indrawn breath the third time, but he only backed up against the metal shelving and banged the cuffs. On the fourth try, the weakened metal bent enough for him to slip free.

Immediately, Hana poured soda over his reddened and blistered wrists. He sighed with relief. Then he rinsed his wrists in the industrial sink. Hana bound the worst of the blisters on his left wrist, then she looked down at him. One wrist was blue and swollen from his self-inflicted wound and now the other one had acid scarring.

But Ernie only winked. "Good thing I'm better with my feet. Come on."

Hana followed her sensei. They'd heard movement a ways down the corridor, so they had very little time to plan. Hana knew Zach must be on the way... she looked down at her watch. "Fifty-five minutes, Ernie," she said.

"I'm going for Takeo." He paused at the door. "Hana, come with me. If we run now, we can all get away."

She looked at him sadly. "And go where? You know Kai will never stop until he has Takeo and I'm dead."

Ernie shook his head at her. "You really don't know, do you?" He leaned forward and emphasized, his electric silver eyes boring into her, "Kai went to such lengths to get you arrested for one simple reason: He can't kill you. He wants you out of his way, but he still loves you. If you have to face him in combat, that's your only advantage. Use it for all it's worth."

Outside in the corridor, Ernie hurried up the circular stairs while Hana snatched a hood and nylon wind jacket and put them on. Not a great disguise, but maybe sufficient to at least get her near enough to figure out what Kai was planning. As she walked, she kept an eye out for a discarded weapon: preferably a katana.

If Ernie was right, maybe Kai would for once fight fair and face her in equal combat. But she'd be at an extreme disadvantage, not only because he was a better swordsman, but if Zach came with the blade, she'd be facing a death match against the best sword ever made . . . if she could somehow stop Zach from engaging him first.

Outside, Zach had the flywheel open and was heaving up the heavy hatch when he heard a masculine cry of outrage. He looked up.

He saw Takeo kick Ross repeatedly, struggling wildly. Ross set Takeo down abruptly, shaking his wrist. A drop of blood drizzled down his arm and Zach realized Takeo had actually bitten him. Ross reached toward Takeo's arm to stop him, but the child twisted free and ran back toward the windmill.

Not sure whether to laugh or scold, Zach caught the determined little guy with one arm when Takeo tensed to jump down toward the open hatch. "This will be very dangerous, Takeo. If you're there, your mother will be thinking of you, not her own safety." Besides, Zach thought but didn't say, the boy didn't need to see his parents locked in mortal combat. He was as sure as he could be that either Hana or Kai would be dead before nightfall—unless he could, in some improbable fashion, avert their fight and neutralize Kai.

Takeo had pulled back his leg to kick him, when a blessedly familiar voice said, "Takeo! Mind your manners." Scowling, his little face a tiny version of Hana's when she was angry, Takeo turned toward the new arrival.

To Zach's huge relief, he looked up and saw Ernie.

* * *

Hana had never been down this corridor. She was walking against the flow of traffic, trying to see the end when she saw Kai's lieutenant approaching. All Kai's men had an air of finality, as if they knew they would die this night. But like the samurai of old, they were protecting their fiefdom and their shogun and they would fight to the death.

Hana doubted if Kai had warned them they had less than an hour to die gloriously in battle or ignominiously in an explosion set by their own leader. But because so many of them had begun looking at her suspiciously, she had no choice but to turn around and go with the flow. However, even hooded and wearing a shapeless jacket, she was apparently quite distinctive, because the lieutenant pushed through his men and grabbed her arm.

"Kai said you'd find a way to confront him. He's waiting."

He dragged her up the corridor.

Outside, Ernie carried a squirming Takeo, ignoring his protests, to the fence perimeter. The Rangers and deputies had built a makeshift bridge of heavy logs suspended from the oak tree to make it easier to get past the electricity. Ernie was tall enough to put Takeo on the bridge. He patted the boy's rear. "Go, Takeo. Your mother has one last battle to fight, and then she'll be with you for a very long time. If you promise to be good and stay with that nice lady—" Ernie smiled and gave a cheery wave to Abigail—"I'll be able to go back and help her. Okay?"

Reluctantly, Takeo climbed down the tree into Abby's waiting arms.

As he climbed down a metal ladder embedded in the limestone, Zach knew he only had about fifteen minutes left before the designated time to cut the power. Ross followed him down, and in the dimly-lit tunnel that seemed to have been carved into solid limestone, they saw two tracks leading away around a curve. They heard what sounded like metal wheels clattering. Down the other way, they heard the shouts of men preparing for battle. It was a universal sound Zach had heard many times before.

As soon as Ross had made it to the ground, Zach pointed toward the tracks stretching away into the distance. Ross shook his head fiercely, pointing at his watch, giving every indication he wanted to follow Zach.

Zach shook his head right back and whispered, "They don't know you're here. Do some intel before they get everything away and figure out how to intercept them. It's obvious they're wheeling all the evidence away. I'd go myself, but I have the katana and I have to get to Hana." When Ross still hesitated, Zach said more loudly, "That's an order, Ross. My dad gave me authority to lead this op."

Ross scoffed, "Surveillance only. We both know he didn't plan an incursion tonight. Who died and made you God?"

"Ask Emm that question once you get home unscathed." Without wasting time with more argument, Zach kept to the edge of the corridor as much as possible and sidled toward the sounds of activity. But he was relieved to glance over his shoulder and see Ross heading the other way.

Zach moved fast and he moved quiet. He made it some way up the tunnel to what appeared to be a crude roundhouse. Inside were carts that looked a lot like mine cars, some disabled and in repair, but a couple still sat on the tracks and were full of various types of drug-making equipment. Workers in white coats, filthy now as they sweated and loaded, labored over the carts. One finished his load and pushed a cart toward him. Zach ducked around the corner behind a rough outcropping. When the cart approached, Zach waited until the worker was even with him and gave the man a karate chop on the back of the head. He fell limp, half in the cart. Zach lifted up his dead weight, putting him on top of the scales and centrifuges.

He did the same with the second worker bee. While he worked, a radio crackled with a harsh inquiry in Japanese. Zach knew one Japanese word and, depressing the talk button, he used it: *"Hai!"* He knew that meant "yes." The radio went silent. Zach stuck it in his belt, feeling like a carthorse with everything he was carrying. He put the *talk* button on silent, then hovered indecisively in the corridor for a second.

He knew better than to take the katana straight to Kai. But where would he stash it? He was still considering when a man lunged at him around the corner. He was dressed in black, wearing a hood, and armed to the teeth. He barreled toward Zach to engage, but Zach had other ideas. He was taller and used his height to his advantage.

He lifted the katana out of his harness and held it high above the man's head. "Want this?"

When the man reached for it, Zach kicked him square in the solar plexus. With a horrid sound between a grunt and a whine, the man fell down on the floor of the cavern, knocked unconscious. Zach was dragging him up the corridor to the roundhouse when his gaze fell on the man's katana sheathed to his back.

Inside the cavern, Hana didn't react when Kai ripped off her hood. Their gazes locked. For a moment six years in the making, Hana stared at the father of her child. From her thoughts to her lips, the words took sound and form before she could stop them. "Don't make me do this, Kai. For Takeo's sake, I don't want to kill you. And if you kill me, he'll never forgive you."

Kai's beautifully shaped mouth took on an ugly slant. "I won't kill you, Hana. But I can leave you so scarred your handsome, rich lover won't be able to look at you." They'd reached the ring. Kai nodded at his men. One handed her his own katana.

Making a mockery of the courtesy, Kai glanced at his watch. Hana checked her dial, too, and she realized Kai was deliberately delaying his own escape to run out the clock.

He lifted the middle rope surrounding the martial-arts ring to allow her to scoot inside. She did so, but then she looked out at the men in various positions of stealth and defense, still building barricades and readying weapons.

They knew the attack was coming. Kai wanted to be seen by the Rangers when they got inside the cavern because he was timing his escape to engage them a few minutes before the bomb blew. Hence, the barricades, with his men manning them. The other end of the corridor obviously led to another exit.

He'd planned this, too, to kill as many of the combined law enforcement forces as possible. And he wanted Zach to arrive in time to see her scarred for life...

While Kai climbed in the ring, she said loudly in Japanese, "He's wired the clean room to blow with enough chemicals to cave in this cavern." She glanced at her watch. "Forty-five minutes is all you have to live. He's betrayed you all. Escape while you can."

Kai mocked, "Yes, run." He pulled his own katana off his back, the wickedly sharp edge gleaming even in the dim lighting. "I would have told you all. It's for them, not us." He looked at Hana, lifting his blade in a mocking salute, with a bow so slight it was insulting.

"Your lover's afraid, Hana. Where is he? My spotters tell me he was in the pasture and disappeared."

"You haven't asked me about Ernie, have you?" she mocked back, making her own travesty of a salute. "He's escaped, Kai. He has Takeo safe. That's the only reason he came. He played you like a fool. You'll never hold your son again!"

Then she was unable to say more, barely averting Kai's angry lunge as he engaged her. She lifted the blade just in time to defend herself against his right-hand downward slash. Deflecting the steel, she brought her own up in the left-hand upward slice, but he beat her blade away. At the same time, he spun aside so quickly that he was in position to strike her unprotected left side before she could raise a defense.

She felt the blade graze her, ripping a gash in her clothes and slicing into her rib cage, but not deep enough to do any real damage. She began to bleed. But she'd been expecting it when she saw him spin, and given his warning, she knew he'd be going for her face next. Ignoring the pain in her side, Hana lifted the katana with the blade pointing straight up and slammed it sideways as he made a swipe at her cheek.

With a *hiss*, their steel engaged in a stalemate, their blades entangled at the hilt.

Time seemed suspended, and even the men who were preparing for what could well be the last battle of their lives, paused to watch the duel. For *duel* it was; there simply was no other word.

When Zach finally crept around the corner, having disabled two more of Kai's men as he came, he saw not just a duel, but a battle to the death: The same battle he'd seen in his nightmares. He saw the shiny blood on Hana's side and no apparent marks on Kai. Instinctively, he pulled his pistol, even knowing firing it would reveal his position. He also knew it was only about five more minutes before the power was cut.

As he watched, Hana appeared to stumble as she moved backward, weakened on her left side.

His heart thudding in panic, Zach steadied his aim against the side of the cavern and prepared to fire at Kai's exposed back.

Chapter 16

Outside, John's little army had deployed as he'd instructed. Men were strategically placed all around the grounds—some as backup in the trees and shrubs outside the fence, others massing in several incursion points that would essentially cover the entire possible egress from any window or door of the house.

John, looking at his watch, stood next to the guy with the cutting torch. Zach had refused to take a radio in case it gave away his position, and John had doubted it would work anyway if there was a stone cavern beneath the house. So to coordinate, they could only operate on the original schedule. 0600 ticked to 12 on his watch. He lowered his hand in a slashing movement. The torch cut and they saw the few lights in the house go off. The faint humming in the current fed through the wrought iron died. Just to be sure, John tossed a twig at the fencing. It bounced harmlessly with no sparks.

"Move!" John yelled, and his men poured in, some from the oak tree, others from the rear, pulling out an entire section of fencing with their four-wheel drive truck. And the welder cut a neat square in the fencing near John, allowing the rest of them to stream inside.

Ross had followed the tracks around a long, curving descent. He heard the sound of water as he neared a growing light and knew he must be near the exit. Just in case, he pulled his Glock as he rounded the last curve. A railed mine car was being efficiently unloaded, the workers so intent they didn't see him. Bags were being piled into what looked like a jet boat, idling on a curve of the Colorado, the driver occasionally firing it up to keep it from drifting in the rough water.

With one glance, Ross saw that the cave had been tunneled to this wide bend in a way nature never intended. Even the cliffside cut had been concealed, by the look of the heavy branches tossed to the side of the exit.

Ross stepped up directly behind them. "Your hands up. You're under arrest." The driver bleated and gunned the motor. With two shots, Ross took out the two rear engines, leaving the boat adrift. The two workers on the riverbank didn't even put up a fight. They both held up their hands.

Ross cuffed them together. Then he ripped a radio from the belt of one of them and dialed the frequency he knew.

Inside the ring, Hana was too busy fighting for her life to notice anything outside this little square of reality. She didn't see Zach's hand shaking as he hesitated, his aim true at Kai's back. She deflected yet another of Kai's strikes, but so weakly this time that her blade trembled.

Zach knew if he pulled the trigger, killing her enemy from behind, she'd never forgive him. He also knew it was a coward's act. Any cop who shot a man in the back faced a battery of investigation, no matter the circumstances. But the bitter truth was that his own safety wasn't in imminent danger. Kai didn't even have a gun.

But it wasn't the reality of law-enforcement protocol that stayed his hand.

It was love for Hana.

He loved her exactly as she was, with flaws of vanity and insecurity and stubbornness, counterweighted by pride and honor and bravery. He could not adore her for those gifts, and then deny her the right to use them. He put the gun back in his holster.

This was her destiny, bestowed on her by the honor of many Nakatomis. It was a choice a direct descendant of William Barrett Travis could understand. If he had to watch her die to share that destiny with her, he would do so.

But he could better arm her. Just as he turned toward the rear, he felt something hard and vicious conk him in the skull. He fell, a roaring in his ears, and then he knew nothing. The time on his watch clicked past 0600 but he didn't see it. Or note that he was searched and relieved of his grenades.

* * *

Inside the armored truck, which had been pulled for safety deeper into the trees, Takeo—with several sentries guarding him—was having so much fun watching all the monitors and fancy gauges he forgot to be mad. He comprehended, as only a child of the digital age could, that these weird uniformed men had access to devices even his father lacked. He kept up a spate of questions to the tech operator. That young man tried to answer patiently as he listened to his audible, viewed his visuals, and then recorded and tweaked his equipment as necessary.

Finally, as 0600 came and went, Abigail gently pulled Takeo next to her on the seat. "Let the man do his work, little boy. He's going to help save your mama, so we mustn't distract him." She patted the "little boy's" shoulder awkwardly when he glared at her.

"I'm not little," he said sullenly. "I know how to fight." He scooted farther away on the seat. "My mama told me not to talk to strangers." Folding his arms over his chest, he stared over her head.

Her hand shrinking away, Abigail cleared her throat a bit uneasily. That stalwart lady, having faced down international drug dealers, murderers, and the occasional lying lover, looked at Takeo as if he had two heads. No glib words would come; for once in her life she was totally at a loss.

Outside, John's men approached the compound in crouching, zigzag patterns, expecting fire to rain down on them from every position. No response but eerie quiet. When they reached the house, they saw metal shutters lowered over every possible opening. They tried firing at the bottom where the latches should be, but dangerous ricochets made them stop.

"Holy hell," John muttered. "This stuff is bulletproof." He grabbed the radio at his belt, but before he could call for the cutting torch, it crackled.

A familiar voice said through static: "John?—there? It's Ro—"

John tweaked his radio and Ross's voice came in more clearly. "I'm here, Ross. Have y'all set off the flash bangs and tear gas? We're trying to get inside, but the bastard's wrapped up tight behind heavy metal shutters."

"Forget the front of the house," Ross said more clearly. "Go to the old windmill. There's a hatch that leads straight down. A left takes you to a hole in the hillside to the Colorado. He was loading everything to make a clean getaway. There's a jet boat drifting downstream loaded with evidence. I disabled it. A right takes you into the main cavern." John looked at the head of the Travis County SWAT team. He nodded and used his own radio to call for a chopper.

"Where's Zach?" John demanded. He, along with the rest of his team who obeyed his arm wave toward the windmill, ran as fast as he could away from the house toward the whirring blades of the old-fashioned water windmill.

"He went the other way. I haven't heard any gunfire or explosions. He went to find Hana."

"Why hasn't he deployed the grenades?" John's heart was beating fast now, and not with exertion.

"I don't know," Ross said curtly. "I'll make my way back into the main cavern from this end as soon as someone takes these guys into custody. Over and out."

Meanwhile, once Ernie was sure Takeo was safe with Abigail, he'd given her a cheery wave and moved back toward the hatch. He hesitated. The entire cavern would soon be crawling with law-enforcement personnel and he knew Zach must already be there, doing what he could to help Hana.

Ernie had debated following, but he knew his skill set was most valuable in another area. It would aid the entire incursion more than just another set of... feet. Ruefully, Ernie looked down at his hands in the growing light, hoping he could type.

Then he turned toward his own bedroom window. He'd planned this, just in case, during one of Kai's drills. Ernie drew back his long leg and kicked high and true. The bolts he'd loosened at the bottom gave way as the metal bent. Another couple of kicks and he could squeeze inside.

Inside the ring, Kai had just made a lucky strike at Hana's right cheekbone, enough to barely graze her, when his movement in the ring led him around enough to see Zach's inert form and his jubilant sentry, his hand cradling an obviously sore stomach, standing over him. Breathing heavily, Kai stepped back, allowing Hana to swipe at the blood on her face with her sleeve. "Do you want to stop? Do you yield Takeo and the blade to me?"

"You can cut off my nose and both my ears, but I yield to you neither," she said between deep breaths. She was breathing more quickly than he was.

He turned away, hiding his smile of glee. If his men could hold off the approaching cops and Rangers—he glanced at his watch—for another twenty minutes, he should be able to get away with his cash just as the bomb blew, burying them all. He'd save as many of his men as he could, but they had sworn loyalty to him until death, and he would hold them to it. He already had plans in motion to get Takeo back. There had been a flicker of light when the power was cut, and then the backup solar generator came on, powering only the interior of the house and the most strategic lighting and systems inside the cavern.

The assault had begun. Their timing was perfect.

Kai looked around to be sure his men were in position, but then frowned. He saw the barricades, but no one peeking above them. He peered down the corridor, expecting to see rifles braced against the cave walls, but there was nothing. He saw no evidence of activity except for the three guards around the prone Ranger.

Kai was perturbed, wondering if he'd forgotten part of his own strategy, but for now he was too busy to chastise the laggards. As for Hana . . . of her fate he would not think. He'd rather leave her marked for life, missing her son, than leave her to be killed in the cave-in, but for now, the blade had to be his priority.

He jumped down from the ring, ordering his men to keep Hana where she was. Several AK-47s pointed in her direction, but she was bent over, her hands on her knees, gasping for breath, and scarcely seemed to notice.

Then Kai was standing over Zach's inert form. He kicked him in the side. Zach groaned, and his eyes opened, uncannily blue in the blacking on his face. He blinked rapidly and then focused on Kai's face.

For good measure, Kai kicked him again. "Give me the blade, or die."

Zach sat up, groaning, and pulled the red-wrapped katana from the side of his harness. He offered it to Kai, as if terrified. Kai noted his guns were missing and he saw the grenades his men had moved out of Zach's reach. He accepted the blade, totally distracted by the feel of it. A split-second later Kai realized his men had missed one of

Zach's defenses when they frisked him because he'd been lying on his back.

With a speed that shocked Kai, Zach pulled a wicked knife from his back sheath and stabbed the knife in Kai's black-slippered foot. He drew it out to stab again, but one of his men grabbed the knife first.

Immediately, guns pointed at Zach from every quarter, and the knife was turned back on him.

But Kai held up his hand. "No! It's just a scratch. I want him to watch what I do to her. Guard him." They hauled Zach to his feet, guns jabbing into him from both sides. The man Zach had disabled earlier was on his right, half turned so he could watch the action in the ring.

Despite his bravado, Kai limped slightly as he walked back toward Hana. As he went, he removed the red silk from the katana, baring the unremarkable black-lacquered sheath.

Just as he reached the ring and bent to climb inside, Zach stomped his foot down on the foot of the man to his right, simultaneously jabbing his elbow into his other assailant's side. When both men stumbled, the assault rifles lowering, he wrenched the real Nakatomi blade from his old foe's sheath. With him bent in pain, it was easy to grab.

He yelled, "Hana! Catch!" and tossed the heavy blade into the ring.

It landed at Hana's feet. Then everything happened at once.

Inside the ring, Hana looked up, seeing Zach for the first time. She realized Zach must have switched the blades when he'd fought with Kai's second in command, knowing the man would return to his master. She saw Kai limping and Zach grabbing at an assault rifle. She tried to warn him about the bomb, but before she could speak, Zach was too busy to listen. He was struggling with both his assailants, managing to kick one rifle away, but the other moved dangerously close to his side. Then a third man walked up behind him and whacked him on the skull with the butt of his gun. Again, Zach went down, and this time he stayed down.

Hana looked at the black sheath at her feet, the hilt slightly exposed as it loosened in its casing when it landed. She recognized it immediately and was able to grab it and unsheathe it just as Kai climbed through the ropes.

Hana only had time for one worried look at Zach's long form before Kai was inside the ring.

He was white with fury, and she saw from his expression that he, too, had read Zach's switch too late to stop it. He drew the katana in his hand free of a very similar-looking sheath. It was a good blade, but not remarkable.

He looked at Hana, and finally, there was death in his eyes. "Give me the blade, you bitch."

With her family's legacy in her grasp, Hana stood straight, stronger and somewhat rested. "Come and get it." The blade gleamed as she held it in one capable hand.

John and his men were moving as quietly as they could down the corridor toward the noise they could hear. He'd sent five deputies in the other direction to relieve Ross, but most of his force would be needed to fight against Kai and his men.

John was still worried because he saw no evidence of either tear gas or flash bangs. That meant Zach had been captured, killed, or disabled.

His cheek working, John pulled off his gas mask. At his gesture, they all removed their masks. Moving even more stealthily, they separated into two forces, one along each wall.

They'd only gone a short way around another curve when they saw black-garbed men walking toward them. The Rangers raised their guns and to their shock, the men—silent as wraiths—dropped their own weapons one by one at their feet and raised their hands.

What the hell? John wondered. He counted. Must be twenty of them. At least. They seemed very eager to be taken into custody, moving as one toward the left entrance, in a way that made John suspicious.

Like they wanted to escape the cavern. . . .

Inside the ring, Hana raised the blade, gripping it with both hands in the classic samurai pose: arms bent, knees slightly flexed, preparing to strike.

Kai moved fluidly despite a slight limp, and faked a right-hand downward diagonal, spinning at the last minute on his good foot to morph into a side strike toward her rib cage.

This time, Hana read him and leaped sideways, at the same time striking back underhanded to catch his blade and force it upward. The two blades rang loudly in the cavern, but Kai's vibrated slightly. Hana's held true. Before he had time to recover, she used her blocking momentum to continue in the same direction with a strike at his nearest appendage—his leg, extended in his lunge. He moved to block her strike, but a split-second too late. She felt the Nakatomi blade penetrate the meat of his thigh before he stumbled out of range.

He faltered, blood oozing, shiny but still dark, on the nylon of his tight pants. He backed away another step, limping on his bad foot.

Hana looked down and saw that his foot had opened too, and he was leaving bloody footprints with every step. The blade drooped slightly in her slack grip. "Stop, Kai. This is enough. They're coming. Give yourself up. If you do, I promise I'll bring Takeo to see you in prison."

Immediately, his own slightly lowered blade raised to strike. She should have known better than to tell him that, but there was no time to say anything more.

Only then did she realize how he'd been holding back. Wounded, bleeding from two spots, he weaved a wall of impregnable steel with his inferior blade. She backed up, studying his timing. She didn't dare look away, even for an instant, but she thought she heard sounds down the corridor.

She moved left, right, blocking his furious blows at her side and even one upward diagonal that would have cleaved her in two. The Nakatomi blade sang as its tensile strength caught and deflected the force of his two-handed blows. Still, while the steel rang true, only by backing up each time could she fully fend off the strikes by lengthening his range.

Then she was against the ropes. She had no more room to move.

Even Kai was gasping now. Only she heard his puff of venom, "If I die, you die . . ."

He'd heard the men arriving too.

She lifted the blade just in time to block his full body blow aimed at her midsection. His own steel glanced off hers, and his blade bounced away, cutting into her sleeve as it went.

Vaguely, Hana sensed frantic activity all around, but she had no time for anything but to stare at the twisted, perspiring face of her son's father. She sensed the Rangers had the upper hand even though she didn't dare peek, but one look in Kai's dead, dark eyes and she knew.

Just as she'd predicted, either he died or she died.

There was no compromise.

Regrouping the last of her energy, Hana, for the first time in her life, used one of Kai's underhanded tricks. As he gripped his hilt more tightly, raising his sword for a final head strike—arms bent, blade lifted high—she brought her own booted heel down, hard, on his wounded foot, which he'd had to brace to gain power for the blow.

His elbows lost some of their strength as he stumbled slightly. The blade fell toward her.

Smoothly, she used the movement she'd made to stomp his foot to gather all the power in her body in the upward right diagonal, her strongest stroke. Leaning slightly toward her and off balance, Kai still tried to block, but her powerful steel glanced off his sword and struck true. The Nakatomi katana, like the five-body blade it was, cleaved Kai from his hip in one stroke, diagonally upward through gristle, muscle and bone, excising organs and intestines as it sliced. Her perfect cut exited at the clavicle on the opposite side of his body. His blade fell to the mat.

A strange look of shock on his face, he fell apart before her eyes, the upper left part of his body moving in one direction, the right half going the opposite way in a greasy slither. He was dead before he hit the ground. In pieces. Quite literally. Blood jetted in a growing pool, forcing Hana to jump back to avoid it.

She fell to one knee, panting so hard she had to lean on the blade to help support herself or fall into the red mess oozing into the mat. Then Zach was there, using antiseptic wipes at her cheek and arm. It stung, but revived her enough to smile at him.

A bright smile showed her white teeth. "You saved my life by getting me the blade. And you stabbed Kai too? Didn't you? In the foot?"

Zach only nodded.

Finally, still panting, she looked around. To her shock, she was stared at from every quarter. All types of law-enforcement personnel gawked at her: deputies, SWAT, Texas Rangers. She was puzzled why they looked at her so strangely. But equally odd, she didn't see any of Kai's men. She hadn't heard a single shot . . .

Her gaze found John Travis. He stood, one foot propped behind him on the cave wall, and she got the feeling he'd been watching her battle Kai for some time. He was too far away for her to clearly see his expression, but she knew from his body language that he was moved, somehow. His motions seemed a bit sluggish and he finally pushed himself away from the wall and started rounding up his men and waving them toward the cave exit down the tunnel.

Then she surged to her feet. "My God! The bomb." She looked at her watch, but it had fallen off during the sword fight. She knew they couldn't have more than a couple of minutes.

Zach said, "I know. They tried to disable it, but none of us are bomb experts. Kai's men all bailed when they realized Kai was going to let them die. They unplugged the damn thing, but it had some kind of wireless backup and came back online. We gotta get the hell out of here. We only have two minutes or so."

Hana bit her lip, looking down at what remained of Takeo's father.

Pulling her away, Zach growled, "Leave the bastard. He'll be buried, all right. By his own hand. What's more appropriate than that?"

Zach was helping her out of the ring when the backup lights went out. Then they heard another generator kick in. In a split second, it went out too. Someone yelled from the direction of the clean room, "The counter's gone dark! The bomb's disabled!"

Then a voice came over the intercom. A blessedly familiar voice that said, sounding uncannily like David Bowie: "Rangers, deputies, and Nakatomi: This is Major Tom to ground control. It's safe to leave the capsule. All systems compromised. No bombs for you today, Kai the Magnificent." Then Ernie's voice took on its normal tone. "I hope you guys brought lots of flashlights."

And in the dark, an exhausted Hana took full advantage. To rest, to live. To love. Why else had she fought so hard?

Grabbing Zach's hand, she pulled him into her arms. She groped for his head to cup it in her palms. She felt his own lumps, and then she was kissing him, for she knew without him she wouldn't be here.

Somewhere, God really can open a window.

And in that moment, the last of the shutters dropped away from her heart. For she knew that Zach could have killed Kai from a distance if he'd chosen to.

But he'd let her fight her own battles, understanding, finally, that she not only had that right, but the obligation.

And that, to Hana Nakatomi, was true love.

In the aftermath, after they recovered over ten million in cash, arrested fifty people, and confiscated all of Kai's assets, destroying many kilos of various designer drugs. The operation was deemed one of the most successful ever undertaken in central Texas against the drug trade.

After their initial conflict, Takeo and Abigail Doyle became fast friends. Abby had helped foil the men who surrounded their armored car in an attempt to take back Takeo. She coolly provided cover while the young tech guy took advantage of their armor and puncture-proof tires to simply drive away from the rain of bullets.

By the time they returned some time later, John's Rangers had rounded up the last of Kai's men, including the would-be kidnappers.

The bomb was carefully disabled by the bomb squad, and the last of the cavern's contents, including Kai's remains, were cleared away. He was buried in an unmarked grave. Only Hana, Takeo, and Ernie, along with Zach and John Travis, were in attendance at the brief service. Takeo put flowers on his father's grave, clutching his mother's hand tightly.

Jiji's funeral was small too, but with joy the order of the day, instead of sorrow.

Ernie had explained things to the boy. Takeo was very young, but he'd been tutored in life by Jiji literally since he could talk. He understood that his father was a bad man and wanted to kill his mother, so his mother had been forced to defend herself. Nevertheless, John arranged family counseling for both of them.

Abigail came around to Hana's new home regularly. Ernie had been released from his immunity agreement with full pardons for all offenses, current and past. He'd started calling Abigail on various pretenses. She tried to avoid him when she could for the simple reason that he unnerved her. She'd never known a man like him, as she confided to Hana and Mary.

Best of all, to Zach at least, John had agreed to let Hana and Takeo move in to their huge family mansion.

He'd been reluctant at first. During the delicious meal Consuela cooked for all the family after the funerals, Zach had whispered something to his father. John had looked at Hana and Takeo, then away.

Hana knew what they were discussing. Zach was aware she and Takeo had nowhere to go but Ernie's. Her former sensei had offered to take them in, but he was a bachelor, with a bachelor's lifestyle. So Zach asked his father to let them stay and informed him he and Hana were engaged.

Despite the engagement, John remained reluctant about the arrangement. His reaction put a pall over the entire meal. Hana stood and reached out to take Takeo away, but Mary Travis threw her napkin down on the table and straightened to her full height.

She looked down at her husband. "John William Barrett Travis, I seldom ask you for anything. And demand less. Today I'm not asking. They're both staying. It's my house too."

When John's face set into lines that put Mount Rushmore to shame, Mary's expression turned so severe that, for the first time, she showed her age. "Unless, of course, you'd rather I petition to make it only my house. In court."

John's mouth dropped open.

Zach too was stunned. His staying grip on Hana's hand went slack.

Hana glanced between John and Mary, seeing the power dynamic and wondering if she was interpreting it correctly. Had Mrs. Travis just threatened divorce?

Mary didn't even glance their way. Her steady blue gaze held her husband's. She didn't bother lowering her voice, either, as if she wanted both Zach and Hana to hear her next comments. "Look at him, John. Really look at him. He loves her. For the first time in his life he's found a girl he can be happy with. And he's not an easy match. Will you deny him that? And put her and her child in danger?"

Zach grabbed Hana's hand again strongly and pulled her to stand next to his mother.

Mary put her arm around Hana. "Besides, we have a wedding to plan." She enfolded Takeo too into their embrace. He wasn't particularly appreciative, however, and soon scampered away to pet one of the Belgian *Malinois* still on duty outside.

Then Zach moved to stand next to his father, extending his arm toward both women, as if to a vista. "Don't you see it, Dad?"

John was clueless. At first. Closing his open mouth, he gulped. "See what?"

"They're a lot alike. Other than their coloring."

Silhouetted by the commodious hall and creamy walls, black and white marble at their feet, the two women were both tall, slim, and regal. Even their bone structure, fine noses, high cheekbones and perfect mouths, were similar. But it was the steady character, strength allied with the clarity of logic and compassion, in their eyes of blue and black that really defined them as soul sisters.

It was as if blinkers came off John's eyes. "Holy shit... I never, that is, I didn't know—"

Despite being so moved that her heart was thrumming, Hana had to smile. "I'm not just a perp anymore?"

And John Travis sighed heavily. "You might as well stay, then. Now, follow me. I'm not as stupid as I sometimes seem. I knew this was coming." He beckoned and they all followed him into the study.

Inside a long display case with discreet lighting and temperature control, lay the Nakatoni katana. Except it was no longer denoted as *Attributed to Masamune, believed to be the Nakatomi family katana*. Now the label read *On loan from owners Hana and Takeo Nakatomi*.

Hana's eyes filled with tears as she looked at her future father-in-law.

"When you're ready, we'll change the name to Nakatomi-Travis. You don't mind loaning it to the museum once in a while, do you?"

Her voice thick with tears, she teased, "Why not Travis-Nakatomi?"

Zach laughed as his father's face turned red.

Hana kissed John's cheek. Realizing she'd been teasing him, he patted her hand.

Mary laughed too, then caught her husband's arm and dragged him from the study. As the door slowly closed, they heard her teasing, "Did it make your joints flare up to write such a big check, darling?" And then sounds of kissing, interspersed with Mary's, "I love you, you old softie."

Then the door closed completely, muffling their voices.

Inside the study, Hana's eyes were still moist as she looked up at her fiancé. "He really bought out his partners? To gift the blade to me and Takeo?"

Zach goaded her. "As long as your name is Travis."

She tilted her head to the side. "Who knows? Maybe I'll decide to start my own gang. The Nakatomi-Travis Westside Ninjas."

Zach kissed her to shut her up, then drew back and looked at her seriously. "My dad has the strongest sense of right and wrong of anyone I've ever known. He and the guys got into the cavern in time to watch the last of your fight with Kai. He saw then in full, living color, like no argument could ever persuade him, that you belong to the blade, as much as it belongs to you. So he bought all his partners out. I knew, but I wanted him to tell you."

Hana smiled at him luminously, her black eyes as soft as the nights that awaited them. "I only have one request, darling." She kissed his neck, one beating vein on each side, nibbling with tongue and teeth. When his breathing had quickened, she pulled back and smiled. "For the wedding ceremony, promise me you'll come in a towel wrap?"

And there, with the Nakatomi katana safely in its case, Hana pledged her troth to her fiancé in the age-old way of her ancestors.

A stray ray of sunlight came through the study window, reflecting off the priceless blade. It still held minute amounts of blood and tears, though they could not be seen. For now, it rested, having assured the safety of its next generation.

This time, it reflected back no battles of mayhem and murder, only love and devotion in the soft images of the entwined couple.

It was the blade, after all, that had united them in times of strife. Now, it would continue its reign in peacetime as a legacy of two proud families born of the sword. As Masamune himself had intended when he tempered it repeatedly, the Nakatomi katana had helped forge a new destiny.

And somewhere, both Jiji and William Barrett Travis smiled.

Have you read the first of Colleen Shannon's Texas Rangers books? *Foster Justice* **is available now wherever ebooks are sold!**

One Riot, One Ranger...

That's the Texas Ranger motto, but when Chad Foster's rebellious brother goes missing, it's time to put his elite training to use investigating a crime that strikes much closer to home. Turning Los Angeles inside out to retrieve Trey and save their ranch from a ruthless land grab is a no brainer, even if it puts his badge at risk. His only lead is a heart-stoppingly sensuous exotic dancer with a very tempting butterfly tattoo, the woman who helped scam his brother out of their ranch. But staying on top of this redhead's every suggestive word and sensual move means putting his case—and his heart—right in the line of fire...

A Texas Ranger, complete with quarter horse, is as out of place in downtown L.A. as a lawman is in the bed of a suspect, but with both their lives at risk, Chad has to put his trust in the one woman who could bring him down for good, and pray that somehow hard evidence is really just a pack of lies...

"Intense romantic suspense with a sexy edge."
—Tanya Anne Crosby
New York Times bestselling author

A TEXAS RANGERS NOVEL

COLLEEN SHANNON
FOSTER JUSTICE

Don't miss any of Colleen Shannon's Texas Rangers books. *Sinclair Justice* is available now wherever ebooks are sold!

Ranger Proud, Ranger Strong...

Texas Rangers swear to uphold the law to the letter. But Captain Ross Sinclair isn't about to play by the rules to destroy a major human trafficking cartel—especially now that the only chance to break this case just strode into his life with attitude as long as her gorgeous legs. Heiress Emm Rothschild is taking names and raising hell as she searches for her abducted sister and niece. And the evidence this wild-child turns up sets off a lethal chain of events—challenging Ross to keep her reckless determination and seductive daring up close and dangerously personal...

Now a blindsiding betrayal has Emm heading straight into harm's way. And Ross will have to put his badge and career on the line to get justice—and prove to the woman he loves that a Ranger's word is a forever bond...

"Intense romantic suspense with a sexy edge."
—*New York Times* bestselling author
Tanya Anne Crosby on *Foster Justice*

Visit us at www.kensingtonbooks.com

COLLEEN SHANNON

A TEXAS RANGERS NOVEL

SINCLAIR JUSTICE

Colleen Shannon grew up in West Texas where the skies are as limitless as the tales told by its many colorful residents. Surrounded by oil men, lawyers, and drillers in a community that has produced two presidents and many national leaders and businessmen, Colleen grew up reading and writing stories of every kind. After college when she married and was expecting her first child, she used a scrap computer to write her first romance. She sold it herself in less than a year, and at the age of twenty-six began a new career and never looked back. The strength of her first book led to her nomination by Romantic Times as Best New Historical Author. She went on to win or be nominated for many other awards, and her fifteen single title releases have appeared on numerous bestseller lists. She has well over a million books in print.

Her newest series, focused on the modern Texas Rangers, is from Kensington. Colleen's ancestor, a Texas Ranger, was one of the first people buried in Brown County cemetery, Texas. Another one of her ancestors was a signatory to the Texas Declaration of Independence.

Learn more about Colleen and her novels at colleenshannonauthor.com.